Sincerely Yours

Cover Design: Dean Roth
Cover Art Copyright 2000 www.arttoday.com

Town Book Press
255 East Broad Street
Westfield, NJ   07090

Town Book Press is an imprint of The Town Book Store of Westfield, Inc., an independent bookstore established in 1934.

ISBN 1-892657-10-4

Printed in the United States of America
First Trade Printing: September 2000

10 9 8 7 6 5 4 3 2 1

Lovingly Inscribed
to
Ed, Gerry, Judy, Christina, and Amy

Sincerely Yours

by Gertrude Wood

Gertrude Wood

Town Book Press
Westfield, NJ

1

Alex Southerick paced the floor in the cramped quarters of his den. He was a man of medium height and build, neither homely nor handsome, with light brown hair tapered in an old-fashioned barber cut. 'Average' was stamped all over his appearance, right down to his white shirt and charcoal-gray slacks. His career accomplishments, however, were well above the ordinary. In twenty years he had made seven corporate moves, and he was now a vice-president at Kinnelac Corporation, a company with worldwide subsidiaries.

Alex claimed that his brain worked when his feet walked. He tackled both business and personal quandaries while striding back and forth with measured gait. When he had requested a spacious office before accepting his latest position, his colleagues thought he was concerned with prestige, but what he really wanted was enough room to pace and think in seclusion. He had learned early in his junior executive years that treading up and down corridors was guaranteed to label him eccentric.

In his own home, his usual location for pacing was the long center hall, but right now, on a Sunday afternoon, he was in his small den instead. Since he was supposed to be addressing the family Christmas cards, he did not want Marcia to see him ambling in the hallway with furrowed brow. Poor Barkle, the family's big English sheepdog who was accustomed to following Alex back and forth in the long hall, had to scramble for position each time Alex turned a corner. Barkle peered out through the shaggy hair that covered his eyes, but even though he watched for stop signs, his thickset body was too bulky for the area, and he bumped his bottom at every swerve.

When Alex had volunteered, the week before, to write out the annual Christmas cards, Marcia was astounded. For the past 22 Christmases she had sandwiched card-writing in between shopping and decorating, gift-wrapping and menu-planning. She was so delighted to exclude at least one holiday activity that she had said 'yes' at once, asking no questions about Alex's unprecedented interest. She had made one offhand suggestion: "I always write a brief note on cards to old friends. You might want to do the same."

Today Alex had closed the den door—generally left open when he worked on Kinnelac contracts—slamming it noisily for Marcia to hear and understand his wish not to be disturbed.

Now, after innumerable circuits of the room, Alex finally sat down at his desk, picked up his monogrammed pen, and wrote:

December 10, 1982

Dear Friends:

I know this will sound strange as a Christmas-card note, but I'm going to ask you a tremendous favor. I am trying to get $10,000 together immediately. To do this, I am writing ten couples and asking each to lend me $1,000. For personal reasons, I don't want to borrow this money from a bank or lending institution.

I want the money for only one month. I will return it on or before January 10, with interest at the current Treasury Department rate. There is no time for further communication, and no time to make up a loan contract. *If you can possibly see your way clear to sending me $1,000 within the next two or three days, I will appreciate it immensely and repay it promptly. Please send it to my office address (card enclosed).*

With best wishes to you and your family for a happy holiday season,

Sincerely yours,
Alex

As an afterthought he added:

P.S. Please do not telephone me for additional details, as I cannot disclose any other information about the loan.

His solemn face erupted in a smile. He was sure that no one could guess why he wanted the money. "But now comes the hard part," said Alex aloud. He gave his one-dog audience a soft nudge with his foot, and rambled around the room a few more times. Barkle emitted a grunt of objection, but heaved himself up and followed. Then Alex sat down once again at his desk, and removed the Christmas-card list from a top drawer. 324 names and addresses.

First he scanned the pages quickly; then he studied each of the 324 names, crossing out entries thoughtfully, and scribbling notations in the margins. After this preliminary analysis, the list was reduced to 87. Another process of elimination left him with 34 names. Concentrating intensely, with a slight frown and a synchronous faint smile, he took another hour to produce his finished list of ten names.

With a sigh he got up from his desk and walked across the luxurious rug to the window, gazing at the wooded land he referred to as 'The Acreage.'

The acreage had been discovered by Alex and Marcia in the suburbs of Chicago two winters ago, after they had searched for years to find the ideal lot for a custom-built residence. Every few years during their marriage, Alex had secured a better job, and they had moved to a different part of the country. After their most recent move, they had dusted off their bulky file of sketches and watched their self-designed contemporary ranch materialize.

The completed house was everything they wanted it to be, but they could not say the same about the mortgage. From the day they had started making plans until the day the builders began to hammer, prices had escalated, and the house had cost four times as much as they had originally figured. Another timing factor was off: their son and daughter, who were in grade school when building dreams had commenced, were now attending expensive colleges. Olivia had hopes of becoming a research scientist; Earl wanted to study archaeology and earn a doctorate before settling down with pickax and shovel. Olivia and Earl were achieving excellent grades in college, and Alex was determined to help them reach their objectives. Nevertheless, despite a high salary, Alex's savings were miniscule; his bankbook would have shocked both his family and his subordinates.

On this particular day Alex was taken aback when he saw that his acreage was snowswept. Snow was common for December in the outskirts of Chicago, but Alex had been so engrossed in the Christmas-card list that he had not noticed three hours of falling snowflakes. Snow and ice glistened on evergreen branches, and he was glad it was Sunday afternoon so he could drink in the glory of the storm without having to drive in it.

4

After reveling in the beauty for several minutes, Alex went back to his desk and examined the list of ten names with satisfaction. They were all names of couples, they were from ten different states, and they all lived at least 700 miles from Chicago. He did not want anyone showing up at his door, with or without the money, making inquiries. He had tried his best to ensure that none of his ten selected couples had a close friendship among the others.

He had intentionally chosen friends that he had not seen in years. He had also made an earnest effort to judge each couple's approximate income, a difficult criterion because of the infrequent contact. He had dug deep into his memory to recall his friends' annual brief Christmas-card notes about new jobs, transfers, and promotions. He had even searched through back copies of the *Alumni News* for items that might help him to make his ultimate decisions.

Alex stared at the 'Dear Friends' letter he had composed. Then, before picking up a single Christmas card from the boxes stacked on his desk, he telephoned his long-time associate, Humphrey Wattsindorf, and read the note to him. With Humphrey's approval, he was ready at last to write out ten Christmas cards. And, as Marcia had innocently suggested, each card would include a note.

——— ✦ ———

Marcia's fourth call to dinner finally pierced Alex's concentration. Though Marcia was somewhat hurt about the closed door, she respected Alex's obvious desire for privacy, shouting from the hall until he hastily cleared his desk and opened the door.

"Well, how did you make out with the list?" she asked cheerfully, standing in the doorway. "I'm frazzled. I decorated the living room—except for the tree—and I wrapped

23 gifts. I organized the food and the guest list for our Christmas party, and made two of the hors d'oeuvres. And I put a pot roast on to simmer a couple of hours ago." She was a short, slender woman who looked appealing even though she wore no makeup, and had her naturally curly hair pinned straight back.

"I addressed ten cards," he said sheepishly.

Marcia could not hide her astonishment at this meager output. "You've been closeted in here for over six hours and you've written only ten cards?" The question ended in a high squeak.

But, my dear, he thought, you have no way of knowing that I had to make an extremely judicious selection. I had to pick couples who fell into specific categories. Aloud he said, "I admit I'm a bit slow at this sort of thing. Now that I've gotten the hang of it, the other 314 will go much faster, I promise you."

"Did you write these people lengthy notes?" she asked.

"No, they were short," he replied, squirming uneasily.

Marcia stepped inside the room, mainly to observe if Sunday newspapers strewn around the den would belie the inference that he had been working on Christmas cards the entire time. But the place was tidy, and on his desk were ten addressed cards, all sealed and stamped. As she turned them over curiously, she saw that the names started with various letters of the alphabet, not all A's and B's. What a peculiar way to do the cards, she thought.

"Alex," she said, "how come you're skipping around like this? Here's a B, and this one is a Z! How will you remember what cards you've done?"

"That's one thing I don't have to worry about," he answered. "I made a list, but I'll remember without consulting it."

His smile—was it cunning, self-assured, or bordering on gleeful? Did he sound guarded? Marcia wasn't sure. She had never seen her husband look so sly. After 22 years of marriage, was there a facet of his personality that she did not know? Unable to interpret his odd grin, she resorted to triteness: "You look like the cat that swallowed the canary."

"No," he said. "The canary is still very much alive."

Marcia decided to forgo comment on his enigmatic remark, though she was bewildered when they both left the room. Continuing her speculations, Marcia resolved not to make an issue of the afternoon fiasco. Criticism might give Alex a handy excuse to decline the rest of the card-writing stint and to foist it back on her. In the middle of her 'holiday busies,' as she called them, her mind full of shirt sizes and canape recipes, she was more than willing to accept erratic behavior if the job got done.

"How about a glass of Chablis after all that hard work?" she asked with a mischievous titter.

Alex was relieved that she had changed the subject.

"After dinner, I'll write faster," he said, smiling broadly. Marcia wondered how he could look so enormously pleased with himself when he had accomplished so little.

Mr. & Mrs. Alex Southerick
2612 Kendalpark Lane
Aranda, IL 61015

Dr. and Mrs. Quentin Lisenbod
12 Yardley Ave.
Willow Run, Pa. 17586

2

Emily was exhausted. She had spent seven hours poring over the hundreds of wallpaper patterns available in browns and beiges. Shopping marathons took their tolls, even from Emily's extraordinary supply of daily energy. She pulled her car into the driveway, and thought about her doctor-husband's easy life.

He's sitting there gabbing to people during all those office hours, while I'm hiking from store to store finding everything we need for a ten-room house. And planning the family's wardrobes to boot. Not that he appreciates it. He'd be content to wear recycled burlap bags if I let him.

She had launched her current redecoration project because she was bored with the greens and purples she had chosen for the living room barely two years before. Emily replaced drapes and furnishings as casually as others changed their hats or shoes.

Tiring or not, shopping was Emily's favorite diversion. Spring, summer, winter, fall, she bought clothes for everyone in the family, even though price tags were still attached to much of the apparel from the season before. Surplus rings and necklaces lay dormant for years in hand-carved jewelry boxes. In addition, she filled the house with collections: spoons, plates, buttons, bells, paintings, and figurines. She shopped endlessly for such collectibles, and then was obliged to shop for furniture to accommodate them.

Emily arrived home with no bundles to show as visible fruits of her labor. She took the stacked envelopes out of the mailbox, and entered the house with weary steps, glancing indifferently at the letters and Christmas cards. Then the words PRIVATE SALE, in bold-faced type on a thick catalog, miraculously revived her. Visions of the things she would buy tomorrow danced giddily in her head.

Nevertheless, she was glad she had assigned the house-keeper to cook dinner that evening instead of dusting. Chippy worked four hours every weekday, her chores varying according to Emily's daily whims. But most of the time, Chippy dusted; and because of that, Emily treated her with deference. It was difficult to keep help that was willing to face the monotony of repeatedly dusting Emily's collections.

Tonight, after bookmarking her catalog, Emily noticed that the house was unusually quiet. Before determining the whereabouts of her nine-year-old son Rupert, who normally produced more than enough background noise, she decided to open the pile of Christmas cards. She settled down in an elegant Queen Anne chair and picked up her letter-opener, gazing fondly for a moment at its golden handle laden with cherubs and fourteen-carat rosebuds. Then she started slitting open envelopes with businesslike efficiency. The third card she read was from Alex and Marcia Southerick. *'I am writing ten couples and asking each to lend me $1,000...'*

Sincerely Yours

Emily jumped up so quickly that Queen Anne's cabriole legs trembled. The rest of the holiday cards were forgotten. Seething, Emily prepared herself for battle.

Just when I'm redecorating the living room, my softy husband will want to send Alex Southerick $1,000. Over my dead body! I'll tell Doc a thing or two or three.

⸺ ◆ ⸺

Quentin was exhausted. He had spent seven hours resuscitating and bandaging an accident victim who had died anyway. Earlier in the day he had told a man of thirty, the father of four children, that his cancer was terminal. The patient had begged for the truth bravely, but had broken down when the doctor revealed it. Quentin felt inadequate at times like these, not realizing that his gentle approach, his concern, or simply his steadying presence, were substantial comforts to the people whose lives he touched.

The images of what he perceived as the day's failures were still fresh in his mind as he entered the house and took off his shapeless old felt hat. His shoulders slightly bowed, he was hanging up his coat when Emily appeared in the vestibule.

"Wait till you see the latest thing in Christmas greetings," she said, not bothering with 'hello.' "Alex Southerick had the nerve to ask us for $1,000, right on his Christmas card. Sacrilegious, I call it! Just because you're a doctor, people think we're millionaires."

Quentin felt too withered to react strongly. "I'm sure he has a good reason for asking," he said.

"Good reason, ha! He won't even tell the reason. It's a deep dark secret."

Chippy announced that dinner was ready, and Quentin felt rescued, at least temporarily. He knew that a minor interruption like eating would not silence Emily for long.

"Where's Rupert?" he asked. He always looked forward to the demonstrative greetings of his lively young son, the only child at home now that his two grown daughters were away.

"He's not feeling well. He's staying upstairs in bed."

Quentin looked anxious and headed for the stairs, but Emily said, "Never mind Rupert. You can examine him after dinner. He's not dying, he's watching television."

She brought the Southericks' Christmas card to the dinner table, saying, "Read this before you start your soup." She allowed him a minute before spewing her wrath. "Isn't that the height of gall? I know we were friends when they lived three blocks up the street, but they moved away years ago, and they have visited us exactly twice since. I warned you over and over not to get social with your patients, but you wouldn't listen to me. Though I admit Alex and Marcia Southerick started it by inviting us to that big bash they had on New Year's Eve. Probably expected a discount on their medical bills. Huh!"

How she prattles on, thought Quentin. He shut his eyes for a moment and put his hand to his forehead as if this discourse were giving him a headache. Aloud he said, in a reminiscing tone, "The Southericks came to my office when patients were hard to come by, and they stayed with me until they moved."

"Well, they weren't sick much," Emily said. To her, a loyal patient was one who had innumerable ailments, or who had the grace to be a hypochondriac.

"I thought you liked Alex and Marcia. Personally, I'm quite fond of them."

11

"They were fine when they lived here, but I don't like people who capitalize on friendship by asking for money. They go down in my estimation right then and there."

"They aren't asking for money *per se*; they're merely asking to borrow it for a month."

"Bah humbug! We'd be kissing $1,000 good-bye, that's what. Anyone who has the audacity to ask old friends for money outright like that would be brazen enough to keep it."

"I don't think that's fair to say, and what's more, I think we should send it."

Emily's voice became shriller. "I knew you'd say that! It's typical of you! Like that $500 church donation you made. Let the church sell off those high-priced stained-glass windows and put in regular windows like everyone else... But at least we're doing better since I took over handling our checkbook. That was the greatest decision we ever made—our financial position has improved 100 percent." Emily had improved it by disregarding any and all requests for contributions, however noble the cause; the doctor had previously been munificent to many charities. She would have thrown the Southericks' card away if she could have been sure that Alex would never mention the loan again. Ordinarily she spotted and discarded direct-mail solicitations without opening the envelopes.

"Now we have much more money to spend on our-selves," she went on, "and that's as it should be. We work hard for it, why shouldn't we be the ones to spend it?"

That's using the editorial 'we,' thought Quentin with a small rueful smile. "Well, how would you respond to the note?" he asked, a hint of resignation creeping into his tone. "At the very least it deserves the courtesy of an answer. We are their friends, or so they thought, anyway."

"Oh, that part's easy. I'll think up a good excuse. I'll say our daughter Gwendolyn is going to premedical school, everybody knows that costs a fortune. And my father had a stroke—his therapy is most expensive."

"But we aren't paying for that."

"Did I say we were?"

"No, but the implication was there."

"Of course, Doc, that's the reason for bringing it up."

Though normally slow to anger, Quentin was chafed whenever Emily called him Doc, probably because she employed it as a synonym for stupid. Quentin had no aversion to others greeting him with 'Hello Doc'; he rather liked the informal reference to his chosen profession. But Emily could say the identical two words and give his abbreviated title the connotation of a cartoon character.

He had asked her several times not to use the word. However, this time he did not repeat the request, but said reasonably, "Emmy, why don't we mail a check. It would be so much simpler. It sounds odd to say we can't afford it, when we're getting the money right back. No matter what excuse you give, Alex will know the truth is that we don't want to make the loan, or else we don't believe him when he says he'll return it in a month. He must have seen on his last visit that my practice had increased considerably— he knows perfectly well that we can afford to lend him $1,000 just for a month."

"Just for a month! Just for a month! That's all you can say!" shrieked Emily. Though Quentin heard her raucous voice often, it still made him wince.

Emily paused to reload her ammunition, then continued with full steam: "This is a terrible time for anyone to be asking for money—did you forget that I'm redecorating the living room? You're not as solvent as you think. The bill for the new Oriental rug hasn't come in yet. And if you have $1,000 to throw away that I don't know about, I'll buy a wool coat I passed up in Oppenheim's Department Store. You aren't thinking of *our* needs. You'd rather let Alex

Southerick have the money. And what is he to us? A former patient, that's all. In a month I could have $1,000
spent four times over."

Amen! thought Quentin. I can't dispute that statement. "This isn't in the same category as spending
money—you keep forgetting it's nothing but a loan," he
said quietly. He had given up noisy squabbles with Emily
long ago.

"Don't use that bedside manner with me, Doc," Emily
yelled. "*You* keep forgetting we might not get the money
back."

Quentin rose abruptly from his chair. "I'm going
upstairs to look at Rupert," he announced. He stopped in
the hall to fumble in his overcoat pocket for a spacecraft
toy he had bought for Rupert, who had a passionate desire
to become an astronaut.

When Quentin came downstairs much later, Emily was
still drinking coffee and plotting her moves. "All right,
Doc," she said, "if you think it sounds strange to say your
general expenses are high, we can tell Alex Southerick his
timing is poor, a few weeks before Christmas. That would
sound plausible to most people. I could write something
like 'It's a shame you need it right now, I'd send it in a
minute, but I'm caught short because I bought my wife a
sapphire bracelet and silver fox jacket for Christmas."

Quentin started to speak, but Emily quickly interrupted. "No, that's not a lie. You always say I should Christ-
mas-shop for myself because I know best what I want, so
this year I did; I've already ordered the jacket and bracelet.
And here's another thing I want to point out—did you see
Alex's business card? It says 'Vice-president in Charge of
Marketing.' In other words, he has a much better job than
he had when he lived here—yet he has to borrow money
from his friends? We've progressed too, but are we asking
our friends for money? What's the matter with Alex? Can't

handle his job, or his personal life, or both? Do you want to lend money to someone who is that irresponsible?"

The telephone halted Emily's attack on Alex Southerick, and Quentin was grateful to hear the ring even though he was tired and he knew it would probably mean a house call.

Could the doctor come over immediately for an emergency? A pregnant woman was having a hemorrhage.

Quentin hurriedly picked up his bag, kept handy by the front door. Since Emily had not made any inquiries, he called over his shoulder, "Rupert's stomach is off, nothing serious," as he rushed out of the house.

Quentin was constantly being lauded for making house calls, by his colleagues as well as his patients. The praise gave him no satisfaction, however, because he privately questioned his motives.

At the outset, when he started practicing, he had offered house calls as a lure to attract reluctant patients. Although he had taken over a retired physician's practice, many people had switched to experienced local doctors rather than come to a young upstart, fresh out of medical school, who looked like Norman Rockwell's freckled all-American boy-next-door. Rebuilding the practice was a struggle; he had made house calls because the established doctors in the area had discontinued this service.

Now, after many years, he had a practice almost too big for one man to handle. But he had not abolished house calls. It was true that he hated to inconvenience his patients, especially the elderly ones who were unable to drive. Aside from that he felt morally compelled to handle emergencies, because the nearest Emergency Room was forty minutes away. Nevertheless, he was aware that house calls served other ends: they provided extra money to satisfy Emily's lavish tastes, and they got him out of the house

15

and away from his wife's petty indignations. Quentin was not sure which of these factors was his primary motivation.

———— ⚔✦⚔ ————

In the beginning months of marriage, Quentin had tried to describe his professional experiences to Emily, especially his feelings about his patients—how torn up he felt inside, for example, when a youth was brought in after a diving accident, paralyzed from the waist down. He discovered that Emily's chief interest—in fact, her sole interest—was the size of the medical fee. 'How long will he be in treatment?' was not the sympathetic question Quentin originally supposed; it could be translated into 'How much will you be able to charge?'

Why had he not noticed her brazen materialism when they were dating? Had she purposefully hidden her real character under the sheath of glamour that had entranced him?

During the years of internship, Quentin had not seen many women wearing anything but white uniforms and tired faces. When he met Emily, a medical librarian, she had seemed chic and dynamic. Although her separate features were not pretty, she knew how to use makeup so that her finished appearance was attractive. Quentin admired her flair with clothes as well as her vivacity. They were married in four months, their wedding hastened by Quentin's acquisition of a practice 1,200 miles away from their families.

Before leaving, Quentin hosted a 'Lucky Me' party, because he had found a glamorous bride and a genuine practice in such short order. He was exhilarated by the prospect of working side by side with his energetic wife, who had no experience in accounting but was nonetheless eager to tackle the business duties in his office.

He soon found that Emily's avid interest in bookkeeping was confined to the column marked 'income.' From the start the newlyweds wrangled about Quentin's fees, which Emily insisted were too nominal.

Quentin tried to teach Emily compassion, but either it was an unteachable subject, or she was an impossible student. He stopped trying eventually, but before he had quite given up hope, Emily was pregnant. When Gwendolyn arrived, Quentin felt such joy in parenthood that the disillusionment of his marriage was relatively reduced.

When another daughter, Cynthia, was born a year later, Quentin rejoiced anew. And Emily, with her seemingly inexhaustible energy, did a remarkable job of ordering and record-keeping, even with two babies to attend. And through the countless phases of nursing and bottle-feeding, teething and diaper rashes, Emily did not miss a single billing.

The marriage continued to be tempestuous, however, with the worst controversies still about money. Occasionally Quentin decided to revoke a fee for a family he knew to be going through financial hardship. Whenever he told Emily to omit a charge, there was an explosion.

"You have absolutely no business head," she fumed. "If we leave it up to you, everybody in town will be healthy as a horse, and we'll be in the poorhouse."

After a while, when Quentin felt that fee-cancellation was justified, he did not mention it to Emily, but simply informed the patient, "You will receive monthly statements; just disregard them."

This strategy did not provide deliverance from Emily's caustic tongue. Emily complained interminably about non-payments, and made uncharitable commands: "Stop treating those duds, the Hunnerts; they don't pay their bills." Quentin ignored her for months, but when she bluntly announced one day that she was going to send the deadbeats' bills to a collection agency, he was forced to confess. Emily became doubly enraged, not only because he had told specific persons not to pay, but because he had withheld the information from her.

When their days were not stormy, they were cloudy. The office waiting room held either too many patients, or too few, somehow never attaining the mystery number that would suit Emily. The old account books were wide and cumbersome; the new ones had columns that were too nar-row to accommodate her figures. If it was raining, people would track mud into the office; if it was sunny, the bright light would ruin the draperies. When Quentin stopped to chat, he should be tending to business; if he did not talk, then he never paid her any attention.

In this no-win environment, Quentin gradually paid less and less heed to his wife's commentaries. If God can't produce the right amount of sunshine to meet with Emily's approval, he thought, what can I expect to accomplish? He found solace in his growing daughters, and in his burgeon-ing practice.

By the time Rupert was born, eleven years after Cyn-thia, Emily was able to retire from the office, and Quentin hired a shy, middle-aged widow, Mrs. Islas, to replace her. He welcomed the freedom to direct his pleasant new employee to stop billing indigent patients; he had no inkling that poor Mrs. Islas silently bore the wrath of Emily's ire. Whenever Emily swept into the room and demanded to inspect the books, Mrs. Islas' fingers began to shake. Emily's sharp eyes missed nothing, and when Emily inquired 'didn't such-and-such family pay yet?' Mrs. Islas quaked when she admitted she was no longer billing them.

"Don't you quit billing the Kearshans just because Doc tells you to," ordered Emily sternly. "They can get the money from welfare or disability... or somewhere. That's their problem. Why should we lose out? The doctor has rendered his services, and we should be paid, first and fore-most."

Mrs. Islas did not argue, but she felt her allegiance belonged to the doctor. She said 'yes ma'am' but continued to do Quentin's bidding, only to be admonished by Emily again the following month. Timorous about reporting these encounters to the doctor, Mrs. Islas lived in constant fear of losing her position.

But Emily was too shrewd to discuss Mrs. Islas with Quentin. Though she badgered the hapless woman at regular intervals, she spent most of her time shopping. During the years that she had worked in her husband's office, she had been left with little time to shop. On the day she left the job, she embarked on a buying spree that Quentin was sure should be noted in the *Book of World Records*. The vigor he had admired when he first met Emily was now used to assuage her previous frustrations. In six months she amassed a collection of art, china, and furniture that would have taken an average shopper twenty years to accumulate.

What disheartened Quentin the most was that none of this assortment of purchases appeared to give Emily any real pleasure. She never returned from a store looking jubilant because she had acquired an object she liked. She was more wont to be petulant because nothing was ever exactly right. "If only I could find the matching piece," she would fret; or "How I wish this had been available in chartreuse." And Quentin would think, if I saw her just once with her face lit up, bubbling over something she had bought, it might be worth the price.

In the meantime, increasing house calls had steadily curtailed the Lisenbods' social life. The doctor was busy even on Wednesdays, when he had no office hours; and if he had an unforeseen respite, he preferred to spend it with his youngsters rather than attend social events. Emily often went to parties alone, explaining, "My husband is out on calls." She also joined women's card clubs, and took trips back home with the children.

"Quentin lives for his patients—he doesn't care whether I come or go," she would grumble to her bridge friends. Quentin cared more than she thought, but in the opposite way she would have liked: he wished she would go more frequently. When she was away on a trip, he dismissed the housekeeper and ate mediocre but restful meals of cold cereal or sandwiches. He enjoyed the tranquil interludes more than Emily enjoyed the vacationing.

——— ✦ ———

After cramming the house with clothes and collectibles, Emily coveted a larger home. She had run out of space. Walls were covered; closets and corners and cupboards were full. Quentin would have thought nothing of finding artwork attached to the ceilings. Emily carped that he did not care one whit about her imposing collections. It was true; Quentin considered them to be disposable doodads.

"Is this a home or a museum?" Quentin asked once, whereupon Emily told him peevishly that he had no feel for beauty.

Her own barometer for measuring beauty was associated with the size of the price tag. "Isn't this an exquisite red-winged blackbird? It cost $300."

When she could not persuade him that the accessories added splendor to their home, she tried to convince him that they were wise investments. "These articles go up in value, you know. Next year this Camellia will be worth twice as much."

Quentin remained unimpressed. Nor did he have any wish to buy a bigger house to lodge the investments. Would Emily use the extra room to spread out her paraphernalia more tastefully, or would she gather more objects until the larger, new house became as congested as the old one? As he expected, the latter speculation came to pass. Emily found a ten-room colonial mansion, and within a year after they moved they were living in a bigger and better museum.

His objections to her purchases were mild, however, because he did not care what she did with the money he earned, as long as the children were well-tended and their education was secure. He was apathetic regarding the house, but he was adamant about his downtown office. He declined Emily's repeated offers to decorate his reception room, because he thought it would be unethical to give his patients headaches the minute they walked in the door.

At home Emily played a *carte blanche* role. Quentin assumed that the new house pleased her, since she had selected it by herself. But when a guest remarked, "This is a splendid house," Quentin heard Emily respond, "I'd like it better if the windows were larger, and the bedrooms were two feet wider."

Later, when he asked her why she did not search longer if the house was not completely satisfactory, his query unleashed a vitriolic reply: "Why can't you tell what's wrong with places! I have eyes, I can see that any house could be improved. You wouldn't give a hoot if you lived in a tent! Your being so lackadaisical means you're not making any effort to grow. If it weren't for me, Doc, do you know where we'd be? We'd be living in our old house with threadbare rugs and worn-out sofas. Why, you'd never buy a new suit if I didn't throw out the old one. You don't really want anything!"

At this moment I just want peace, thought Quentin. To achieve it, he said no more.

But Quentin had become mindlessly accustomed to Emily, and he endured her ways with little pain. The overwhelming tragedy in his life, haunting his soul even when he was busy, involved his second child, his daughter Cynthia. Where was she now? The only time he had ever been sorry he was a doctor was when sixteen-year-old Cynthia had taken packets of drugs from his office and distributed them to friends in her high-school class. Two years later, on the evening of her eighteenth birthday, she had left home.

He had relived that grim night a thousand times. He remembered how jittery Cynthia had been at the dinner table. Her dark hair was unkempt; her dungarees were wrinkled and frayed. She had run upstairs right after picking nervously at her supper. Then Emily had brought out an elaborately adorned birthday cake, and called her to come down. Just as Emily and Rupert were lighting the candles, Cynthia entered the room with a large suitcase.

"I'm eighteen now and I'm leaving," she said in a breathless monotone.

The ample size of her carrying-bag made her thin short frame seem tinier than its five-foot-one reality. She did not look happy at the prospect of gaining her independence; she looked more like a scared young doe.

Emily glared at her, and then asked, "Would you like a piece of your birthday cake before you go?", as if Cynthia were going to the corner store for a soda.

"No, thanks," said Cynthia in that same lusterless voice. "Good-bye."

Seven-year-old Rupert, to whom birthday cake was still one of life's Important Happenings, implored, "Aw, c'mon, Cynthia, you have to blow out the candles." He jumped up and handed her a small, crudely wrapped package. "I made you a present," he said. "Happy birthday!" He stood first

22

on one foot and then the other, waiting impatiently for her to open it.

"Thanks a lot, Rupie," said Cynthia. She was unable to control a teardrop rolling down her cheek. She put down her bag and unwrapped a little ring that Rupert had formed out of wire. Slipping it on her shaking finger, she kissed him and hugged him so hard that he had to catch his breath.

Quentin, who until then had been stunned into silence, suddenly leaped out of his chair. His customary composure had vanished. "What do you mean, good-bye?" he shouted. "Where are you going? You'll be graduating from high school in four months!"

"Dad, there's not a chance I could make graduation. I'm failing three subjects."

Every detail of the scene was permanently etched in Quentin's memory. Emily was standing at the table, where she had risen to cut the showy birthday cake, its festive look now incongruous. "If you leave now, young lady," she cried, "don't come crawling back here when you have no place else to go. You've been nothing but trouble these past two years with your pot-smoking and your zero school-marks and that spaced-out boyfriend who used to hang around here with his bloodshot eyes."

Like a musical score reaching a crescendo, Emily's voice swelled as she proceeded. "And actually stealing drugs from your own father! I'm ashamed that I raised a daughter who would do such things. Now you say you're leaving before you graduate. Do you think you're qualified for a job? Don't you know you need a high-school diploma to do *anything?*" She was waving the cake knife around in the air as she yelled, but she never left her place at the table.

Answering none of the questions, Cynthia said a second soft "good-bye" and started for the door. Quentin ran after her.

"Cynthia, please, can't we talk? Can't we work something out?" And as she kept walking, he said agitatedly, "Let me give you some money if you're hellbent on leaving. And please, tell me, where on earth are you going?"

There was the faintest glimmer of a smile. "Dad, I'll get by."

Then he had followed her out the door and received another shock. Josh, Cynthia's infamous boyfriend, was sitting in a dilapidated old car in front of the house. He was wearing a dirty sweatshirt, torn at the neck, and he was looking smug and smoking a cigarette. The boy had always appeared to be under the influence of drugs or alcohol. For the past six months Quentin had not seen Josh at all, and he had assumed that Cynthia was no longer dating him.

Josh sat there smoking, his eyes half closed. He did not say 'hello.' He did not get out of the car to help Cynthia with her heavy suitcase. Earsplitting rock music blared from the radio.

Cynthia opened the back door, and Quentin put her baggage in the car. He was used to feeling helpless, when patients died or illnesses were beyond treatment, but he had never before felt so overcome with defeat. Almost in a trance, he hugged Cynthia and pleaded, "Promise you'll call me and keep in touch."

She made no promises. She kept her eyes cast down, as though she were afraid to see her father's face. "Good-bye, Dad." She already sounded far away.

The car drove off with a sickening screech. If Josh had been a green-headed Martian in a saucer-shaped UFO, the scene could not have seemed more unreal to Quentin.

He felt like the victim of a hit-and-run driver, left on the street to die. He stared at his right hand. He could not believe that he had placed his beloved daughter's luggage in that character's automobile. I'm an accessory to the crime, he thought. Why didn't I pull her away and shout, 'No, no, you can't go'?— Because she's eighteen, that's why. She could go.

When he came indoors, choking back a sob, life was continuing serenely. Emily and Rupert were eating Cynthia's birthday cake. A large piece of cake had been put at his place at the table, as if nothing had happened and Cynthia would be back any minute for her party.

Quentin could understand seven-year-old Rupert: at that age, a big cream-filled birthday cake would take momentary precedence over a grown sister going away. Rupert had witnessed his sister Gwendolyn departing for college with much luggage, and subsequently returning home for holidays. No doubt he perceived little difference with Cynthia's leave-taking. But Emily? Emily—Cynthia's mother—was sitting there munching her lost daughter's birthday cake and ordering Rupert to take his elbows off the table. Quentin gaped at the absurd spectacle, then trudged up the stairs to his bedroom, closed the door, and wept.

— ·— ▪◆▪ —· —

When the family heard from Cynthia after a year, her letter was a mishmash of incoherence, a dismal testimony of continued drug abuse. There was a post-office box address in New York City, and Quentin had written her a long, loving letter, explaining that he would be more than willing to send her to any rehabilitation center of her choice. He had included one of the most difficult sen-

25

tences he had ever composed: *'If it would please you, I will be glad to send Josh too.'*

There was no reply. Had Cynthia resented his well-meaning offer? Maybe he had not made it clear that he loved her just as she was, but wanted desperately for her to be happy. His carefully worded second letter was returned, marked 'Left No Address.' A terse, impersonal notice, rubber-stamped on the envelope by a postal employee, but to Quentin those three ink-smudged words were ominous. They kept repeating in his brain, like a nightmare recording that could not be erased.

Several months after that, Cynthia had called him from a pay phone during office hours, saying she had moved but giving him no address when he asked. When he blurted out, "Cynthia, what are you doing? Are you all right?", she evaded his questions and rushed to end the call. "I just phoned to see how everyone is. 'Bye, Dad. Tell Rupie I'm wearing his ring." That was all. Was she holding back tears? Or was he projecting his own sorrow and imagining a slight catch in her voice?

Emily had seemingly managed to put Cynthia out of her consciousness, an attitude that Quentin could not fathom. Despite the lack of certain wifely attributes, Emily had been a good mother to the children—listening to them, watching over their activities, and disciplining them when necessary. She played no favorites in shopping to locate the clothes and other articles that each girl preferred. As for Cynthia's and Gwendolyn's separate bedrooms, they were decorated in equally tasteless profusion.

Yet when Quentin wanted to discuss Cynthia, Emily was able to say, coldly, "It was Cynthia's choice to walk out of our lives. She is no longer a daughter of mine." In fact, Emily had made a suggestion, appalling to Quentin, that they remove Cynthia's name from their wills.

At a large benefit party for the local hospital, Quentin overheard Emily telling a stranger that she had only two children. When he questioned her about it later, she retorted, "What did you want me to say? 'Oh, yes, I also have a pot-head daughter who shacks up with her boyfriend in New York City'? I suppose if Cynthia walked in here right this minute, you'd kill the fatted calf and have a party."

"For the return of my daughter," said Quentin, almost in a whisper, "you bet I would."

"It's not going to happen, Doc, so stop dreaming. I have put Cynthia out of my mind, and you would be wise to do the same."

Quentin drove home slowly after his house call. His pregnant patient had lost her first baby, a girl, in her sixth month. He had treated the distraught woman, and sent her to the hospital; then he had stayed with her there for another hour. Although he had not lost any children before birth, he felt that he understood the heartbreak of losing a daughter.

As he approached his house, he saw that lights were still on in Emily's room and Emily's bathroom. He did not want to face Emily just then. He was thankful that tonight was not bridge night, which would have meant walking past the living room and greeting ten or eleven smiling women whose names he had forgotten. He parked the car in front of the house and sat there. He decided to wait until Emily's lights went out.

He peered up and down the street at the yards and houses decorated for Christmas. Santa Claus was leaning heavily on the chimney next door, resting from his steep climb to the rooftop without a flying sleigh.

Sincerely Yours

Quentin's thoughts drifted to Alex Southerick's Christmas card.

I wonder why Alex needs $10,000. Maybe he's doing something he always wanted to do. Some special quest. I hope he makes it.

Poor Alex. I could have sent you the money easily if you had asked me before I became successful. That might sound like a contradiction, but in the old days I wasn't besieged with patients and I handled the checkbook myself.

Quentin considered sending a check to Alex from his office account. He knew that a personal loan did not belong in his medical records, and that it would confuse the balances for Mrs. Islas as well as for his tax accountant. And would it be worth the furor later when Emily discovered the entry, as she inevitably would? She knew the details of his income and outgo better than he did. He was aware that she periodically examined his business books and check stubs.

Strangely, through all the years of spending and screaming, Quentin had not once contemplated divorce from Emily. In his practice he had deemed many illnesses to be psychosomatic, either caused or aggravated by home upsets of one kind or another; and he had made an almost subconscious decision not to subject his children to the traumatic experience of separated parents.

And now Cynthia was gone, perhaps forever. The last time he had heard from her was four months ago, and she had said, "This is Cyn. Oh, that's my new nickname. You can spell it s-i-n if you like; wouldn't that be appropriate?" Her hollow, self-deprecatory laugh still rang in his ears. If only it had been a joyful laugh, his frequent recollection of it would not hurt so much. He ached to see her and talk to her at length. He was adept at sorting out problems for his patients. Numerous people sought him out for advice about

28

their trials. How had he failed his own daughter? If she were seriously addicted, how had she hidden it from him, a doctor? He had cautioned other parents about the telltale signs of drug abuse, and yet he had not noticed them in Cynthia.

He reviewed his mistakes. He had judged Cynthia to be an inquisitive teenager who had tried smoking marijuana experimentally a couple of times. When she had taken drugs from his office, he had blamed excessive influence from her associates. Then, when Josh stopped coming to the house, he had jumped to the conclusion that Cynthia's temporary fixation with 'the wrong crowd' was over. It was clear that he had never accurately assessed the depth of his daughter's affliction. Not even in his most abject moments had he foreseen any rash moves like the one Cynthia had made.

Firstborn daughter Gwendolyn had been a precocious child; she was now a brilliant polymath in her world of academia. She would soon be graduating from college, and she had already been accepted to medical school. It was no fault of Gwendolyn's that she had consistently outperformed her sister Cynthia. In school Gwendolyn had earned straight A's seemingly without trying, while Cynthia hovered between C's and D's.

But Cynthia was smart too, in her own way. She showed me up when she was five years old and I was at my wits' end trying to put her doll carriage together. That pint-sized rascal picked up my tools and assembled it herself.

And just last year, when we couldn't get a locksmith, she fixed the front-door lock. I can fix a broken arm, but I couldn't fix that wretched lock.

No wonder she had all A's in her Auto Mechanics course. Her teacher said she was the brightest student he ever had. But then she failed math and English and history.

Had they praised Gwendolyn too often? Had they compared too much? Did Cynthia simply give up trying to compete with her gifted sister? Quentin recalled hearing Emily make a few comments to relatives about Gwendolyn: "She was writing sonnets at nine." "When she was in the fourth grade, she could read Shakespeare." But such pronouncements were rare, and he had not felt that they were overdone. Had he been too nearsighted to notice whether these occasional remarks made in front of Cynthia were discouraging to the child? It seemed to him that as a youngster Cynthia had laughed and frolicked much more than studious Gwendolyn.

If I favored either one of my daughters, I think it was Cynthia. When she was little I held her and hugged her twice as much as Gwendolyn. Perhaps it was because Cynthia was always there, ready to be bounced or piggy-backed, while Gwendolyn was in a corner with a dozen books...

After a while he looked up and saw that the house was dark. Even the electric Christmas candles in the windows had been extinguished. He pulled the car into the garage and closed the garage door slowly, taking care to make no sound.

Like a man who has been out late for illicit reasons, he took his shoes off and crept stealthily up the stairs. He reached his own room, his sole haven for at-home peacefulness. When Gwendolyn had vacated this room for a college dormitory, he had suggested that he use the room himself. He told Emily that she might like separate bedrooms so she would not be disturbed when he came home from late night calls. She had not minded at all. Her answer was, "Of course I'll have to redecorate our two rooms."

His initial hope was that his room would not be papered in red cabbage roses like the ones that bedecked their joint bedroom. What he gazed at now was a wallpaper that he

30

Gertrude Wood

was sure a salesperson had sold to Emily as the quintessence of masculinity. It showed repeated hunting scenes: a tight-lipped man pointing his gun, and a dog retrieving a dead bird of some kind, over and over again in a dull gray-and-brown pattern, the dogs relentlessly carrying their birds around the walls, and across the matching draperies and bedspread. Quentin loathed hunting. He loathed the wall-paper. Given a choice, he would have settled for red cabbage roses.

The first thing he did whenever he entered his room was to declare a no-hunting zone by turning down the dead-bird bedspread. Underneath was a plain gray blanket.

He had just started to take off his socks when he heard Emily's footsteps. She sometimes popped in, when she heard Quentin come home, to voice a few neglected thoughts. He groaned under his breath when he heard the familiar knock, followed by the opening of the door.

"And furthermore," she said, as if he had never left, "if you'll read Alex Southerick's note over and think about it, you'll see that there's something mighty peculiar about the wording. Alex wants the money with no signatures or loan contract. What if he drops dead in the meantime? Nobody would know we loaned him any money. Did you consider that? You have patients dying all the time, and then come the hassles trying to get their bills paid. You should think a little, Doc."

Quentin squared his shoulders and sat taller on the bed. "I have a surprise for you, my dear," he said. "I have been thinking more than a little. I have been thinking a whole lot. The letter from Alex Southerick, and your reaction to it, have caused me to take a good hard look at my objec-tives. It turns out that I agree with you that we need every cent of money we have. Right now, I have neither the strength nor the inclination to fight you on secondary

31

issues. Therefore, you win about Alex Southerick, and you may write him anything you wish."

This statement brought a triumphant little smile to Emily's lips; she appeared quite satisfied. But Quentin continued to speak. "In the past you have bought whatever you wanted to sit on, step on, wear, or collect. Plates and spoons we hang up and don't eat with, and bells we don't ring. You won our discussion about moving into this overgrown house. A house full of glass tulips and bug-eyed blue jays. You have always won every debate, partly because you're a screamer and I'm not, but mostly because I never really cared very much."

Emily was hardly listening to Quentin. Her goal had been reached; her mind was busy contriving a note full of excuses to send to Alex Southerick. But she came to attention when Quentin's speech took on an authoritative quality she had not heard since the first year of their marriage.

"*This* time, however, I care a great deal. And I am telling you in advance, don't bother to argue with what I am about to say." Quentin spoke slowly, underlining the words with his voice. "I'm glad you have ample clothing to keep you warm through the next decade or two, because there won't be any money for you to spend on new garments for a long time. The venture I have decided on will be costly, so the rest of your redecorating will also have to be forgotten or postponed indefinitely. I am acutely aware that even after spending piles of money, my undertaking might not be successful. You don't need to point that out to me. I am going ahead with it in any case, and you will not change my mind if you holler from now till doomsday. Listening to you invent one excuse after another for Alex Southerick made me resolve not to accept any arguments whatsoever about this. If my income isn't adequate, we may even have to cash in some of our valuable birdies."

Emily stared. Quentin went on.

"Tomorrow I am hiring full-time private detectives to try to locate our beloved daughter Cynthia. New York is a vast city, and it could take years..." He paused and lowered his eyes. "Or it could be never," he said huskily. "But maybe they will find her, and maybe—just a slight, possible, glorious maybe—she will be ready to come home. And then my fervent hope is that we can save her."

Armies of words marched up to Emily's throat and were swallowed, fallen soldiers in her Pyrrhic victory.

Quentin still talked.

"After I find Cynthia, I might open up a clinic for drug addicts. Who knows? I have to do first things first."

It was so curious to see Emily open-mouthed yet speechless.

Mr. and Mrs. Bartholomew Rambell
443 Appledale St.
Danview, N.C.
28724

3

Bart hated mail. No matter how humdrum, mail raised his blood pressure and aggravated his ulcers. Sometimes it made him chew his fingernails. To help keep his anatomy intact, Lilibeth scheduled her activities so that she could arrive home before him, scoop up the day's mail, and dispose of all but the most harmless-looking circulars.

Bart suspected everybody of everything. He said sales brochures were Communist plots to promote foreign merchandise. Increased sales of goods from overseas would cause mass domestic unemployment, which in turn would make the American public more vulnerable to subversive suggestions.

When Lilibeth pooh-poohed such ideas, Bart said she was incredibly simple-minded. In his more tolerant moods, he called her 'Miss Naivety,' or 'Lili-hoopoe,' after the hoopoe, a European bird that is particularly easy to catch. But when his irritation was intense, he lectured. He avowed that Lilibeth's brain was incapable of grasping the intricacies of direct-mail advertising and media programming.

Lilibeth was a Phi Beta Kappa member, but Bart maintained that this distinction had not given her the key to proper judgment of the evils around her. "Go back to your Brownie Scouts," he would say when Lilibeth refused to endorse his bleak views of humanity. "You hit the appropriate age level when you decided to work with them."

Brownie-level Lilibeth managed a smooth-running household of six persons, as well as a towering load of volunteer responsibilities. In her spare time she handled the family bills and kept a balanced checkbook. She had freed Bart from these latter duties when she became pregnant with her first daughter, Natalie, and left her laboratory-research position to be a homemaker.

In the early years of the Rambells' marriage, before Lilibeth initiated her mail-scooping regimen, every incoming piece of mail that Bart surveyed brought forth a caustic remark:

"Here's a 'free check' for $300 off any used car in The Auto Man's lot. They forgot to mention that they added $300 to last week's prices in order to send us this gigantic discount."

"This is a cheapie—only $975 per person for a two-day investment seminar given by a group of prominent economists. A real steal—and that's a superlative choice of words. They don't know any more about risking my money than I do. Listen to their initial gem of advice: invest a wad of money in their course, although you can read the same material in books and magazines."

"Look here, a form letter from our Congressman. He is gathering opinions from us, his plebeian constituents, to enable him to vote according to our desires. Actually he will vote according to the best way to get reelected. Just remember one thing, Lilibeth: everyone is out for himself— *Numero Uno.*"

He likened health-food companies to the hawkers of yesteryear, who stood on street corners and yodeled the praises of a bottled panacea guaranteed to cure diabetes, rheumatism, tuberculosis, and athlete's foot. "If you poured some on your head, it would take care of baldness too," said Bart. "But nowadays, as the populace becomes more educated, so do the peddlers. The pills and the schemes have to get more and more sophisticated, so that even highly intelligent people will swallow both."

Lilibeth sometimes agreed with Bart's evaluation of the mail, but said little, because any small word of agreement encouraged an hour-long dissertation on the omnipresence of wickedness. Lilibeth had a one-sentence personal philosophy: why think the worst when one can think the best? When she asked Bart that question, however, he answered impatiently, "Because you have to be aware of what's going on, to avoid being duped. Your approach is overly simplistic. You are a textbook model of what the racketeers and the Communists want: individuals who don't think much, and let events happen by default. Wars, crime, dictatorships—people like you close their eyes to the blatant clues in their mailboxes, or on television. They believe iniquities will vanish of their own accord."

After six or seven years of expostulation brought on by the daily mail, Lilibeth started, in gradual steps, to get rid of most of the mail while Bart was at work. She always left the monthly bills and one or two selected letters on the hall table, so that Bart would not accuse the mailman of skipping the house altogether. She did not bring up the subject of mail unless she needed a response to an invitation.

Bart did not seem to miss wading through profuse quantities of mail. Perhaps he thought his name had been removed from mailing lists because he and Lilibeth were not customers. More likely his attention was focused on significant events that happened during the same year that Lilibeth started her mail-disappearing act: a second daughter, Edith, was born; and Bart was promoted to loan manager of the bank where he worked.

When the volume of mail tripled in December, Lilibeth made no effort to conceal the abundant Christmas cards. She hung photocopied newsletters on the kitchen bulletin board, and she made displays out of the cards, even though they gave rise to sarcasm from her husband.

"Can't you see that this card madness is nothing but commercial propaganda? It's phony!" he declared, year after year. "The presidents of the card companies printing these religious-looking cards—they probably don't even believe in God! What they believe in is making money. That's what Christmas is all about—the stores making money on you and millions of other gimps."

Bart's iconoclastic views about Christmas did not ruffle Lilibeth's composure. And Bart, despite his ranting and raving, always relented and bought superb Christmas gifts for Lilibeth and the children. Although he insisted that Christmas had become totally commercialized, he had no desire to sadden the members of his beloved family on a day that gave them so much joy. "I wasn't hypnotized by the hoopla," he would explain as he distributed the packages. "I'm glad to buy you presents any day of the year."

Though it was not consciously planned as an antidote for Bart's paranoia, Lilibeth kept balance in her life by involving herself in volunteer work. Here she met men and women with optimistic attitudes that were more in tune with her own.

In Girl Scouting she had advanced along with her four daughters. She had started out as a Brownie leader, with trepidation, when Natalie had pleaded to join a troop and there were no leaders in the area. Natalie was now fifteen and a senior Girl Scout with prospects of future leadership. Edith, twelve, had dropped out of Scouting after five years because she wanted to pursue sports.

Sincerely Yours

Winifred, at ten, liked to study nature and earn Girl Scout badges, though she shunned her schoolwork; and six-year-old Denise had recently become the fourth Rambell to begin Scout life as a Brownie. Lilibeth was leading Denise's troop for the same reason she had initiated her Scouting career: a dearth of volunteers. But during the intervening years she had changed her status from novice to expert, and today she served as a state officer as well.

Bart often spoke disparagingly about Lilibeth's volunteer services. When she joined the local Rescue Squad as a telephone dispatcher, working four hours a week to handle emergency calls, he said, "Those people love to race through town and make everybody get out of their way, while their lights flash and their sirens scream. It's a kind of power, it's their sort of excitement."

Lilibeth knew that her fellow Squad members were motivated by compassion, but she also knew that nothing she could say would alter Bart's sentiments.

—•— ▆◆▊ —•—

Rushing home from an afternoon Girl Scout meeting, Lilibeth was dismayed by the lateness of the hour and the large amount of mail stuffed in her mailbox. Bart's job seldom deviated from its nine-to-five pattern; she knew she had only a few minutes to hide the bulk of the mail before Bart arrived home. But as she dropped her armload of envelopes on the living-room sofa, she could see Christmas cards sliding out from between the catalogs. She delighted in the annual exchange of greetings between old friends, and she could not resist the temptation to open some cards.

She heard Bart's car in the driveway just as she was reading the novel message on Alex and Marcia Souther-ick's card. At first she was speed-reading, anticipating the customary 'happy holiday' tidings. Then she became so intrigued she did not even bother to shove the other mail into a cupboard. '...*I don't want to borrow this money from a bank...*' She was still studying the note when Bart strode into the living room.

"What happened?" he bellowed, staring at the envelopes and circulars that surrounded his wife. He was no longer accustomed to seeing such a heap of mail in his own home. "Did you open a branch post office?"

Lilibeth thought the Southericks' Christmas card would be a perfect distraction. "Look at this," she said, evading his questions.

Bart read the note. He let out a long, low whistle. "So smart old Alex Southerick is bankrupt," he commented. "But if he's so strapped he doesn't have $10,000 of his own, how can he get it by January 10th?"

"He must have investments that are coming due early in the new year."

"Why the hocus-pocus then? If this is legitimate, why doesn't he say, 'I have a sizable certificate reaching maturity in January'?"

"I guess he prefers to keep his financial affairs to himself. Or it could be for something so profitable he knows others would want to get in on it, and for some reason he can't let anyone else take part. And he doesn't like to say 'no' to his friends."

"Lili-hoopoe, I know you think everyone is as pure as the driven snow, but I smell a rat. I don't like the fact that he doesn't tell us why he wants the money—my kids need braces, or my wife needs a liver transplant. And I don't care one bit for this injunction that no one should ask any questions."

"There again," said Lilibeth, "some people regard their medical history as confidential. Anyway, it's not material—he says the money will be returned in a month."

"Yeah sure, they always say they'll pay it back right away. How else are they going to get you to lend it? Remember when the paper-boy borrowed ten dollars for a skateboard? He looked up at you and promised that you could take a portion of it out of his paper-money for the next twenty weeks. Two weeks later he quit the paper route and we never saw him again. It wasn't a large sum, it was the principle of the thing. In any case, this letter isn't legal. It doesn't even include a full signature, just 'Alex.' Could be Alex Whatchamacallit for all a court would know."

"But the other side of the Christmas card is signed 'Alex and Marcia Southerick.' That would clarify who Alex is."

"No, Miss Naivety, the note itself has to have the complete signature. Alex and Marcia Southerick are only wishing you a Merry Christmas, and Alex Anonymous is pledging to return the money."

"I don't see why it's not legal. The whole note is written in his handwriting," Lilibeth said.

"You assume it is. You don't really know. It's not notarized. It could be his wife's handwriting. Could be one of the children, or his secretary. We don't know who's been writing out their Christmas cards all these years."

"You went to college with Alex; don't you recall his handwriting?"

"Oh come on, from over twenty years ago? Do you recall the penmanship of *your* classmates?"

"No, I don't. That was silly," she admitted. "Now that you mention it, this *is* a different handwriting from other years' cards. But our jabbering about legality and signatures and handwriting is academic. As if we would ever take our old friends into court! Besides, I know that Marcia would never let Alex do anything crooked. She's as straight as an arrow."

"What do you mean, 'let'? She might not know a single thing about it. Alex enclosed his business card and wants the money sent to his office, not to his home. That sounds to me as if Marcia has not been informed of this little loan. Wives don't necessarily know what illegal tricks their husbands might be up to."

"I'm sure Alex's loan is not illegal in any way," said Lilibeth. "But I do wonder why he sent this request to us. He must have lots of closer friends."

"For once you're thinking. We haven't seen these old buddies for five years, since my last class reunion. And how about relatives? Alex has at least two sisters, and I think a brother. Doesn't one of them live near him in Chicago? That's another indication that this note isn't on the up-and-up. Alex doesn't want to bilk his intimate friends and relatives."

Lilibeth was sorry she had asked. "It's possible he doesn't want associates in his vicinity to hear that he's in a bind. We're far away and not in frequent touch, so it doesn't matter as much that we know."

"You mean it doesn't matter as much that we get taken. Honey, at the bank I hear about loads of white-collar charlatans. I'm coping with mortgage interest and embezzlement while you're picking wildflowers with the Brownies. I can say with authority that this letter has all the earmarks of a racket.

"Let's say a number of couples send him a thousand bucks, no loan contract, no anything. Then comes January, February, March, and nobody gets a dime back. Alex is in Chicago, and his victims are in various parts of the country, like us here in North Carolina. Laws vary from state to state, and it seems like a pain in the neck to sue somebody from a distance. And most people wouldn't want to broadcast that they were rooked so easily—makes them sound dense. Then another thought strikes—hey, the lawyer will probably charge more than the $1,000 he's trying to retrieve. Therefore, all things considered, they'll sit back and do nothing.

"But let's suppose one or two couples start suit proceedings, or go to a claims court. Do you think this brief note on a Christmas card would hold up? I can just hear the judge: 'You mean to say you sent off a $1,000 loan with no signed agreement for repayment?' You'd probably be committed to a mental institution. And Alex already knows all this. Don't forget, he was our valedictorian, he was the top brain in a college class of over 2000. And when you think about it, this is a pretty ingenious ruse."

Bart shook his head, clucked his disapproval, and went on. "Imagine that, brilliant Alex Southerick involved in a fraud. It ties in with a piece I read in last month's *Magazine of Banking*, that a large percentage of criminals have high IQ's and are classified as 'gifted.' The article said they have the intelligence and imagination to either improve the world, or carry off a spectacular crime.

"Alex is in the genius category; he could easily fabricate a clever operation. Before graduation, the class elected him 'Most Likely to Succeed,' but I don't think anyone thought that he'd use his intellect to succeed as a con man. But what could be shrewder than inveigling a thousand bucks from everybody on his Christmas-card list? Neat way to make a cool $200,000."

"Bart, it says right here he's asking only ten couples, and he only needs $10,000."

"Lili-hoopoe, you are impossible! It could say anything! Swindlers are not famous for their honesty. But even if he's small potatoes, and the total he's trying to hoodwink is only $10,000, it's clearly not on the level."

"It's not clear to *me*. Personally, I can't see Alex in the role of an impostor."

"You, my dear, could not see anyone in the role of an impostor. If you had to identify a thief in a police lineup, you'd say the whole row looked like Snow White and the Seven Dwarfs. If you're ever selected for jury duty, you should beg off on the grounds that you were born with implanted rose-colored glasses. But facts are facts, and this note from Alex does not stand up to scrutiny by a normal person." He sat thinking for a moment, and then he added, "I never could put my finger on it, but years ago I thought there was something out-of-the-way about Alex. He had a peculiar expression around his mouth."

Lilibeth was tired of hearing an old friend degraded. "I can see we're not sending a check," she said resignedly. "But in my opinion Alex needs some money, plain and simple. And I don't agree with you about Alex's mouth—I thought he had a fine mouth."

"Naturally. You'd probably say that Al Capone had soulful eyes and lovely matching crow's feet."

Lilibeth dismissed the remark. "How do we handle our Christmas card to the Southericks?"

"Send a card right back with an ordinary note—they'll think it crossed in the mail. Better do it tonight so that not too much time passes."

Lilibeth followed instructions, but she could not transmit her customary élan as she wrote in an expressionless manner on a glittering Christmas card:

Dear Marcia and Alex,

Hope things are going well for you and your family. We have no big news this year. The children are growing up fast. I can't believe my 'baby' had her sixth birthday last week. We are in fine health. Have a Merry Christmas.

She signed and sealed it, but she felt like a hypocrite. After a minute she opened the card, re-read it, threw it in the wastebasket, and wrote another card omitting the sentence *'Hope things are going well for you and your family.'*

On the night Lilibeth wrote the return Christmas card to the Southericks, she suffered a rare case of insomnia. Her mind raced as she lay in bed.

What a typical reaction from Bart! He could read wrong-doing between every line of Alex Southerick's letter. Why is Bart so suspicious of everything? What's the difference if Christmas-card manufacturers believe in God or not? Can't Bart see that a vast amount of good comes out of people sending joyful greetings to each other?

Lilibeth tossed and turned and found herself thinking about Bart in relation to dogs.

"Poochie's your soul-mate," he had told her more than once when talking about the family's mongrel pet. Poochie had never been known to bark at anyone; in fact, much to Bart's disgust, he was ready to frolic with every passer-by. Poochie broke all the rules of dogdom and even nuzzled mailmen.

With the exception of Poochie, Bart's skepticism about humanity extended to animals. In addition to enjoining Lilibeth and the children not to talk to strangers, Bart was forever cautioning them not to pet stray dogs.

Lilibeth claimed that a wagging tail and a cute expression were reliable indicators of a dog's friendly nature. Bart said he could probably line up cute dogs from here to China that had bitten witless mortals who had supposed the doggies were too lovable to be nasty.

"What about that dainty little Pekingese monster that almost took off my leg?" he asked during one of many discussions with the same theme.

"She was so sharp she could tell with one glance that you didn't like her," defended Lilibeth.

"True, I disliked her, but at least I didn't express my lack of devotion by chomping off her leg. She was sharp all right, mostly in the teeth area. And, she was wagging her tail fast and furiously the whole time she was sinking her fangs into my flesh. You can't trust a wagging tail any more than you can trust a beaming salesman."

"Well, I've lived this long without being bitten by a dog or hit over the head by a salesman," Lilibeth responded.

"Don't plan on living to a ripe old age, if you don't mend your habits. This country is getting worse by the hour."

"It does seem as if there are more housebreakers these days," Lilibeth conceded. Bart was heartened. Perhaps I'm making progress—she's becoming more informed, he thought.

Lilibeth continued, "That's why I've stopped reading the newspapers—they're full of violence."

Bart moaned as she went on, "But anyhow, animals don't change. I'm sure the percentage of mean dogs to nice dogs is the same as it ever was. Mostly nice."

"Mostly mean," said Bart.

—————————

Instead of counting sheep to get to sleep, I'll count Bart's good points. Most people have seen only his cynical side, because that's the part of his temperament that's in the foreground. They haven't seen him sitting up until three o'clock in the morning with a croupy baby, or placating a scared little girl on the way to the dentist's chair.

He has always been a dedicated father, and he tries strenuously to protect the girls—and me—from harm. Of course he overdoes it—he worries about every breath we take—but that's better than if he didn't care at all. How cheerfully our daughters take him in stride, even when they differ with him. They know instinctively that he loves them, and that he would like the world to be devoid of bandits and mean dogs just for them.

Bart could answer a resounding 'yes' to the familiar query, 'Do you know where your children are tonight?' He willingly chauffeured his daughters to their evening activities, relieving Lilibeth who handled the daytime stint.

He was attentive to his daughters in other ways as well. Convinced of the demoralizing effect of watching too much television, he planned what he felt were more healthful pursuits. He believed that many television programs were created by anti-morality groups that glorified depravity; or by money-hungry moguls who concerned themselves exclusively with profits, without any regard for the nation's moral structure. His solutions included family ping-pong contests, old-fashioned taffy pulls, and multi-level word games around the corn-popper.

A-plus for fatherhood. Next good-point sheep: Bart rates tops for fidelity. I've gained a lot of weight, and I know I should trim off these extra pounds, but Bart never ogles other women.

Now in her mid-forties, Lilibeth had a matronly build that made her seem older. She wore her hair in a short, straight bob, which had been an attractive hairstyle before her face had become rounded with the excess weight. Her hair, figure, and wardrobe combined to make her look like a woman who had given up on beauty and opted for easy-care.

When first meeting Bart and Lilibeth, a newcomer might have wondered what Bart saw in this dowdyish creature. Bart was, without question, the more good-looking of the two. He retained a trim physique, and a head of thick wavy hair, with a slight graying at the temples that added dignity to his appearance. The same amount of gray in Lilibeth's hair added nothing but age to her looks.

Next sheep: Bart is a steady worker and a responsible provider. Not once did I have to get a job and shunt the girls off on baby-sitters. I worked for a couple of years before I got pregnant with Natalie, and Bart asked me to stay home and tend to the baby, which is precisely what I wanted to do. And we owned nothing. 'Home' was a sweltering fourth-floor walk-up in the heart of Memphis, Tennessee.

Lilibeth's mind drifted back to Alex Southerick, for it was in Memphis that Bart and Alex had renewed their college friendship, and Lilibeth had met Alex and Marcia Southerick for the first time. The relationship had flourished, and the two couples had seen each other often while they all lived there.

It was a long time ago, but I'll never forget the fun we had. The baseball games and the home-cooked spaghetti dinners, heaps of spaghetti but very little meat. And the gutter-balls when we bowled. And rushing to the movies before the prices changed at four o'clock. Two young married couples with plenty of energy but no money. One Sunday afternoon in the park the four of us together had barely enough money to buy two hot dogs, so we bought them and split them in half. Split our sides, too, laughing! I can still hear Alex saying, "We just ate our total assets." And Bart said, "Oh, I thought they were hot dogs." My, how we roared. Alex had a better job than Bart, but he already had two kids to support.

And as soon as Marcia found out I was pregnant, she gave me stacks of booties and blankets and little sleepers that Olivia had outgrown. Those baby clothes were a tremendous help.

What warmhearted friends, Alex and Marcia Southerick. I hope they're not having serious financial troubles, and I do wish Bart would lend Alex the thousand dollars he wants.

But Bart is a good person. His pessimism is hard to take sometimes, but his redeeming qualities make up for it. I love him, even though he may think I'm cooking up a foul message in the alphabet soup. No, I forgot—I'm much too naive to contrive a sinister plot. My foul message in the soup would be spelled f-o-w-l. But beware of any restaurant that serves alphabet soup! Bart should be glad he married me. He needs a woman who doesn't take him too seriously.

The next marital conversation that Lilibeth retraced in her memory evoked a smile. She had made a facetious remark to Bart: "It's lucky you weren't rich when we met, or you'd surely have suspected that I might marry you for your money, or that I might be working as an undercover agent for the I.R.S."

"I have to confess," he replied, "that I did try to analyze any possible ulterior motives."

"What ulterior motives could there have been?" she squeaked in astonishment. "You didn't have two nickels to rub together back then. Didn't you consider that my inspiration might be love?"

"Oh yes; I meant in *addition* to love."

This dialogue went back ten years or more, and the remembrance of it caused Lilibeth to chuckle. The last virtue she counted on her list of good-point sheep was "He's a wonderful lover." In the dim light of a tiny night-lamp, she glanced over to see if Bart was still awake.

———❈———

On the night Lilibeth wrote the return Christmas card to the Southericks, Bart had one of his frequent attacks of insomnia.

What a typical reaction from Lilibeth! She couldn't read a single thing between the lines of Alex Southerick's note. She would have plopped a $1,000 check in an envelope and mailed it, without using a bit of logic.

Why is Lilibeth so naive? I can't even persuade her that it's downright dangerous to open the door to strangers.

Bart had equipped his home with an intercom system so that any door could be answered while it remained locked. After learning the caller's identity, and peering through a peephole, the homeowner could either unbar the door or not. Bart clipped stories out of the newspapers that described rapes and robberies of women who had unlocked their doors for men purporting to be from authentic companies. He discussed these accounts with Lilibeth at great length, emphasizing that many of the perpetrators were wearing the proper uniforms. But Lilibeth still allowed entry to anyone who rang the doorbell, disregarding both the intercom and the peephole. She didn't do this to nettle Bart; for her it was a reflex action to open the door when the chimes sounded. She hospitably invited into the living room various salespeople, survey-takers, and religious devotees. On a hot day she would offer these unknown visitors iced tea or fruit juice. When Bart exploded, she would defend her actions: "It must be onerous to have a job traipsing from house to house like that. I'm only being polite."

"Be as polite as you want, over the intercom," retorted Bart despairingly. He was convinced that, one way or another, she would come to a dire end.

Years after the speakers had been installed, he came home from work one day to find a short dark man vacuuming his living room. The man was wearing an oversized green-and-orange plaid cap that came down to his eyes, and was perspiring as he worked.

"Oh, this is Mr. Parsonet, dear," said Lilibeth blithely. "He wants us to buy a vacuum cleaner." Bart managed to control himself, but his face became so red and distorted with the strain that Mr. Parsonet, sensing that he was somewhat unwelcome, gathered up his cleaning accessories and hastened away.

"Lilibeth, I have asked you repeatedly not to allow strangers into this house," said Bart in a stern voice.

"I know, dear, but he was such an amiable man," Lilibeth explained. Seeking to divert Bart from his wrath, she kept talking. "Did you see how clean our parlor rug is? It was a smooth-running vacuum."

"It could have been a smooth-running robbery."

"Oh, Bart, anybody could see that Mr. Parsonet was a vacuum-cleaner salesman. The first thing he did was hand me a printed identification card from his company, with his picture on it. An excellent photo, looked exactly like him, big plaid cap and all. And he had this vacuuming equipment right there next to him, on the stoop, when he rang the bell."

"Can't you comprehend that it could have been an empty vacuum shell containing a gun or a knife in place of a motor? It could also be a handy place to store jewelry and sterling silver after he had you dead or unconscious or tied up somewhere."

"Bart, you're so excitable. Didn't you notice—he had an honest face, and a lovely smile."

"The country's richest crooks are probably grinning from ear to ear," replied Bart sourly.

Remembering that episode, Bart sighed now in the semi-darkness of the bedroom.

Heaven knows, I've tried my darndest to teach her, enlighten her, open her eyes!

Bart was not getting sleepy. Thoughts about Lilibeth kept running through his head, keeping him awake.

I have to acknowledge that it was her air of wide-eyed innocence that attracted me to her from the beginning. She was the only real live ingenue I had ever met. What I didn't know was that, in Lilibeth's case, it was more than an air of innocence, it was every bone and cell in her body. I didn't know she would never become more circumspect, regardless of age. She still has the trusting outlook of a five-year-old. Our daughters are more alert to corruption than their mother.

Then came the anxieties common to chronic insomniacs.

If I died tomorrow, what would become of her? There are connivers out there who prey on gullible widows. She'd probably lose this house and everything in it within a year. Look how she fell instantly for Alex Southerick's little game.

Bart liked to think that he and Lilibeth had a symbiotic relationship.

I believe my perception pays off—for instance, tonight I was able to expose Alex's strategy and keep us from losing $1,000.

And we sure have to save our pennies to put four children through college.

Lilibeth should be glad she married me—she needs me to protect her. Some of my admonitions must sink in a bit, even if only subliminally. Perhaps it's thanks to me that she has survived to age 45.

But there are days when I need Lilibeth's optimism, just to keep going. If I come home feeling down, she makes me feel alive again, because she's always up; I can count on it. She can be lighthearted in the midst of all the vicious happenings in the news. Her mind doesn't seem to be able to center on what's wrong with the world.

Lilibeth's overtrustfulness is hard to take sometimes, but except for that, she's a treasure. As a mother, she's matchless. She has gotten heavier in the last dozen years, but somehow she still looks good to me. I guess it's that warm, pleasant expression of hers—not one low thought in her head, and it shows right on her face.

I couldn't ask for a better bed partner either... I wonder if she understands that the reason I don't want any harm to come to her is that I dearly love her.

Lilibeth had turned around to peek at Bart just as he was turning toward her.

Mr. & Mrs. Alex Southerick
2612 Kendalpark Lane
Aranda, IL 61015

Mr. and Mrs. Sidney Tullew
7075 Valley St.
Edmonfield, N.Y.
       12403

4

Snowflakes fell on dancing couples and made them neither wet nor white as they swirled around the shadowy Sin-
gles Dance floor. The dry warm snowflakes of light came
not from clouded skies, but from a mirrored rotating globe
in the center of the ceiling. Corner pin spots sometimes
colored the snowflakes red or blue or green; and all the
while the band played sentimental music, and the lead
singer cooed about love and roses, June and moonlight. In
this euphonious setting, Sidney Tullew was smitten by the
angelic face that belonged to Vivian.

Brighter lights during intermission revealed that an
earthly body was attached to the angel face. Vivian was a
divorcee whose plumpish curves were controlled with a
tight girdle. Her ash brown hair was worn close to her head
in tiny tight curls that would not quiver in a hurricane.
She had on a drab brown print dress that was adequate
though not stylish, and the costume jewelry that she wore
with it was a jangling distraction. But when she blinked
her big wondering eyes, she blanked out every other feature
and created an aura of angelic innocence.

52

Sidney, a widower, appeared deceptively youthful. His baldness was offset by his smooth, unwrinkled complexion. His well-fitted slacks were pressed to sharp precision, and his striped tie held a perfect knot. Within a year, this pair, in their middle forties, were married. Their first anniversary was coming up soon, and Sidney still regarded Vivian as an angel whose halo was always in place.

── ═♦═ ──

Sidney was a sensible man who possessed his fair share of brains, yet he was unaware that he was a frequent victim of wifely gerrymandering. For Vivian, it was automatic to parry whenever she was asked a direct question. If on a Saturday morning Sidney said, "Good morning. How are you feeling today?" she would reply, "Oh, not bad," her voice controlled to express neither apathy nor enthusiasm. The unspoken query was, "What did you have in mind?" If Sidney suggested that she help him scrape wallpaper, Vivian had an excruciating backache; but if later in the day he invited her to go swimming, her unpredictable spine was much better. ("The pain must have been brought on by early-morning humidity.") Her body's moving parts could recover or deteriorate rapidly to suit the circumstances.

Vivian and Sidney had both sold their former separate homes, and invested the proceeds in a Victorian mansion that was a potential pearl but needed much renovation. As a consequence Vivian's back (knee, wrist, shoulder) relapsed into many encore disablements.

"I'll rub your back with liniment if you like, or perhaps bed-rest is the best healer," said Sidney lovingly as he went to stain doors or dig gardens by himself. He was pleased if Vivian limped out of the bedroom an hour later and said feebly that she thought she could manage driving over to the mall to buy a new dress.

Sincerely Yours

"Glad you're feeling up to it, sweetheart," he'd be likely to say.

At other times, Vivian gazed up at him with those beautiful baby-blue eyes and sweetly offered to lend assistance, as on one Sunday when Sidney was painting the intricate wooden gingerbread on the porch. Throughout months of exhaustive house-hunting, Sidney had been captivated by Victorian architecture, and Vivian had consented to buy a house with that design, knowing that she would not ever have anything to do with its toilsome upkeep. But on this particular Sunday she 'helped' for almost thirty minutes, dribbling paint while swishing an over-laden brush sloppily in all directions.

Sidney responded on cue. "Never mind, darling, I'll do it alone," he said, eyeing the mess she had made, and the section that would have to be redone. Then he painted for the rest of the day, while Vivian manicured her fingernails and read the Sunday newspapers. New at this game, Sidney was none the wiser.

But week after week and month after month, Vivian never raised her voice or changed its honeyed tone. And Sidney found it hard to imagine why her former husband had left anyone as sweet-tempered as Vivian.

———❖———

Vivian had taken a lengthy course in the Art of Deviousness from her mother, and she had learned her lessons well. When Vivian was fifteen, her mother had advised, "There's no need to fight with a husband. There's more than one way to skin a cat. Remember those words when you get married. If you don't like to cook, don't fuss and complain about it—just burn the supper or stir up a few rank concoctions for him to eat. Ketchup in the chocolate sauce, garlic in the plum cobbler—you name it. And for

54

yourself, always have a little snack before dinner." Mother and daughter giggled, and Mama continued, "You'll find he'll take you out to eat quite often. If you bake one delicious cherry pie, you'll be in a hot kitchen making cherry pies for the rest of your life." Until this revelation, Vivian had believed that her mother lacked natural cooking ability; she had had no inkling that the family's habituation of restaurants was the result of meals that were intentionally atrocious.

Mama and Vivian laughed uproariously at this confession, and Mama gave the moral of the story: "Don't nag or scream about anything; bear in mind that you can calmly rule the roost however you like. You can do what you want, and have what you want, and yet you can be a gracious lady instead of a raucous fishwife."

Many confidences were shared by Mama during Vivian's formative years. "What a man doesn't know doesn't hurt him," declared Mom. "You know how your father insists on having pure maple syrup from Vermont for his pancakes? That stuff is not only expensive, it's hard to find. To this day Daddy's not aware that I bought one single jar of Vermont maple syrup years ago, and ever since then I've been pouring any old brand of supermarket syrup into the same container. By now he probably wouldn't know the taste of real maple syrup if he had some. He still tells people he won't eat any other topping on his pancakes, because maple syrup reminds him of his carefree boyhood days in Vermont."

Gales of laughter followed every such disclosure.

One subject was not covered when Vivian was an adolescent. Mama waited until three weeks before young Vivian's first marriage to enlighten her virgin daughter about the handiest tool in marital management: sex.

Mama had her own version of sex education: "If you want something badly—a fur coat, or a new appliance—

just hold back until you get it. Sex is the most powerful negotiating agent in the world." She finished with a sly wink, and her final words of wisdom: "Be generous only when he's generous."

Vivian—still a teenager on her wedding day—concluded that her mother's formulas for a blissful marriage were effective. The proof was in front of her: her mother and father never argued, whereas her friends' parents seemed to be squabbling constantly.

Thus, after her honeymoon, Vivian quietly contrived to be a mediocre cook. She added liberal amounts of tabasco sauce to her entrées; for dessert she mixed scoops of horseradish with vanilla ice cream. Restaurants were not affordable in the beginning years of her marriage, so in self-defense, neophyte husband Wayne volunteered more and more of his services in the kitchen. He shopped for food and taught himself how to stew and steam and simmer it. In time he was reconciled to his place at the stove. Vivian praised his cookery talents again and again while she feasted on his stuffed breast of veal and chicken à la king.

Wayne would have been astonished to hear that the eight-member Edmonfield Canasta Club rated Vivian as a superfine chef because she turned out savory quiches and soufflés for the occasional club luncheons. But that was as far as Vivian went. She did not entertain at large functions—for these, she was always a guest but never a hostess. She wangled repeated invitations from the same set of party-givers, continually promising to have the gang over for a brunch (cocktail party, holiday bash) as soon as her bursitis was better (the floors were varnished, the chairs were slipcovered).

Eventually she sent fifty invitations to a grand party that she cancelled a few days before the given date by feigning a minor accident. For the next three days she read magazines and watched television, with her self-bandaged 'sprained ankle' elevated on a hassock, while sympathetic friends stopped in with casseroles. She smiled widely at these visitors; indeed, she was barely able to keep from laughing out loud. Everyone, including Wayne, commented on her sunny disposition after such an untimely mishap. And no one noticed that she did not set a future date for her party.

———————

Vivian embraced deviousness so wholeheartedly that she used indirect overtures in matters where they served no practical purpose. If she wanted to go to the movies, she would say to Wayne, "You look as if you're carrying a load of bricks on your shoulders. You ought to relax for a couple of hours." Then, with the eagerness of an impulsive thought, she would exclaim, "I have a great idea—why don't we take in a movie?"

Wayne favored movies and would probably have answered 'yes' had she simply suggested "Let's go to the movies tonight." But the size of the issue at hand was immaterial; she liked to think her adroitness was responsible for all fruits, whether grapes or watermelons.

———————

As a newlywed, Vivian held a lackluster clerical position, which she left when she became pregnant a year after her marriage. Then motherhood, accentuated by the birth of a second son a year later, gave her scant time for anything except child-rearing. It was impossible to be devious with babies—when an infant gave a direct cry for a diaper change, Vivian was forced to give a direct response.

When Wayne was home, however, she maneuvered him into taking care of many of the children's needs without making straightforward requests. "I feel a cold coming on, so I'm trying to stay away from the baby"—delivered with an affected sneeze or sniffle—worked wonders with two o'clock feedings.

As sons Gordon and Scott grew from babies to boys, they received detailed instructions for handling Daddy. When nine-year-old Gordon wanted a bicycle, Mommy counseled, "Tell your father you'd like a deluxe ten-speed bicycle with fancy lights and brakes. You can show him a picture that we'll cut out of a catalog. He'll jump to compromise on an ordinary bicycle, and that way you'll get what you wanted in the first place, instead of a flat 'no'."

This was in line with Vivian's personal tactics: if she wanted to vacation at a nearby lake resort, she pretended to pine after world cruises; then her final selection of a close-to-home bungalow seemed like a most reasonable concession.

It was true that Vivian's ruses helped Scott and Gordon to acquire toys and bicycles as children, but if they could have foreseen the future, they would have relinquished all such childhood advantages to save themselves from later becoming puppets in the same hands.

When the boys became teenagers, Vivian calmly controlled their social activities from behind the scenes. "They shouldn't get serious with anyone till they're through with college," she said to Wayne in the low-pitched, mellifluous cadence that always put her listeners off guard.

Casual dates were allowed, but as soon as either son showed a spark of steady interest in a girl, she didn't stand a chance. While Gordon was upstairs studying, Vivian would tell Lois on the phone that he was out with Bernadette. When Lois snubbed Gordon the next day, he had no idea why. Several other young ladies in her sons' lives met the same fate.

As for Vivian, she suffered no pangs of conscience, not even when steaming open and discarding occasional love-letters addressed to her handsome offspring. "My sons' happiness comes first," she rationalized. "Everything I do for them is for their own good."

Wayne was oblivious to the household shenanigans. After a few years as a machinist, he had opened a small tool-and-die shop. Busy with operation schedules during the day, he took care of bookkeeping at home in the evenings, and his mind was full of labor rates and material costs.

He also had less time to spend in the kitchen. Vivian had long since established her reputation as a non-cook, and the family easily fell into her preconceived pattern of eating many meals in restaurants.

There was one significant domain, however, where Vivian was foiled. When she tried to use sex as a method of negotiation, Wayne was often too tired to care. He turned around and fell asleep, promptly accepting a 'no' that was meant to be conditional.

Vivian reached her zenith and her Waterloo with the same episode.

She had asked Wayne more than once to remove a towering hemlock tree that he had planted many years before, near the dining-room window. For years Wayne had fostered the tree, raving over it as it grew to be lofty and well-proportioned. In dry weather, he dragged out the garden hose after work, and watered his hemlock. Photographing it in the summer, with the boys standing next to it, was a ritual. But when the stately evergreen began to obscure the dining-room lighting, Vivian's dislike for the tree expanded as rapidly as the branches.

Sincerely Yours

"Wayne, the dining room is wall-to-wall dreary with that hulking tree standing smack in front of the window," she remonstrated for the third consecutive year. "Will you please chop it down, or have a tree surgeon remove it?"

"I'm sorry, Viv," answered Wayne, "but I've told you before, I love that tree too much. I've fed it, and watered it, and watched it grow from a sapling. I could never destroy such a majestic living thing. Have you observed that every branch of that hemlock is absolutely symmetrical?"

"I've observed that every branch gets wider and wider, and takes away more and more light. It's getting hard to observe the knives and forks."

"I'll tell you what—let's install extra fixtures in the dining room, and buy a larger chandelier. If you like, we can put indirect lighting near the ceiling to lighten up the room in the daytime. I'll do anything except cut down that tree." Wayne's voice was emphatic.

Vivian said no more, but the next day she took matters into her own hands. She drove to an out-of-town hardware store—where she wouldn't be recognized—and purchased a potent weed-killer. She mixed up a solution ten times stronger than that recommended for weeds, and poured the concoction at the base of the tree, then continued to pour many gallons of it in the soil around the tree, farther and farther out, until she had inundated a ten-foot-diameter circle. Then she found the garden sprayer and soaked the foliage.

Suddenly the once-sturdy tree was doing poorly; its branches were wilting, and the needles were turning brown at the edges.

"My hemlock looks as if it's dying," Wayne told Vivian with visible distress. "I can't figure out why; it's always been exceptionally hearty."

60

"I'm so sorry," she replied smoothly. "I know how much you love that tree."

"I'm going to give it a feeding," he said in a troubled tone. "I'll drive over to the nursery and see if they have a product specifically for evergreens." When he came back he spent the rest of the afternoon studying directions and feeding the tree.

The following week—the tree having shown no improvement—he took foliage samples to a county agricultural station for professional advice. The experts' joint opinion was that the tree was dying from an overdose of chemicals, and that it was already beyond help. Wayne found this impossible to believe. He pressed further with an expensive soil analysis. When the results furnished undeniable proof, he was beset with self-recrimination; he assumed that, despite his customary precautions, the weed-killer he had sprayed on the nearby lawn had drifted in the wind to the tree's foliage.

"I took such pains not to get anywhere near that tree," he repeated over and over, shaking his head. "And I didn't spray when it was breezy."

He slumped into a chair, and Vivian rubbed the back of his neck consolingly. "I'm sure you did everything you could," she soothed.

Wayne leaned back and took her hand. "I feel like I've lost a very dear old friend," he said. "Thanks for caring."

There probably never would have been a divorce if Wayne had not come home sick from the shop several months later at two o'clock in the afternoon. The cars parked in the driveway told him that this was Vivian's Canasta Club day. Rather than disturb his wife and her guests, he decided to enter the house through the back porch door, from which he could get to a bedroom unseen.

Rollicking laughter from the dining room greeted him as he opened the porch door. Then, as the mirth subsided, he heard Vivian's voice. She was evidently telling a humorous story.

"So we owe the brightness of this room to my ingenuity," she said, and the women laughed again. "To this day Wayne doesn't know that I poisoned the high-and-mighty hemlock tree. I wailed right along with him at the funeral." More laughter.

Wayne felt nauseated. His head was spinning. He knew he had a fever, and he wondered if he was delirious. Had he actually heard what he thought he had heard? He stumbled to the bedroom and collapsed on the bed. He stayed home sick for three days with influenza, and throughout that time he found it hard to endure Vivian's solicitous touch as she nursed him.

The first day the fever was gone, Wayne sat up in bed and asked for a divorce. Vivian stared at him and said, "I'd better take your temperature."

"No, I'm not that sick any more," assured Wayne. "I'm a bit shaky, but mentally I'm fine."

Vivian looked thunderstruck. "B-but why?" she stuttered. "What's wrong? I've always been a good wife! We don't even fight, like all the other couples we know." Feeling a surge of weakness, she sank into an armchair. "Let's talk it over," she said. She spoke jerkily, with little breaths between words. "All problems have solutions."

"In this case, the problem is that I don't like the way you arrive at solutions."

She seemed baffled, so he told her that he had overheard her sidesplitting version of 'The Killing of the Tree.' "It's bad enough that you knew how much I wanted to preserve that tree. But the things I can't get over are: first, the

62

deception; and second, the hilarity—your thinking that the whole incident was really very funny. Not a bit of remorse. And you allowed me to think I had destroyed the tree myself through carelessness. The false guilt made me twice as miserable—another belly laugh, right? I'll never again believe you are sincere about anything. My only regret is that it has taken me this long to wise up." He scanned the angelic face that denied the craftiness of the brain it shielded. Even now, he thought, she still strikes me as a woman I could trust around the world with the family silver.

Vivian, for her part, could not understand why Wayne considered her offense so grave. After all, it was only a tree, and there were a dozen others on the property. And wasn't her placid disposition of the conflict preferable to loud ugly wrangles about the tree? Didn't he give her any credit for keeping the marriage tranquil?

With practice, Vivian had outclassed even her mother, and had become the champion soft-spoken, non-argumentative wife. She had rated her marriage, quite accurately, on a par with her parents' Happy Marriage; the flaw was that she and her mother both measured happiness in noise decibels.

For the rest of her days Vivian would think the real cause of her marital failure was that Wayne loved a tree more than he loved her. "There's nobody on earth but you who would perform an autopsy on a tree," she told him with sullen disgust.

⋯ ⋙✦⋘ ⋯

Vivian detested living alone. Her sons were away— Gordon was in law school, and Scott had decided to hitchhike across the country, though she had heard he intended to return and live with his father. She weighed and rejected an invitation to move back with her parents, who had retired to Florida. And her only sibling, a brother, owned small bachelor quarters 600 miles away. Even her aging Persian cat was poor company—she lived behind the sofa except at mealtime. Vivian figured that her best recourse was to actively seek another husband.

Though Wayne had given her the house, she knew she would have to get a job to support herself. She had been an excellent student in high school, but she had married at nineteen and had acquired no special skills. After much deliberation, she decided to take a course in real estate. She passed her realty test a few weeks before the dance where she met Sidney Tullew, the man who would become her second husband. She and Sidney were married a year after their first rumba, and by then she was ranked as a leading salesperson in her territory. Within a month of the wedding she was honored at a symposium for members of the Million Dollar Club, a recognition for listing or selling two million dollars worth of real estate in one year. Though she had worked hard for this achievement, she had also benefitted from an asset that required no effort: her guileless countenance that influenced people to believe everything she said.

From the onset of her selling career she had extended her mother's theory about husbands to embody 'What a client doesn't know doesn't hurt him.' When driving prospective buyers to see houses, she took circuitous routes so that crumbling neighborhoods were not seen until long after moving day. With local customers who were acquainted with the various neighborhoods, she sometimes commented on dilapidated houses they passed: "See that small gray clapboard house on the right—the one with the peeling paint? I heard through the grapevine that it sold last month for six figures." This served to enhance the value of the house she wanted to unload.

She also kept undercover the fact that the city planned to build an elementary school on a wooded tract located behind a long row of houses, one of which she sold to an elderly couple who cherished the peaceful serenity of the forest-like background.

"It's a lovely restful place to spend your golden years," Vivian concurred, knowing the trees would soon be leveled.

The following day, she blithely applied the upcoming school as a selling point when showing a house in the same row to a young couple with preschool children.

Thus it was that Vivian, in little more than a year, rose to membership in the distinctive Million Dollar Club, made up of the finest real-estate salespeople in Edmonfield. And Sidney, a forthright agent for office furniture who knew nothing about his wife's methodology, was exceedingly proud of his choice of mate when Vivian was introduced at the dinner as 'the most likable salesperson anyone would ever want to meet.'

As a realtor, Vivian could more or less set her own hours. Since her marriage to Sidney she had voluntarily reduced her work commitments, and she compensated for scattered evening appointments by going to the office later in the morning. Early in the day she did a superficial job of straightening the house; any substantial housekeeping was on a par with her cooking, inferior by design, with Sidney unflaggingly correcting the deficiencies.

One thing she did before leaving for work was to sort the mail. She placed bills to pay, and letters to be answered, in neat manila file folders. She invariably culled several items to withhold from Sidney, because she might want to broach him deviously about invitations or furniture markdowns and the like.

On the morning of December 14th, the heap of mail consisted mostly of Christmas cards. Vivian glanced at her watch and decided to quickly open the cards before setting out for the office. She stopped when she came upon the note from Alex Southerick. *'...I am writing ten couples and asking each to lend me $1,000...'*

Well, well, my husband's devoted pal Alex Southerick! $1,000! I certainly don't want to participate in a crazy deal like this. Anyway, we put everything we had into buying and fixing this run-down house. And we've already agreed on getting a small tree, and using our old Christmas decorations this year.

Vivian knew that her husband and Alex Southerick had been good friends for years. At one time they had been employed by the same company as co-directors of production. They had lunched with each other daily, worked on the same committees, and traveled together when attending conventions. Although both men had changed occupations since then, they had remained friends, sometimes even meeting for dinner in an airport when their paths crossed.

Sidney had recently remarked to Vivian, "When we get settled I'd like to look up my old friend Alex Southerick. I haven't caught up with him for almost five years. I know you'd like him, and his wife also. Alex is a prince, smart as a whip, but down-to-earth." Vivian had listened to many such accolades about Alex, but so far her sole contact had been to write the Southericks a polite thank-you letter for a generous wedding gift.

Vivian reread the curious request handwritten on Alex's Christmas card.

I most assuredly do not want to lend Alex Southerick any money. Why should we? I haven't even met the man. If he needs $10,000 in a hurry, he'd better start writing some more letters; I don't want to get involved. Besides, we don't have any surplus funds; we have to make roof repairs, and do our Christmas shopping. And I don't like the way he wants to set up this loan—no papers or contracts. How can Sidney refer to him as a brilliant administrator? If I sold houses like that, I'd be out of a job in a week.

But if I show this card to Sidney, he'll send a check by special delivery in the next mail. He wouldn't care if it were our last dollar; he's like that. And he's awfully fond of Alex.

Let me see, what can I say to Sidney. I could tell Sidney that a woman at work heard that Kinnelac might be bought by a foreign company. That would place Alex's job in jeopardy and lessen our chances of getting the money back. No, Sidney would be doubly inclined to make the loan because he'd feel sorry for Alex.

Here's an idea— Greta from my office used to be a close friend of Marcia's when the Southericks lived here. I could say that Greta dropped a couple of hints that Alex has become a compulsive gambler. Then I could go on to say, that's no doubt why he's suddenly short of cash! Alex claims he'll have $10,000 back in a month, and that fits in with the story. Gamblers always think that they're going to win. Alex's note sounds so queer that I'm certain Sidney will fall for the whole thing. And it wouldn't be likely to stir up feelings of compassion, since Sidney abhors gambling.

What I'd really like to do is tear this card up and throw it away, but Sidney would notice if there was no Christmas card from Alex Southerick. He'd probably call him up. Not only that, there might be a reference to the loan in the future. Sidney might see Alex about a sale some day.

Wait a second— a long time ago Sidney mentioned that in the spring he may be assigned the entire midwest region—and that would include Chicago. Kinnelac's headquarters! How stupid of me not to think of it before!

Sincerely Yours

If Sidney gets Chicago, I'll urge him to sell his line of office furniture to Kinnelac by going straight to Alex. If we had loaned him money, he might feel obligated... And what an account that would be! Kinnelac is huge. They must have to replace furniture by the carload. And if this new assignment for Sidney comes to pass, we might have to move to the Chicago area eventually. What a plus to be buddies with a vice-president of Kinnelac! Yes, I think the possibilities here are worth the investment, even though the terms are weird.

After dinner that evening, Vivian asked, "Sidney darling, would you like to go over the Christmas cards we received today? There's a request for a loan from your old friend Alex Southerick. I put that one on top."

Sidney snatched the top card and read Alex's note with intense concern. Then he spoke cautiously. "I realize this is a rather unusual way to borrow. And I know we've put our capital into this house, and we don't have much of a balance left. But Alex has been a good friend for years, and I would very much like to send him a check if it's all right with you."

"Of course, dear, I think you're right to support your friends," affirmed Vivian with an engaging smile.

"What a sweetheart you are to accept this so readily!" exclaimed Sidney. He jumped up from his lounge chair to hug her. "And just before Christmas, too, when we both need extra money. You're so understanding—honestly, darling, you're wonderful."

Vivian silently agreed with his assessment of her. If she played her cards well, she was sure she could make this marriage better than her first.

Mr. & Mrs. Alex Southerick
2612 Kendalpark Lane
Aranda, IL 61015

Mr. and Mrs. Chester Kovent
33 Franciscan Drive
Ondilee, Ariz.
86037

5

Pamela stacked the day's mail neatly, above and to the left of Chester's dinner plate, just as Chester wanted it.

She was philosophical about Chester's contention that all the mail belonged to him, even if addressed to 'Mr. and Mrs. Chester Kovent.' She found it amusing, rather than demeaning, that she was permitted to open letters only if they were addressed to her alone. She saw the mail after dinner anyway, so she did not consider this brief denial important.

She was playing parcheesi with eight-year-old Nicholas when Chester arrived home from work and brushed her lightly on the cheek with his lips at almost the same instant that he asked, "What's for supper?"

"Shrimp and rice curry, fixed the way you like it," she replied cheerily, getting up from the game in the middle of her turn.

Chester wanted his dinner the moment he walked in the door. Since Pamela was home by two o'clock from her part-time secretarial job, she felt no hardship in having the meal ready. The dining-room table was always set by mid-afternoon, with pretty dishes and place mats.

Chester was a large man, with broad shoulders and a muscular physique that accurately reflected his hearty appetite. A factory production manager, he was voluble most of the day; but by dinner-time he was so ravenous that eating took precedence over conversation. Pamela was reticent by nature; thus young Nicky monopolized the table-talk in the Kovent household.

After dinner, it was Chester's habit to read the mail while Nicky went off to play, and Pamela put the leftovers away and prepared to serve dessert. This between-courses routine was usually quiet, but tonight, just as Pamela started to whip cream, Chester let out such an earsplitting whoop of laughter that she dropped the electric beater. Blobs of cream flew from the whirring blades to the window, the cabinets, and the countertop.

Chester yelled from the dining room, "Pamela, come here, this you've gotta see." Still laughing, he handed her the Southericks' Christmas card, with Alex's singular request for a quick loan. Pamela read it through twice and handed it back to him. She remembered their friends Alex and Marcia Southerick very well, from college days.

"What's funny about this?" she asked, looking puzzled.

"What's funny? Where's your sense of humor? Didn't you see the note? 'I am trying to get $10,000 together immediately.' Here's this guy who was valedictorian of our college class, voted 'Most Intelligent' and all that bull. Here he is, so broke he has to ask ten friends for a lousy thousand bucks. *That's* what's funny."

"Just because a man needs money, I don't think that's humorous," ventured Pamela.

"It is if the fella was top dog all through school. And if he was voted 'Most Likely to Succeed'." At that he went into another convulsion.

"But why? It strikes me that makes it more pathetic. I don't recall that Alex was nasty or conceited about being at the head of our class."

"Maybe I didn't tell you about the time I asked him if I could copy his math homework." Chester's tone was sarcastic. "He said it would be more *productive* if the two of us scheduled periods after classes to work on equations, then I could really master them. Roundabout way of saying 'no.' Said some rot about having a natural gift for mathematics, and he would share it by helping me in the evenings. Hah! Thought he was smarter than me and he was gonna teach *me*, the captain of the football team. I never forgave him for that."

"I think that was a very kind offer," said Pamela softly.

"Oh, you do, huh? Well, to show you my heart's in the right place, I'm gonna be Mr. Nice Guy this turn. I'm gonna send him a thousand bucks tonight, real speedy." Chester could not stop laughing. "I want to show him that the old dumbbell who couldn't do geometry can send him $1,000 and think nothing of it. How about a sweet little note with it, 'Need any more, call me.' This is one of the best things that's ever happened to me."

Pamela opened her mouth to speak, but Chester went on. "And don't think I won't mention it at our class reunion this spring. I'll wait till there's a bunch of people around. 'Hey, Alex, I hope that loan I sent you was enough. Do you need any more money'?"

Pamela flushed with embarrassment. "Oh, Chester, please don't do that!" she implored. "He wants the money sent to his office—that means Marcia may not know about the loan. Besides, it will be paid off and forgotten by then."

"Not forgotten by me!" Chester thundered. "I'll never forget it. I'll bring it up every time I see the man, to my dying day. Mr. Big Shot Southerick is gonna remember that *he* needed *me*." He howled uproariously. "Boy, I can't wait to go to that reunion in April!"

Pamela brought out a bowl of almond custard pudding. She called Nicky, and was relieved when he brought a model car to the table to chatter about. After dessert, Chester picked up Alex Southerick's Christmas card and started to laugh again as he went downstairs to the recreation room in their large split-level home. In the evenings, while Pamela cleaned up the kitchen, he liked to practice shots on his slate-top billiard table.

Pamela heard the familiar clicks of the ivory balls snapping against each other. But tonight the noise was diminished by Chester's resounding laughter; and at every guffaw, Pamela's tears dropped silently into the dishwater.

⋯ ⋯

Pamela could still hear Chester laughing in the back of her tortured mind as she packed her suitcases the next morning. She had been awake most of the night, agonizing about the mammoth decision she had made while washing the supper dishes. A dozen splintered sections of her life had tumbled into place, and all at once she knew that she did not want to be married to a man who laughed between billiard shots because 'Most Likely to Succeed' was not succeeding.

But she was trembling with fear that was almost impossible to bear. She was afraid to talk to a lawyer, afraid to take her son out into the world to be raised by a single parent. The tasks ahead of her seemed monstrous: she would have to find a full-time position and an inexpensive apartment. More formidable than anything else, she would have to explain her move to her mother and young Nicky. Today she had taken the day off from work, but she knew that sooner or later she would have to cope with questions

72

from her co-workers. Her trepidation mounted when she envisioned the shocked faces. She had never confided her deepest feelings to anyone; in fact, she had suppressed them even from herself.

Pamela had been fearful of things all her life, including common activities like driving over bridges, riding in elevators, and climbing small heights. She shivered whenever Chester raised his normally loud voice to a shout, even if the shouting was not directed at her. "You name a fear, she's got it," Chester always said about his panphobic wife. Taking a critical action like this—leaving a man she had been married to for 23 years—was so foreign to her disposition that every step terrified her.

She was aware that relatives and business associates regarded Chester and her as a well-suited, good-looking couple. Not that there were a great many friends and relatives to ponder. Pamela's mother, a widow, had a small apartment in a neighboring town. An aunt, an uncle, and two cousins lived in Maryland; Pamela had seen them but once, at her wedding. Chester's parents were both dead, and his two unmarried sisters lived in a mobile home about a hundred miles away. Once a year Pamela invited them to a sumptuous Sunday dinner that she slaved over for hours; they always accepted, but never reciprocated.

The Kovents' college chums had become Christmas-card friends, scattered around the country. Local friends were sparse, due partly to Pamela's bashfulness, and partly to Chester's inclination to go through life without close companions. If Pamela suggested a social evening with others, Chester would say, "Nah, I just wanna relax with the TV and a coupla cans of beer." Now and then he brought a colleague home for dinner to talk business, without giving advance notice to Pamela, who did not complain but scurried about, taking extra food out of the freezer.

Sincerely Yours

Tess was an office friend of Pamela's, but when Pamela invited Tess and her husband over for an evening, the two men played pool in the recreation room while their wives chatted upstairs; and when Pamela and Chester went to Tess and Otto's house, the husbands watched sports on television, and the women talked about recipes. Pamela never had the feeling that four friends were enjoying an evening together, but rather that two men who happened to be thrown together were tolerating the interval until their wives finished visiting.

Pamela thought back to the lighthearted years at college, where she and Chester had met Alex Southerick and his girlfriend Marcia. They had double-dated, and had also shared their company as part of larger groups at fraternity dances. Alex had been a congenial gentleman, but Pamela had an especially warm feeling toward Marcia. Gregarious Marcia had made a practice of subtly bringing Pamela into discussions; thus Pamela, without knowing the reason, had felt at ease with Marcia. She thought again about the Christmas card.

Oh, I hope the Southericks haven't had a financial catastrophe. They are such a gracious couple. I've always looked forward to seeing them at our class reunions. How can Chester laugh because he thinks they're in trouble?

Come to think of it, Marcia is the only person I've ever been able to speak to freely about anything serious. If she weren't 1,500 miles away, maybe I could talk to her about this situation. I can't bring myself to tell my mother the unpleasant details. She worked like an ox to bring me up, and she was a young widow with no help. All she wanted out of life was my happiness; I feel as if I've failed her.

I know I can't discuss this sort of thing with Tess, either, much as I like her. And the other kids in the office, they think I have it made—with a handsome husband, a healthy son, and an attractive home, what more could I ask? They gaze longingly at

74

*this huge diamond ring Chester bought to replace the miniscule
zircon engagement ring that I didn't want replaced. Not once
have I said a word against Chester, and the compliments I've
given him are the truth—he is generous and he treats me well.
They would never understand how I could give it all up. I'm not
sure I understand it myself.*

Pamela folded her skirts and blouses, and placed them
in one of the plastic bags that she ordinarily used for leaf
collection. She started to cry as she packed Nicky's favorite
toys into cartons. Her eyes fell on a nearby box of Christmas decorations and she wept harder. She picked out one
of the items at the top, a small waterglobe, turned it over
slowly and watched the snow falling on a Christmas
scene—tiny brown animals around a tiny brown stable,
everything turning white. Then she knelt down and prayed
that she was not losing her mind.

———— ≡✦≡ ————

Pamela's father had died when she was two years old,
and she had no recollection of him. Her earliest memory
was a feeling of bewilderment when her preschool playmates talked constantly about daddies. They would say,
'My daddy is strong,' or 'Daddy throws me up in the air and
catches me.' The other children looked at her strangely
when she said she had no daddy, and her mother cried
whenever she asked her about it.

Pamela's mother, widowed at twenty, had never remar-
ried. Nervous and frightened, she had labored night and
day to raise her only child and send her to college. It had
occurred to Pamela many times, after growing up, that her
fatherless upbringing might account for her timidity. It was
obvious that she had inherited many of her mother's char-
acteristics: she was reserved and self-effacing, and not gifted with the ability to express her feelings.

75

Sincerely Yours

When she was in the fourth grade, some classmates had discovered that her middle name was Mary, and they had taunted her relentlessly as 'Mousy Mary.' Though she abhorred the nickname, she thought secretly that it was fitting. Why didn't she ever speak up for herself? In groups, she rarely contributed to the conversation, and she knew that others mistook her meekness for stupidity. She remembered with pain how many people showed surprise when she was listed in the upper ten percent of her high school class. "Pamela!" they exclaimed, in a tone that indicated their amazement that Mousy Mary had been able to accomplish anything.

When Pamela met Chester in college, he seemed to her to be Mr. Strength. A massive football player, he had solid shoulders to lean on. Until then she had not had a dominant person in her life, and she relished the security of relying on Chester for all her decisions, even trivial ones: should she have a soda or a milkshake? Vanilla or chocolate? And Chester was gratified to be the object of her dependence. Pamela was everything he wanted—someone deferential who sought his advice, hung on his every word, and openly admired his brawn.

Chester proposed marriage on graduation night, and Pamela told her mother that she was the luckiest girl alive. From the beginning, she had thought it was unbelievable that a popular football star had noticed her at a crowded college social, calling out to her, 'Hey, little china doll, let's have a dance."

Pamela did resemble a china doll, with her rosebud mouth and sweeping dark eyelashes. She was five-foot-two and slender, and she looked as fragile as a flower petal against Chester's six-foot-four frame. Her hair was mousy colored, but it had a slight wave that was most becoming. Under her yearbook picture was written: 'Her smile could melt an iceberg.'

76

Pamela and Chester waited a year before getting married. The ceremony took place in a small church, followed by a dinner for the few family members, the only type of reception that Pamela's mother could afford. Everyone present said that the charming newlyweds, little China Doll and big Football Hero, were surely destined to live happily ever after.

──── ══╬══ ────

They had been married for two months before Pamela noticed that Chester was laughing at newspaper stories, and she was not. An article headlined 'Actor Playing Cripple Breaks His Back' was top comedy to Chester; and he thought it was a joke when a million-dollar lottery winner reported that his bonanza had given him a severe nervous breakdown.

Pamela did not join in his glee, and she seldom made any reference to Chester's laughter when he was reading the daily news. She offered a word of sympathy for the lottery winner, and Chester said, "You don't appreciate a real farce. Can't you see the funny streak in a guy having a breakdown because he won a million bucks?"

"I can't see anything funny in a person getting ill, no matter what the cause," she replied quietly.

──── ══╬══ ────

Three years later, Pamela was horrified when Chester swaggered home one evening boasting that he had presented an associate's idea to the boss as if it were his own, and had taken full credit for it. The result was a substantial salary increase for Chester.

Sincerely Yours

Pamela sucked in her breath to muster her courage, then said, "Chester, that's not fair. You shouldn't have done that."

"You're the one who's not being fair, criticizing me for striving to get ahead," he countered. "This could put me in line for a promotion. I thought you'd be tickled. I forgot that you don't know the score. Being a secretary in that pocket-sized office keeps you out of touch with the nitty-gritty of business competition. People have to step on people on the way up—that's how it works. Lester would have done the same thing to me, except I wouldn't be so dimwitted as to confide in him or anyone else. The nameplate on *your* desk should say 'Miss Goody Two-Shoes.' But then, you're not going anywhere, or making any effort to advance." Pamela resented the implication that she would betray her co-workers to progress, but she was not brave enough to dispute it.

Three weeks later a smug Chester waved a bonus paycheck in front of Pamela's eyes. He was not feeling any belated regrets. "Put the food away—we're going out to dinner to celebrate," he crowed.

Pamela felt that she should have the integrity to refuse, but she lacked the nerve to give the actual reason. "No, my chicken crepes won't keep—they have to be eaten today," she said, withdrawing into the kitchen. During the meal she could not respond to Chester's attempts to make the occasion festive. When Chester brought out a bottle of champagne he had been saving for a noteworthy event, she said hastily, before he popped the cork, "I don't want any, I have a headache." The next day she had a burning impulse to mail a large amount of cash anonymously to Lester and his wife, but she was afraid that Chester might somehow find out.

The Kovents had lived in a three-room apartment for six years before purchasing their home, a split-level house more than twice the size of their former quarters. Pamela decorated the rooms with conservative charm. She hung her copper molds and copper-bottomed pots in a bright circle around the kitchen, and in the den she covered an entire wall with Chester's football memorabilia. Although the furniture did not conform to any particular period, it was all in good taste, and the effect was restful.

Pamela had a collection of dolls, gathered since childhood, which she displayed in a three-sided glass cabinet in the living room. When she was arranging them she had told Chester that a small antique china doll was her most special one, because he had called Pamela 'China Doll' before he knew her name.

Like her mother, Pamela was industrious; she kept the house spotless. Perhaps because she had always seen her mother cope with the household duties alone, she did not request or expect any assistance from Chester. This was fortunate, as Chester did not think a man should do any work about the house; it would not have entered his mind to wash a dish or a floor. He would not have objected, however, if his wife had chosen not to be employed. But Pamela said, "I'll stay home when we have our family."

Fourteen years elapsed, but no family additions appeared. Pamela yearned to have a baby, but her bashfulness, coupled with Chester's self-assurance, deterred the couple from investigating their infertility. Pamela had long thought that motherhood would be her most fulfilling career, and she was thrilled when she finally became pregnant. She quit her job before Nicky was born, and did not return to work until her son was six years old.

———— ▰◆▰ ————

Pamela was right—parenthood was her forte. After Nicky was born she started to develop more respect for her own opinions, especially in relation to child-rearing. In fact, the first time she considered the possibility of leaving Chester was after a conflict involving Nicky.

Six-year-old Nicky had come home from a game of marbles with his friend, and said that he had picked up some of Stewart's marbles. "I didn't mean to," he whimpered, "but I didn't knock out any cat's-eyes or rainbows."

Pamela was pleased to see an emerging conscience. "Just take them over to Stewart's house and give them back," she said.

"Whaddaya mean?" Chester boomed. "If the kid next door is too slow to pick up his own marbles, that's tough. Grab 'em fast, Nicky, you've gotta learn to nab the winnings and go, and you might as well start young. Tell me, did you win?"

"Yes."

"That's my boy! That's the main thing. The world is loaded with losers. Every night I read in the paper about losers. They're only good for a laugh."

Pamela had a frantic desire to scream out, but her timidity overruled it. She decided to think the issue over calmly, and deal with it when her heart was not pounding in her throat. The following day she told Nicky to return the marbles, stressing that it was wrong to keep them if he didn't shoot them out of the circle. "They really belong to Stewart because you didn't win them," she explained.

"But Daddy said I could keep them," Nicky argued. "And I don't have any that color."

A crying scene evolved before Nicky reluctantly took the marbles next door. Worst of all, Pamela had the feeling that he was obeying the instruction without grasping the lesson.

That night it was Pamela's turn for tears when Nicky, still sullen, informed his father that Mommy had made him return the marbles. Chester raged at Pamela in their son's presence: "You want him to grow up namby-pamby, like you? He's a boy, Pammie, he's got to learn to compete."

Pamela was sure that Nicky's concept of good sportsmanship would be marred forever. Plagued for two days by indecisiveness, she finally dared to see a family counselor. She told him she was thinking of separating from her husband. Then, meekly and ineffectively, she recounted the marble incident. She spoke of Chester's unfair pay raise, and his habit of laughing at the mishaps of strangers in the news. Subconsciously she wanted someone to embolden her to leave Chester so she could raise her son properly.

Instead, she was asked conventional questions about Chester, which she answered truthfully: no, he does not drink to excess; he does not gamble; he has never struck me or beaten me; he has not threatened me; he has not had any extramarital affairs; he does not abuse his son; we do not have financial worries.

Pamela left the office feeling like a petty fault-finder who had belittled a giant paragon of virtue. She had a vague impression that the counselor thought she was feebleminded. He had regarded her strangely when she said, "But I can't stand his sense of humor." He suggested a second session later in the week, but Pamela did not make another appointment.

Guiltily, she made a strenuous effort to center on her husband's commendable attributes as underscored by the counselor's questions. She struggled to block out offensive remarks, and quell her repulsion when Chester laughed about grim news in the papers. One evening he was nearly rolling on the floor because six rangers, with years of specialized firefighting training, had perished in an immense forest fire. "That's a good one, isn't it?" he asked.

Pamela took a deep breath and said, "Chester, I want to ask you a big favor. Please do not read any articles or head-lines aloud to me, no matter how ludicrous you find them."

It was so unlike Pamela to utter even a mild protest that Chester was astonished. "But why? I just wanna share a laugh with you."

"Haven't you ever noticed that I'm not laughing?"

"Sure. Sure, I notice that all the time. Like I always say, you can't see the funny side of life. You don't get enough grins."

"You know I laugh about a lot of little things that hap-pen at the office. I told you about the sprinkler system malfunctioning the other day—there we were, working in the indoor rain. The boss hurried in with umbrellas and opened them up over the paperwork, not us." She laughed at the recollection. "And I often repeat the things that Nicky comes up with. I can't imagine what he learned in first grade, but yesterday he said, 'Mom, give me some of Daddy's seeds, I want to plant them in the garden and grow a baby brother'."

She giggled, and Chester responded with a faint smile. "Yes, I suppose that's funny, in a childish sort of way, but I can see the humor in bigger things than you can. I think I should keep trying, and maybe by degrees I can train you to broaden your sense of humor."

So Pamela's earnest plea went unheeded. Chester kept right on sharing 'hilarious' headlines with his wife, while her inner self kept calling out, 'No! No! Don't train me to be like that!'

The second time Pamela seriously considered divorce was a year later, on the heels of another clash regarding Nicky, when he was in the second grade.

One evening at the dinner-table he announced proudly that he had received a gold star on his spelling paper.

"Wonderful!" said Pamela. Then Nicky added, "I didn't know two words, but I saw them on Carla's paper and that made me remember them."

"You must never look at another child's paper when you're taking a test," said Pamela. "That's wrong, Nicky, because a test is supposed to show the teacher only what *you* have learned. I want you to promise me that you won't ever do that again. We'll talk about it more after dinner."

"Now wait just a minute," Chester intervened. "If you glance around the room while you're thinking, and your eyes happen to light on another kid's paper, that's not your fault. Sometimes you spot a couple words that remind you of something you knew but forgot for that instant. If you happen to see something like that, that's called good luck. I had good luck all through school, and see where I am today."

Pamela, whose face had been reddening with fury throughout this speech, suddenly shrieked, "No, Nicky, that's cheating! You *never* look at anyone else's paper! Keep your eyes straight ahead, or close them when you're thinking!"

Nicky looked up in alarm. His eyes were full of fright and confusion. In all his seven years he had never heard his mother shout. This was a new experience for Chester as well. He roared, "Pamela, are you out of your mind? What's the matter with you?" As if Pamela were the seven-year-old, he commanded, "Go up to the bedroom until you simmer down." She obeyed submissively, her hands quivering. She had grown up in a world of subdued voices, and whenever Chester bellowed, she cringed.

She did not tiptoe downstairs until Chester and Nicky had fallen asleep, fully dressed, in front of the television set. Then she cleaned up the kitchen and dining room in her stocking feet, so as not to wake them.

For a week Pamela thought constantly of divorce. Before Nicky's birth she had been able to close her mind to Chester's lower standards by simply not dwelling on them. But now that her son's character was being molded, she was growing more and more uneasy.

She berated herself for not being more wary in college. Chester had laughed when the quarterback of a rival college had sustained multiple injuries in an accident. When she was appalled by his reaction, he said, "Can't you see what a break this is for our team? We have a better chance at the title!"

She suspected there had been similar occurrences that she had been overly quick to forget. She had been so entranced to find someone to lean on that she had been willing to overlook clear indicants without even sorting them out. How true that love is blind, she thought, blaming her lack of discrimination 25 years ago for her present dilemma.

Putting her own feelings aside, she concentrated on what she deemed best for Nicky. Although he was not shy, he was an introverted child, more like Pamela than Chester. He would rather read a book than play ball; he had neither the interest nor the coordination for sports. Chester, who had been an athlete in both high school and college, played catch with Nicky for hours. Pamela approved, because she felt that Nicky needed masculine vigor in his life to counteract his daily exposure to her own timidity. One minute she would ask herself, am I insecure and fraught with anxieties because I grew up without a father? But the next minute she would think: granted that Nicky should have a father—but is Chester a suitable model? Is Nicky absorbing his dad's ethics while I'm preaching opposing principles? Adding everything up, is Chester a destructive or constructive influence?

After many days of vacillation, Pamela decided that she would be doing Nicky more harm than good by leaving Chester. The marriage stayed intact for another year of similar disagreements, until the day that Alex Southerick's Christmas card arrived. Chester had the biggest laugh of his life, and Pamela finally packed her bags and left.

The first thing Chester noticed when he walked in the front door was the absence of mouth-watering aromas emanating from the kitchen. It was unthinkable for Pamela to be out when he arrived home from work—she always attended to shopping and errands earlier in the day, so that dinner would be ready on time. More annoyed than concerned, he strode into the immaculate kitchen.

There, held in place in the center of the table with a miniature cactus plant, was a sheet of pale lavender stationery on which was written Pamela's note. The words were typical of her, but they were a complete mystery to Chester.

Dear Chester,

I am leaving you, and of course I am taking Nicky with me. I know you are strong and will do fine without me. Take care of your bad knee—if you do the exercises the doctor gave you, I think it will feel much better. You have provided for us very well and given us a lovely home. Thank you for everything.

Pamela

"She's thanking me for everything but she's leaving me?" he said aloud. Such an action was impossible for a man like Chester to fathom. He was not aware of his shortcomings, and Pamela's attempts to point them out had been too feeble to make a dent. He ran up to the bedroom, swung open the closet door, and saw that Pamela's clothing was indeed gone. He raced to the living room. The furniture was there, the watercolors were hanging on the wall, the pillows were in their usual places on the sofa, but yet the room seemed stark. Then he saw with a pang that the three-sided glass display cabinet was empty. All of the dolls had fled.

He went to the telephone and called Pamela's mother. He had guessed correctly—Pamela was staying there until she could find a place to rent. His mother-in-law called Pamela to the phone.

"Pammie, I don't understand what in blazes is going on," Chester sputtered. "One day you're cooking my favorite shrimp-and-rice curry, and the next day you're packing a suitcase and leaving me. You never said you were unhappy or anything! For Pete's sake, will you tell me why you're mad at me?"

"Chester, I'm not mad at you," Pamela started.

"You're not mad at me? *You're not mad at me?* You're happy with me but you decided to leave me for the hell of it?" He was hollering so loudly that Pamela was cowering at the other end of the line.

"We're just two different people," she said shakily.

"Every couple that gets married is made up of two different people. Could they be the same people? Come on, honey, make sense, will ya? And it's almost Christmas! You're crazy about Christmas! I love Nicky and you, China Doll, and I'm worried about you."

Chester had used the pet name 'China Doll' periodically since college, but mostly on special occasions such as anniversaries. Now, the term brought Pamela a rush of memories and tears. She knew that Chester's anxiety about her welfare was genuine. Her whole being was filled with an enveloping sorrow. She felt sorry for Chester, sorry for the way things had turned out, and overwhelmingly sorry because she knew that, in spite of anything she might say, the breakdown of the marriage would always be totally incomprehensible to Chester.

"The Christmas decorations are in the den," she said in a plaintive voice. "I brought them up from the basement Saturday." She paused, and then said haltingly, "Chester, I'm sorry I have to do this."

"And I'm sorry for you! You can't hack it alone. I know from living with you that you don't have the foggiest idea what makes the real world go 'round."

Impulsively she blurted out, "I want to be in my own real world, where people don't lie and cheat and tramp on one another to get promotions and laugh at everyone's misfortunes and steal each other's marbles!"

"You better steal some marbles, 'cause you've lost yours!" he yelled. He did not connect her allusions to the incidents that had haunted her for years. In a lower voice he said, "Honey, there is no world like you're talking about. That's just not how it is. You're out of your head, Pamela." Suddenly he became agitated. "Hey, you're not thinking about committing suicide to get to your own fantasy of heaven, are you?"

His interpretation of her frenzied statement was so far off the mark that it increased her anguish. "No, Chester, nothing like that. I would never do such a thing to Nicky."

"I only thought of it because that's what you're describing. You're not gonna find that stuff here on this earth."

"I have to be able to hold my head up while I'm looking for it. But most of all, I have to teach Nicky to look for it too." She knew he did not have the vaguest notion what she was looking for or talking about.

"Listen, tell me in plain English what's eating you, will ya?"

"Well, I'll try." She deliberated for a few seconds before going on. "Remember when Nicky was six and you told him it was all right to pick up his friend's marbles as long as he won the game?"

"Is that what this is all about? You're holding a grudge 'cause two years ago I told my kid it was good to win? Don't you see that Nicky's too wishy-washy already? He's got to have the attitude of winning and getting ahead, or he's not gonna make it when he gets out there on his own some day. You can talk, you're a woman—a woman can marry a winner to go out and bring home the bacon. You want your kid to be a loser?"

"That's another thing, Chester, you always laugh at losers." Pamela discovered she could assert herself more easily when she was separated by a telephone line. "Like last night. It crushed me when you laughed so hard at our old friends the Southericks, just because they wanted to borrow a little money. Alex and Marcia Southerick are wonderful people, and it isn't funny at all if they're having financial problems. In fact, your prolonged merriment about Alex Southerick was the final blow—that's what helped me get off the fence."

"You missed the joke, as usual," he said, shaking his head. "The comic part is that Alex Southerick was supposed to be the one most likely to succeed in the whole class, and twenty years later he's out grubbing small loans." Even now Chester was snickering. "But you're right, people laugh at losers—but you don't care if Nicky turns out to be a loser? That doesn't add up in my book."

Pamela had long thought that trying to explain her feelings to Chester would be hopeless. Tonight she was sure of it.

"That's about it, Chester, we're not reading and writing the same books."

Confounded by that remark, Chester ignored it and asked abruptly, "How about if you come back just for the holidays? We can have a regular Christmas with Nicky—turkey dinner, carols, toys and games under the tree—like we've always had other years. Nicky's gonna be awful hurt without a real family on Christmas."

Of all Pamela's forebodings, Chester had attacked the darkest one. A sickening fear gripped her as she started to waver. The last thing she wanted to do was to ruin Nicky's Christmas.

But Chester lost his edge as quickly as he had gained it. Encouraged by her hesitation, he said, "Hey, I've got another funny story to tell you about Mousy Mortimer—you know, the guy at the plant who gets all the work nobody else wants to do, and never speaks up. This time the jerk has hit bottom." His tone was contemptuous, and he chuckled.

Tears welled up in Pamela's eyes. She put her hand over the earpiece of the telephone and thought, I don't ever have to listen to another one of Chester's funny stories. A few moments later she raised the phone to her ear and heard jeering laughter.

Sincerely Yours

She said nothing and he repeated, "So how about coming home for Christmas?"

Pamela straightened her spine and said softly, "No, Chester."

"Maybe you'll feel better tomorrow." He said good-bye and dropped the receiver into its cradle with a bang.

"Looney, that's what," he muttered. He would always think that a touch of insanity had caused her to leave him, after he had given her everything.

———— ✠ ————

When Pamela hung up the phone, her mother asked her a question. "No," replied Pamela in a low voice. "I am not going back for Christmas."

Then, in answer to her mother's second question, she said, "No, Mother, this was definitely not a hasty decision."

Mr. & Mrs. Alex Southerick
2612 Kendalpark Lane
Aranda, IL 61015

Season's Greetings USA 20c

Mr. and Mrs. Keith Wendler
85 Buckeye Rd.
Calibon, Okla. 73014

6

"Any mail?"

This was Keith's standard after-work greeting, but it was a perfunctory question. In the busy Wendler household of two working adults and two school-aged children, mail was given little importance. It often lay unopened for a day or two before either Donna or Keith had a chance to look at it.

"There's a bunch of Christmas cards I didn't have time to read. I worked late tonight," replied Donna.

"I'll open them while you're getting supper."

"Good, and will you pin them up on the ribbons I have hanging between the windows? I have a little red bow for each card."

"Pin them up on ribbons? With itty-bitty red bows? You've got to be kidding!"

Donna smiled good-naturedly as she tossed a salad. She set the table and was starting to make gravy when she heard an outcry from Keith. "Wow, look at this one! Alex Southerick wants $1,000."

"Who doesn't?" Donna laughed. "What does he say, 'Merry Christmas, please send $1,000'?"

"Yeah, you got it," Keith answered.

"Hey, I just said that as a joke."

"See for yourself." He held Alex's note up for her to read while she stirred gravy.

"Holy Toledo!" she exclaimed, dropping the spoon, handle and all, into the boiling gravy. "I wonder what's wrong. We haven't seen Alex since my last college reunion."

Suddenly Keith's expression became sinister. "No, *we* haven't. Have *you?*" he asked. "It strikes me as strange for a guy you knew in college to be asking us for a loan. I hardly know the man. Are you supposed to be catching a double meaning here? You send him $1,000, he won't let on about something? What is this, hush money?"

Here we go again, thought Donna, rolling her eyes heavenward. Keith's jealousy was one of his few shortcomings. "There isn't anything to hush, silly," she said. "How ridiculous can you get? This man lives 900 miles away."

"What are you saying, you'd prefer to have affairs with men who are handier? Besides, it isn't unheard of for chief executives like Alex to make business trips all over the country."

Donna stared at him in disbelief. She thought she had become inured to his hurtful suspicions, but this jibe topped all the others. She had no chance for rebuttal, however. With a loud sizzle, the untended gravy boiled over onto the stove; at the same time her two young daughters came rushing in the door with animated descriptions of their soccer practice. Red-cheeked and laughing, they looked like models for a health magazine. Bridget, nine, and Allison, eleven, played soccer on some afternoons; on others they pirouetted gracefully in ballet classes.

The Wendler family never discussed unpleasant topics during meal hours, not even world news if it was somber.

The girls had been instructed in this discipline from the time they learned to talk. If they wanted to tell Mom and Dad about a disagreement at the playground, they did it before or after dinner, not while a meal was in progress. It was better for one's digestive system, said Donna, to 'put on a happy face' when eating. Thus it was normal for Donna and Keith to postpone further debate over Alex Souther-ick's Christmas card.

"Johnny hid Allison's books behind a tree," reported Bridget, snickering. "And when she found them he asked her if he could be her boyfriend."

Allison gave her sister a scathing glare, but in keeping with the rules against quarreling at the table, she quickly switched the subject with a riddle. "Why does an elephant paint his toenails red? So he can hide in the strawberry patch!" Everyone laughed and forgot about Johnny and the books.

After supper there was much scurrying around the house, because Allison and Bridget were going to an overnight birthday party. Excitedly they packed their bathrobes, fluffy slippers, and pajamas, while Mom inter-jected reminders about mundane necessities like tooth-brushes. It was dark outside, so Keith drove his daughters the three blocks to the party.

When he returned, Donna said, in the most nonchalant tone she could muster, "I'm planning to write out Christ-mas cards tonight, and since Alex Southerick needs this money in a hurry, I'd like to know if it's all right to send it to him."

"Oh, we're back to the old boyfriend. No, we're not sending any money to old boyfriends."

"Alex was never my boyfriend, as you are fully aware," Donna replied.

"I'm aware of nothing of the sort. He doesn't know me well enough to ask me for a loan, so it must be *you* that he knows quite intimately. You went out with him, didn't you?"

"Oh, Keith, we went over this before my first class reunion—that was almost twenty years ago. I went out with Alex, but we didn't have a boyfriend-girlfriend relationship. It was platonic, a brother-sister type of understanding and trust. I was used to having that kind of bond with my brothers—I talked over my dates, and everything else, with them. So when I was a naive little freshman, it was a godsend to find a similar relationship far away from home. Alex Southerick helped me over excruciating homesickness.

"But when Alex took me to a game or a movie, he never once kissed me—except maybe on the cheek—and I didn't want him to. I regarded him as a member of my family.

"Did I ever tell you how Alex started dating his wife? Marcia was a friend of mine, and Alex confided to me that he wished she weren't going steady with another fellow, because he'd like to ask her out. I told him she wasn't engaged, why not ask her anyhow. And he did, and she went, and they fell in love.

"If I were attracted to Alex myself, would I have encouraged him to take out Marcia? Can't you get this through your skull? Alex and I liked each other, but in a different way. That's what 'platonic' means."

Keith did not believe that a platonic relationship was even remotely possible. "I never took a girl out that I didn't think about in an amorous way," he said.

"Well, just because you weren't blessed with platonic friendships doesn't mean that they can't exist. You were an only child, so maybe it's difficult for you to understand close brother-sister ties. It's having someone to talk to who truly cares but has no ulterior motives. And Alex Southerick provided me with that type of companionship when I was away from my family for the first time in my life. That's why I'd like to do him this small favor. We have the money, sitting there in our account earning minimum interest. You could earn more on it—Alex says he'll give you the Treasury rate."

"Since when are you interested in high finance? I haven't seen you give a hoot about which bank was paying more on savings. How come this instant spurt of attention now that Alex Southerick needs money?"

"I guess I thought it might persuade you to send it," she replied artlessly. "And getting back to your original statement, Alex obviously regards us both as good friends or he wouldn't have addressed this note to 'Mr. and Mrs.' You and I have sat at the same table with Marcia and Alex at every reunion, and we've stayed at the same motel and had brunch with them the next day. And we spent almost a whole Alumni Weekend in groups that included them. I don't see how you can say that you aren't well acquainted with them. Don't you remember what fun we had when they visited us? I could tell Alex liked you, and I thought you liked him too."

"He was okay, but what I really had in mind was keeping him away from you."

This roiled her. "Oh, you were so busy making sure that Alex didn't open a door for me that you didn't bother to get to know him better. A nicer guy than Alex never lived."

The moment this sentence came out of her mouth she regretted it. She knew what Keith's reaction would be before he spoke a syllable.

"Oh, I'm not nicer than Alex? You married me as second choice after the nicest guy who ever lived married Marcia, right?"

"Keith, you're being asinine. That's an offhand phrase I'd use to describe lots of people, like my father or my brothers. And by the way, when you had that eagle eye on Alex, didn't you see that he's wild about Marcia, just from how he looks at her? That would be clear to a blind bat."

"I happen to think he always had an eye on you, even when he was dating Marcia. All these years later, he doesn't look at you as if he hates you either."

"Of course he doesn't hate me. I'm like a sister to him!"

"And it doesn't stack up that the same little wife who didn't want me to spend $200 on a camera last month is now raring to send this 'casual acquaintance' a thousand bucks."

"I didn't say 'casual,' I said 'platonic'—there's a considerable distinction. But the main point is, we wouldn't be giving Alex any money, or spending a cent. It's nothing but a loan, and a very short-term one at that."

"Hah! No loan contract, no signatures—what guarantee is there of repayment?"

"Alex is too honorable a person not to pay it back," Donna said.

"Oh, he is, huh. Then why doesn't he say he'll return a signed contract? You've only seen him sporadically for the past twenty years, but you know he's bursting with honor. Is he too noble for blackmail? You send him $1,000, he won't tell about the lovers you described in graphic detail to precious Big Brother."

Donna was almost in tears. I can't stand it, she thought. We've gone full circle and we're back to hidden incentives behind this loan.

Keith was not finished. "And what's more, even if nothing went on before this—which I'll never know—I don't want you to advertise your supercongeniality to Alex by rushing this loan out by return mail. Your over-eager cooperation could give him ideas, if he didn't have them already. And one more thing. At the reunion this spring I'd like to sit at a table with somebody else, someone you didn't date in college. Are there any such creatures around?"

96

Donna fled from the room without answering as the tears started to flow. Feeling too heartsick now to address Christmas cards, she escaped to the bedroom.

On nights like this, which she was thankful were occasional, Donna wished that she and Keith had twin beds. The sexual aspect of their marriage was usually rapturous, but tonight she did not want Keith to come near her. She was relieved that he made no contact when he slid into bed a half-hour later. But he kept her awake with recurrent low groans.

Finally she asked, "What's the matter?"

"I can't sleep, picturing you in bed with Alex Southerick."

Donna bolted upright in bed. "*Keith!* I was never in bed with Alex Southerick or anyone else. I've told you repeatedly that I was a virgin when we were married."

Every bone in his body ached to believe her, and yet he could not. "I know, but you're so ravishing, it doesn't seem possible that some brute out there didn't get you. Then there's that famous line that keeps bugging me—is it from Shakespeare?—'the lady doth protest too much'."

"Oh, if I didn't defend myself against your addlebrained slurs, then you'd assume I was innocent? Tell me another one!" She was in no mood to take pleasure in his dubious compliment about her irresistibility.

Keith jumped out of bed and left the room, and Donna let him go without following. Crying softly, she asked herself, what in the world makes him this way? And why do I still love him?

Keith's distress matched Donna's as he retreated to the sofa in the den. She hasn't done one thing even vaguely questionable, he thought. Why does this other part of me suspect every move she makes?

—+—≡◆≡—+—

97

He had not thought about Jeanine for over twenty years. Jeanine, his first love when they were both just seventeen. All he could remember about Jeanine was her habit of shaking her head backward to swing her long blond hair out of her eyes.

Long blond hair something like Donna's. Knockout figure like Donna's too. I hadn't realized that they looked so similar.

The parallels stopped there, however. Jeanine was self-centered, ill-tempered, and demanding. His mother had not liked her, and the more his mother objected to his dating her, the more he wanted her.

He and Jeanine 'went steady' for eight months, then she had told him bluntly that she was going to date Scotty for a while. Was his despair when she left him induced by the loss of Jeanine or by the blow to his ego?

He retraced his other female friendships before his marriage. There was Charlotte, the night-club dancer. He had always been resentful of the entire audience watching her dance, her slim form dressed in scanty sequined outfits.

After that he had taken several women out once or twice, and then had dated only one additional long-term girlfriend.

What was her name again? Oh yes, Albertina, another blonde.

It occurred to him now for the first time that he had dated blondes exclusively. He had read somewhere that if a man had an amicable relationship with his mother, he would be most likely to seek the company of women with a similar appearance. He and his mother, a chubby brunette, had maintained an excellent relationship through the years, but he had never had a single date with anyone who even slightly resembled her.

He ferreted out the memory of still another blonde. When he was eleven years old, gazing out the window of a bus that was transporting his sixth-grade class on a field trip, he had seen his father entering a restaurant with a voluptuous blonde cuddled up on his arm. He had been afraid to tell his mother, and just as apprehensive to confront his father.

It's curious that I've blocked that incident out of my brain. I was tormented by it for months. And I had terrible nightmares. How I detested that blonde, whoever she was! But I haven't given her a conscious thought since I grew up. Even when I introduced my own gorgeous Donna to my parents, I didn't think of that other curvaceous blonde. But wouldn't it be logical to surmise that I'd end up loathing shapely blondes and favoring dumpy brunettes? What's wrong with my head?

Nothing further had developed from his father's peccadillo, at least not to Keith's knowledge. His mother had not changed; she had remained warm and loving. He had always admired his mother's serenity.

Like Donna! That's it, her disposition! I found a woman who has both Jeanine's good looks and my mother's grace... But all this meditation on my ancient history isn't producing grounds for my fierce jealousy of Donna. I know she isn't guilty of my vulgar insults, and I hate myself for condemning her. Why do I hurt her, when I love her so much? I've sworn to myself that I'd never reproach her again, but here I am, worse than ever, over a zany Christmas-card note.

The next day was Saturday. When Donna got up, her pillow still damp, Keith was not in bed. She went downstairs and saw him on the sofa, his long arms and legs curled around to resemble a huge misshapen pretzel. Although he was sound asleep, his face did not look peaceful.

How dull it seemed without Bridget and Allison bouncing down to the kitchen to share giggles and eggs. They would be away until dinner. The wise hostess of the birthday party, anticipating chatter until well past midnight, had planned a waffle feast at noon. Then the party group of ten girls would attend a local drama.

Donna didn't see much of her daughters during the week, and she looked forward to their company on weekends. Today she especially wanted them to be with her, to help lift her morale. She ate a solitary breakfast without appetite, and then started to do routine tasks. It seemed inappropriate for the sun to be sending cheery bright gleams across the furniture. "Hey, sun," she felt like saying, "You don't belong here. This day should be gray."

She wished Bridget and Allison were home to decorate the Christmas tree, which stood devoid of ornaments in the corner of the living room. Its nakedness added to her dejection. No tinsel, no silver angel-top, no strings of colored lights. Stop it, she scolded herself. It's a perfectly nice undecorated Christmas tree. Stop wallowing in gloom. She glanced briefly at the twisted form of her sleeping husband in the adjoining room, and as she dusted books and shelves she found herself contemplating her life with him.

Her mind flashed back to their dating months. In the course of those fun-filled days she had noticed that Keith treated her with extreme possessiveness, but she wasn't perturbed about it then. She construed it to be devotion, and she had to admit that in the beginning she was flattered by it. She had made up a nickname and jokingly called him Zee-Jay, which stood for Zealous-Jealous.

One evening at a dance, an old friend cut in while she was fox-trotting with Keith. Zee-Jay was infuriated, and Donna laughed when he said, "Any guy ever does that in the future had better get primed for a showdown in the parking lot."

Reminiscing now, it was hard for her to believe she had once thought that remark was humorous. His green eyes, it turned out, were not very funny.

As newlyweds, the first manifestation of jealousy occurred when Keith came home from work to find a Western Union messenger in their apartment. Donna was never able to understand how Keith could envision a romantic interlude from the reality of a skinny teen-aged boy, muffled to his ears, with telegram in hand, sniffling and shivering in the front hall where she had invited him in from the cold while she went in search of change for a tip.

A few months later, Donna telephoned Keith to say she had to work overtime. She was mortified when he came storming into her office with fury in his eyes—only to see her sitting demurely at her desk, typing letters, while her boss, a corpulent gentleman with three or four chins, sat a few desks away, scribbling memos and munching potato chips.

Mr. Linderson had not met Keith before. When Donna managed a stammered introduction, he perceived the hostility in the air but misinterpreted the cause. "You must be hungry, Keith," he said. "I'm sure you haven't had any dinner. I apologize for keeping your wife working past her regular quitting time." As he spoke he proffered the half-empty bag of chips.

"Uh, no thanks," mumbled Keith, who had been thoroughly prepared for a tirade, but had not determined what he would say in the event of a faultless scenario.

Looking on, Donna was glad that Mr. Linderson's predominant interest was food, so that he would not suspect what was really in Keith's mind. Much to her embarrassment, her boss then handed her an unexpected dinner allowance and told her to take her 'poor husband' out to dinner at once.

Later, over a bowl of spaghetti and meatballs, a chagrined Keith said, "I'm sorry about tonight, but I love you, and I want you with me every possible second."

Married less than a year, Donna accepted this excuse and dismissed Keith's actions as solicitous affection.

Sincerely Yours

Except for occasional outbursts of unwarranted jealousy, the Wendlers' marriage had gone smoothly. Donna and Keith had agreed to stabilize their finances before having children, and in five years they had sufficient savings to buy a large house in the suburbs of Calibon. The next five years were spent making extensive alterations to their home. Donna, a college art major, sketched structural revisions and built-in furnishings. Keith was skilled with his hands, and he was able to execute her designs. By the time Donna's first pregnancy was planned, the spacious home was finished.

Donna chose to combine motherhood with her job, an arrangement that had proved so satisfactory with her first child that she had kept her position after her second daughter was born. By then she was an expert legal secretary, the occupation she had chosen when she discovered that inexperienced artists were not in demand. Keith had not digressed from his original field, which was electrical engineering.

Before Donna started her current job, Keith had investigated the law firm to make sure that other females were employed there. He went to the office, pretending to need legal assistance. While scrutinizing the personnel, he rambled on and on about complex entanglements with the law. Six months later, at the company Christmas party, Donna worried that someone might recognize her husband and remember his fabricated tale of woe. But everybody appeared to have forgotten him, whether from short memories or tall cocktails.

Donna was thinking about these things while she dusted. She had to smile, but the wan smile vanished quickly. *What can I do about his berserk jealousy? Except for that, Keith is a considerate person. He's somewhat chauvinistic, but*

102

I don't mind that; in fact, I rather like the way he insists on holding my coat and helping me down staircases. He's a real gentleman.

Keith had always concurred with the foremost aspects of women's liberation, such as equal pay for equal work; nevertheless, he conformed to old-fashioned gallantries. He habitually relinquished his seat to a lady on a bus or train, and he was crestfallen when one woman told him, "I can stand on my own two feet as well as you can."

Though Keith rejected cooking and dishwashing (and pinning Christmas cards on ribbons), he readily shared the rest of the housework, with a prepossession for the heavier duties like floor-scrubbing and window-washing. Donna liked to cook and was not particularly enamored with scrubbing floors, hence the distribution of labor suited them both.

As for child-rearing, Keith had nurtured his daughters from the start, often walking or rocking tearful babies in the middle of the night. Though Donna and Keith were conscientious about hiring reliable caretakers for their daughters, they took turns staying home from work whenever the girls went through illnesses that seemed to call for a parent's loving presence.

Jobs and parenthood absorbed the Wendlers' full time and energy. Otherwise they kept their lives uncomplicated. Outings were mostly family affairs with the children—picnics, trips to zoos or museums, and faithful attendance at the girls' soccer games and ballet recitals.

One year Bridget entered a Father's Day contest for first-graders, who took their chewed pencils in hand to write in fifty words or less 'Why My Daddy Is the Greatest.' Bridget wrote:

My Daddy helps me wen I dont no how to add and reads storys and finds my tedy and brings us water and chanjes the sheet wen I spil it and hes not mad and kiss me good nite.

For this breathless sentence she won second prize, which was Dinner for Two at an elegant restaurant, for Daddy and his writer-daughter. But the Greatest Daddy magnanimously brought Mommy and Allison also, so the whole family could acclaim its budding author.

At this juncture, Donna was tidying the den, where Keith was still asleep, and as she harked back to Bridget's little prize-winning entry, she studied her sleeping husband's troubled countenance and impulsively covered him with a warm wool afghan. She smiled at the lumpy knots which were visible proof that Allison had assisted her in attaching the hand-knit afghan squares.

Donna was proud of her daughters. Once in a while, especially when she examined report cards, she wished they held history and geography in as high esteem as play and television. On the plus side, the girls were versatile, self-confident, and dependable. On weekdays they prepared their own breakfasts, not merely pouring packaged cereal from a box, but cooking oatmeal or omelets. Though they were competitive like most siblings, they usually worked and played well together; this year Donna and Keith had dispensed with the services of an after-school sitter.

Our family is in fine fettle, thought Donna, until some event associates me with the opposite sex—a mammoth adventure like calling a serviceman to fix the washing machine.

Donna started to think about the outlandish charges which Keith had leveled at her in years gone by. Sometimes it was no more than a sentence or two, spoken insinuatingly. The words were innocent enough, but they were accented in the wrong places: 'You're going to the library *again?* How long will it take you to select your books *this* trip?' Other allusions were made in a matter-of-fact voice:

'I see you're wearing your new dress to the office.' A wardrobe purchase was often the harbinger of a sly implication.

If I ignore the innuendoes, our life can be sublime for months. Thank goodness the really big episodes aren't frequent. But when Keith comes up with an outright accusation, it's insane. Like this furor last night about Alex Southerick. We can't loan my friend some money because my husband thinks I may have had an affair with him in the past, or am having one right now, or may have one in the future. His suppositions would be comical if I weren't the target.

Until now, she had not given much heed to the unreasonable concessions she had made through the years to keep her marriage compatible. She had sacrificed coveted watercolor lessons because the instructor, a prominent local painter, was a male. At social gatherings she made a practice of talking to women only, and if a man happened to join the group, she concentrated on refraining from smiling. The minute anyone started to tell a joke, she instinctively scanned the room to see if Keith might see her laughing when the punch line was delivered. That reflex stemmed from an incident after the office Christmas party a few years ago, when Keith had remarked disagreeably on the way home that she and Otto had certainly seemed to hit it off well.

"He told me a dumb joke, so I laughed. That's called civility," she had said. But petty conflicts like that disturbed her, and this year she had made an excuse not to attend the annual Christmas celebration. She had decided the party was not worth the inharmony. If she went to a beauty parlor, or bought a new gown before the festivity, Keith wanted to know why she was dressing up.

Her appearance was a common source of dissension. In the first month of marriage, when she put on a nicely fitted sweater to go to the office, she caused as much noise as if she had lighted a stick of dynamite. Since that detonation

Sincerely Yours

she had covered her striking anatomy with loose-fitting
clothing, solely to mollify Keith. She had replaced her
sweaters with flowing blouses, and her dresses were mostly
tent styles, the only kind Keith liked. "You want me to live
in tents, you must think you married Minnehaha," she
quipped.

One evening when they were getting ready to go to a
gala reception given by Keith's company, he kept repeating,
"Don't look too alluring."

After the third repetition she said curtly, "I'm going just
as I am, in this smock, with curlers in my hair."

She was sure Keith would be quick to object, but
instead he said, "Great! And leave off the makeup. Suits
me if those philanderers don't ever see you when you're
really decked out."

Donna could not believe his seriousness. "Do you think
I would actually go to a social function in this get-up?" she
asked.

"I can dream, can't I?" was his counter question, and she
left the room without responding.

When Keith awoke at one o'clock in the afternoon,
Donna forced a weak smile and suggested lunch. She
served it along with prattle about Bridget and Allison, sus-
taining a pleasant atmosphere in routine compliance with
her own mealtime regulations. But she had been thinking
for hours, and she had hammered out exactly what she
wanted to say to Keith after the meal was over. Her reflections had been fraught with ambivalent feelings, and at one
point she had quelled an impulse to run into the den and
pull off the afghan she had previously tucked carefully
around her slumbering husband. Maybe even swat him
with it. But now she was supremely calm.

As soon as Keith finished his coffee, she dropped the aimless chatter and proceeded with her planned speech. She had rehearsed it in her mind so many times that it sounded memorized:

"Keith, I've been thinking very deeply about you and me, and our marriage, and your monstrous jealousy. I've put up with a lot before this, but last night's accusation over a Christmas-card note from Alex Southerick—a man I haven't seen for almost five years—was absolutely the final straw. We've been married 21 years and I haven't wandered farther than the supermarket, and yet you have constantly suspected me of wrongdoing. Well, I'm fed up with being under suspicion because I say 'hello' to the mailman. You'd get mad if I called the firemen over while the house was on fire."

She stopped to catch her breath, then continued. "I'll agree not to send Alex Southerick the money. I'll agree to sit at another table at the class reunion. I'll play Pocahontas and wear tents. But only if you will go for counseling or some other kind of help to straighten yourself out. Something must be out of gear for you to have abominable thoughts about a wife who has always been faithful."

Keith stared at her and sat silent. He looked entranced, like a wide-eyed child watching his first butterfly. Then he got up and walked toward her slowly, still saying nothing. He put his arms around her, then tightened them, and as she returned his embrace she interpreted his reaction as agreement. Wordlessly, he led her to the bedroom, and she decided she could finish cleaning the house tomorrow.

———— ✠ ————

An hour later, lying in bed with one arm around Donna's shoulders, Keith began to talk.

"Before I say anything else I want to stress one paramount truth: I love you, Donna. I love you, I love you, I

Sincerely Yours

love you. And you are 100 percent right—I need help. My translation of Alex Southerick's letter revolted me too, and I sat up until early this morning thinking about it. The problem is with me, not you, and no matter what I say to you hereafter, I want you to be assured that I recognize that. There has to be an explanation for my vile conduct, but I can't figure out what it is. You're terrific for sensing that my vicious jealousy is more like an illness than a thrust at you, though I know I've made you suffer plenty.

"I'm glad you hit me with an ultimatum. That gives me added incentive to master this fixation, although that's what I had resolved to do anyway. It's like an alcoholic's wife getting disgusted and throwing the bum out.

"I know a fellow at work—Vernon—who used to be drunk more than he was sober. His wife endured it for four-teen years, then she finally said, 'Shape up or get out.' He left for one boozy month and then he went to Alcoholics Anonymous. The happy ending is, he's back with his wife and he hasn't had a drink for over four years. A few weeks ago we had a long talk during lunch and he told me he got help at A.A. from a Higher Power. I was impressed, but I did not connect any of this with myself, because I don't drink. But last night I got to thinking that my jealousy was just as debilitating as drinking.

"If I consider addiction as habitual behavior that I can't control, then I think I'm addicted to jealousy, if that's possible. Besides the cruel scenes I've put you through that you already know about, you wouldn't believe the rubbish I've kept to myself—visualizing you having clandestine meetings, or hugging men in the office. Stuff like that."

Donna looked nauseated.

"Don't worry. I knew these sick thoughts were unfounded, yet my mind was tortured by them. I even feel pangs of jealousy when our cat jumps up on your lap."

108

Donna had noticed Keith glowering when she stroked Ebony's sleek black fur, but she had supposed that he did not want the cat to shed hairs on the furniture.

Keith continued, "If other people can overcome drug and alcohol addictions, then I'm determined to conquer my obsession with jealousy. I've never heard of Jealous Maniacs Anonymous, but before going for therapy I'm going to try to get help from Vernon's Higher Power on my own. Vernon didn't go to church when he was drinking, and he still doesn't—he goes to A.A. meetings. But since there are no meetings for people addicted to jealousy, I'm going to start out by going to church with you and the girls tomorrow, and maybe I can get in touch with this Higher Power that way."

Donna's eyes opened wide. Without issuing the invitation so often that it would seem like nagging, she had periodically asked Keith to accompany her to church, especially after their daughters were born.

Keith went on, "Every Sunday you've gone off to church with the children, and I've rolled over in bed without giving a thought as to why I refused to go with you. Well, during the night I brooded over it for hours, and the only reasons I could come up with were pretty superficial. First, pure laziness. It was so pleasurable to sleep late on Sunday, then lounge around in a bathrobe, and not bother to shave unless we were going somewhere. Second, proving by this action—or inaction—that I'm a macho male, and once I make a stand, that's it. A 'he-man' doesn't buckle under and give in to his wife. No, I didn't think that all out on Sunday mornings—I simply went back to sleep— but that's what I believe was buried behind the snores."

Keith sat up in bed. His face was haggard; there were dark circles under his eyes. "Honey, I'm not promising miracles," he said. "I'm sure I can't change overnight. Just as an alcoholic might have a lapse here and there before he's permanently off the sauce, I might backslide a bit too, but at least you'll know I'm aware of my affliction and striving to overcome it. That's step Number One. Vernon says an alcoholic can't get anywhere without admitting he's out of control.

"But I still don't know what has made me a jealous maniac. Even after dredging up the story of my life—and running a movie of it before my eyes—I'm not able to fit earlier happenings into my present failing. At any rate, if I can rectify the fault, I don't think it's very important how I acquired it."

Then he told her about his former girlfriends, and confessed that he had been unduly distrustful of each one. He went on to relate the contretemps involving his father and the nameless shapely blonde.

After a pause he ended by saying, "I also intend to go to the open A.A. meetings with Vernon, as his guest. Don't think I'm demented—it seems feasible to me that a bad mental habit might be licked by the same means as a bad physical habit. Vernon emphasized that one of the A.A. credos is 'one day at a time,' and I aim to apply that concept immediately, today. This is merely one approach, and I could be mistaken about the way I propose to beat this thing. If you don't think I've improved by ninety percent in the next year, then we'll discuss other options. And I've made up trick phrases to use silently on myself when I feel an obnoxious remark coming on."

Donna was crying. "This sounds heavenly, Keith," she eventually managed to say. "But if you have beastly thoughts about me and suppress them—that won't be healthy for us either."

"That's right, and that's why I want a whole year, to work on eliminating the thoughts along with the words. I realize it will take time, and there may be a few unintentional slips. After I've accused you in the past, a logical part of my brain always told me that what I had said wasn't true, but the damage was done; and all the while this perverse side of my mind would be pulling in the opposite direction, urging me to believe the lie.

"One January, I made a New Year's resolution not to ever accuse you of anything again, but it didn't hold up. By February I was back in my old pattern. I can't do it alone, and I'm going to ask for guidance. Lord knows I need it."

Donna was in Keith's arms, weeping openly. Her long blonde hair was spread out like sunrays over Keith's chest. She thought about the card from Alex Southerick that had precipitated her husband's soul-searching.

Thank you, Alex, for helping me once again. You will never know how much your little note affected our lives. Now I wish more than ever that we were sending you the money.

She felt a surge of sorrow because it was Alex Southerick's pressing need of money that had served as the catalyst for this whole awakening. Shouldn't she thank Alex by coming to his aid? But after Keith had gone through such intense self-analysis, it seemed importune to put him to an immediate test by saying, "What about Alex Southerick?"

She tried to mention the loan twice, but the words caught in her throat, and she could not bring herself to say them. Wiping her eyes, she kissed Keith tenderly and got up from the bed. She tied her hair back in a bouncy ponytail and smiled fetchingly, but all she said was, "It's almost time for the girls to come home for supper."

Mr. and Mrs. Samuel Norpeg
90 Plane St.
Los Angeles, Calif. 90042

7

The rusty number 90, with bits of the zero chipped off, looked more like a slightly crooked 9C on the front door of 90 Plane Street in Los Angeles. The undistinguished townhouse bearing this number was the Norpegs' seventh home during nineteen years of marriage. In sharp contrast to the drab house, two resplendent automobiles were frequently parked next to it: Sam's ivory Cadillac limousine, and Roberta's red-upholstered black Mercedes Benz. The Norpegs had been living at this address for almost four years, a long stretch from their perspective. Nevertheless, they did not know anybody else who lived on Plane Street, nor for that matter, anybody else in the entire development of 410 undistinguished townhouses.

Although Sam and Roberta were married to each other, they were married first to their careers. They both worked ten to sixteen hours a day, eating and sleeping only when such bothersome functions became necessary. On some days they seemed unaware of each other's existence; they lived side by side like two peas in a pod, with an amount of interaction comparable to that of the peas.

Sam was a construction engineer who accepted projects in any part of the country. Roberta had not opposed periodic relocations because she had been able to advance her career with every move. Twice she had made a transfer near Sam's job, but in most instances she had resigned her position and found another in her field of selling and setting up computer programs. It had not been difficult to command more pay and expanded territories. She was competent and aggressive, and she brought solid experience to each new employer. In four years with her present company she had become chief Western representative, supervising all sales west of the Mississippi. She appeared to be headed toward the coveted appointment of national sales manager.

Because the Norpegs moved so often and were home so little, they were not selective about the apartments they rented; accessibility to an airport was far more compelling than the architecture of the living quarters. They flew in and out of town constantly, and when they were not traveling, they brought briefcases home, stuffed with paperwork for the late evening.

By some criteria, their marriage was harmonious, because they had no time for quarrels; but neither did they have time for more placid communication. Even sex waited for those rare junctures when all prerequisites converged: they were at home together; they were not beset with job priorities; and they were not physically or mentally drained.

Only once had they discussed the possibility of having children. Roberta said, "I think I'm capable of more elevating feats than changing diapers and tying shoelaces. What I want is to be tops in my career. I can live very well without babies bawling for pacifiers."

Sam was studying a thick sheaf of blueprints for a high-rise office building. His response was short and impartial: "Uh-huh."

"People say, have children, you won't be lonely when you're gray and grizzled," Roberta went on. "But that's not true. Your mother had two sons and three daughters—they've scattered to different states, and there she sits in Georgia, a widow, by herself. And *my* mother—well, my sisters Irma and Lucille live nearby and they visit her a lot—but I don't see her from one year to the next."

After the second "Uh-huh," the Norpegs' non-family was born.

━ ▪◆▪ ━

Roberta had grown up in the tiny village of Clooney, North Dakota, population 370. From early childhood her most impassioned wish had been to escape from Clooney. Even back then she was driven by her aspirations, striving for excellent marks so she could earn a scholarship. During her high-school years she had waited on tables in the town's only restaurant, and by the time she left for college she had saved the money for her clothes, luggage, and air-fare to Texas. The day she flew away from Clooney was the most thrilling day of her life, and she proceeded at once to set the pace for her present work standard by taking on a part-time job as a bank teller while maintaining above-average grades.

When Roberta met Sam he was 26 years old, and he had already seen Singapore, most of Europe, and 37 of the United States. He was an assistant superintendent in construction, his chosen province. His father was a military man, and the Air Force had dictated the family's worldwide changes in residence.

114

Roberta, who had felt shackled in Clooney for most of her life, was awestruck by the globetrotting Sam had done. Added to that were his handsome looks, and, more significant, his goals, which matched hers exactly. He wanted to 'make something of himself,' and to both Sam and Roberta this meant to achieve financial success.

The marriage of Roberta Wiley and Samuel Norpeg, after a year of courtship, embodied their parallel philosophies. Neither wanted to take time out from a full calendar to plan a wedding. Sam had never been in one place long enough to call it 'home,' and Roberta had no desire to be married back in Clooney, North Dakota. A bearded justice-of-the-peace in Houston, Texas, proclaimed Sam and Roberta husband and wife in a five-minute ceremony witnessed by hired strangers. The bride and groom left immediately for a weekend in Acapulco, and informed their parents of the big news by telephone when they returned.

The brevity of the honeymoon was due to Sam's reluctance to neglect his job, a fact that might have disturbed other brides, but made Roberta respect her groom all the more. Since she, too, felt obliged to hurry back to her post—her first job after college—she was in total compliance with their abbreviated travel plans. The newlyweds rushed back to Houston to their first flat. They knew in advance that Sam's project would be completed in a year, so Roberta could see no sense in hanging curtains or draperies.

"We'll just about get them up, and we'll be taking them down again," she said. Hence they lived with bare windows, except for the crumbling dark-green shades that were provided with the apartment. These were kept lowered 24 hours a day, because it was always dark by the time the Norpegs came home from work.

One year later they moved to New Orleans without ever having raised the shades.

Sincerely Yours

Though Roberta was meticulous at the office, in her home she was a slovenly housekeeper. When she was a teenager, her mother used to marvel at how she came forth from 'Piglandia' (as Mom labeled her room) looking as if she had stepped out of a salon instead of a bedroom where her mother claimed she could not find the bed.

But what her mother had considered wild disarray back then was sparkling order compared to Roberta's present home in Los Angeles, where Piglandia reigned on. Spread around the townhouse were unwashed stockings, half-filled coffee cups, moldy pizza crusts still in their square cartons, and numerous unidentified objects. All the rooms featured women's shoes, in every hue and heel. Ashtrays overflowed with the remains of Sam's cigars and Roberta's cigarettes. After nineteen years Sam had yet to see a bathroom without lingerie in the tub and hosiery on the towel-racks.

The massive Mediterranean furniture pieces in the bedroom and living room, purchased when Sam and Roberta were first married, looked tired from their moving-van existence. Bulky and out-of-scale in the small apartment, they were now repositories for any miscellany that needed room.

Sam was by nature tidier than Roberta. He put his shoes in boxes and hung his suits in the closet. But the rest of the conglomeration was too overpowering for a one-man attack. Once in a while he would become disgruntled by the jungle effect, mostly when he wanted a catnap, and the bed and sofa were strewn with Roberta's clothing.

"Can't you leave six inches of free space?" he would ask, and Roberta would compound the muddle by transferring the offending items to the floor.

Yet no one observing Roberta in the course of a business day would have believed that she had emerged from such chaos. Like Cinderella stepping out of the scullery, Roberta in the outside world was preened to princess perfection.

—·—·—✦✦✦·—·—

Sam and Roberta did not generally eat full meals together at home. Sometimes one of them would fry bacon and eggs, or they would share ham sandwiches and cole slaw from a local delicatessen. Sam's early interest in learning to cook had been slowly stifled by stoves covered with messy coffeepots and grimy utensils. And Roberta, born without a quark of culinary inclination, could manage to make a slice of toast look unappetizing. As a result the Norpegs were regular customers at fast-food eateries, which suited their schedules as well as their dispositions.

When they had sufficient time, however, they went out to eat in a fancy restaurant. The occasion afforded them a balanced meal, along with an opportunity to talk to each other. Frequently the discussion turned to what they would do 'some day.' In reality they did not take vacations, but 'some day' Roberta wanted to travel to exotic islands. Sam, who had moved from country to country throughout his life, hoped 'some day' to settle down in a splendid home, though he realized that if it were to remain splendid he had better have the income to pay for an adequate staff. Sam and Roberta agreed that the epitome of the 'success' image they wanted to create was a yacht, crewed and ready for impromptu cruising. Possessing it was considerably more important than sailing it.

But their dreams were set aside; their occupations absorbed them. For the time being it sufficed to spout purposes that were more tangible than their goal of simply wanting to be wealthy.

Sincerely Yours

At their most recent restaurant dinner together, Sam remarked, "I'd be happy if 'some day' you would just clean up the bedroom."

Roberta's eyes came up swiftly from the glazed duckling spread out in front of her. "Why me?" she said with a glower.

"Why you? Because it's 95 percent your junk. My underwear is in the dresser. Or the hamper."

"Well, your shaving stuff isn't. I work as many hours and make as much money as you do. You should be equally responsible for straightening the house, but I'm the one who always takes care of it." By that she meant calling a cleaning service once a month to tunnel through the mountains and form narrow valleys of walking space. "Furthermore, it's not really dirt, just a little clutter."

Sam shuddered at the thought of the 'little clutter,' but he had actually become quite used to disorder. When he had a knotty construction problem on his mind, he would walk through the rooms and step over piles of laundry or newspapers without seeing them. He made no further comment; the succinct dialogue about housekeeping was closed.

Over mint parfaits and demitasse, Sam asked, "Are we going to have a Christmas tree this year?"

"I have no time to shop for one—to say nothing of putting it up. If you want a tree, that's fine, go ahead and do the whole project, but count me out. Don't forget, someone has to dismantle it later. Seems like a lot of wasted energy, doesn't it? At any rate we probably wouldn't have five minutes to look at it."

"I'd look at it if you decorated it."

"Hah! Maybe if I set it smack in the center of the hallway. The only way you'd see it is if you fell over it."

Sam thought, there's plenty to fall over already. But he didn't say it aloud. Then he dismissed the subject entirely when he remembered that he would be going out of town on Christmas night, and would not be at home anyway for the rest of the holiday season.

—·—◼◆◼—·—

Since business seldom took Roberta anywhere in the vicinity of Clooney, North Dakota, she rarely saw her mother or sisters. Bobbie—which was her hometown nickname—had no tolerance for her family's rustic lifestyle. Even occasional phone calls from her mother produced monosyllabic responses that showed little interest in kinship.

Bobbie's last visit home was three years ago, for a few hours during the week before Thanksgiving, when she happened to have an appointment with a customer in North Dakota. Garbed and groomed in her customary rich fashion, she rented a car and drove to Clooney without phoning. Mom would never be outside of town, she thought with disdain.

She was right. Nelly was home, making the mincemeat for Thanksgiving pies in her cheery red-and-white kitchen. In personality, Nelly was the direct opposite of Roberta: she kept her cottage immaculate, but she did not like to dress up, and she never wore makeup. "The way God made my eyes is good enough," she would say.

Still attractive though somewhat plump, Nelly brimmed with smiles at the sight of Roberta. "It's been three years!" she exclaimed joyfully. "You look gorgeous, Bobbie, just like the ladies on television."

Nelly stretched open her arms, but Roberta did not enter them. "You'd look better with some lipstick and a new wardrobe," said Roberta in a flat voice. "And after a diet," she added after giving her mother a second glance.

Nelly disregarded the criticism. "I've been praying every day for you to come see me. You're the answer to my prayers!"

Roberta's scorn was so glaring that Nelly quickly substituted another topic. "Your old friend Tootsie just had a baby. A girl!"

"So what else is new? It's her fourth, or fifth or sixth, isn't it?"

"You two were practically inseparable in high school. I thought you might want to go see her while you're here."

"I barely have a couple of hours, Mom. I have to catch the six-twenty plane back to L.A."

"Tootsie's other little girl is four—she's the most adorable child I've ever seen. She should be a model," declared Nelly, as she held out a taste of mincemeat.

Roberta shook her head to the spoonful of food. "She'll never be a model if she doesn't grow up to have more gumption than her mother has," she said. "There are no modeling agencies out here in the boondocks. All Tootsie knows how to do is have kids."

"Raising children is a good way of life, Bobbie," countered Nelly, licking the spoon clean herself. "You don't know how satisfying it is to watch them spring up. In the beginning they creep, and then they take a wobbly step, and pretty soon they learn to run. They run to you when they fall down, and you can kiss the bruise and put a little bandage on it, and like a magician you can turn tears into smiles. It's not all bad, Bobbie."

"You don't get paid for pasting bandages on kids' elbows, Mom. When I was a teenager I decided what counts. Personally, I like driving to work in my Mercedes. I like wearing designer clothes and eating in exclusive restaurants. I want genuine gold chains, and real diamonds in my earrings, not rhinestones. I'd rather put the smiles on my own face."

Nelly shook her head and sighed. "So where are all these smiles? I haven't seen you smile since you came in. Irma and Lucille are laughing all the time about funny little things the kids have said or done."

"Our outlooks are not comparable, Mom. I need something more sophisticated to laugh about than some kid giving his tooth to the Tooth Fairy."

Nelly started to bring out bowls of tantalizing food, but Roberta insisted she was not hungry, so Nelly went back to filling pie-shells while she talked. "Let me tell you what little Matilda said yesterday. That's Irma's youngest, she's not quite three. Irma and Hiram have a habit of spelling words that they don't want the kids to make out—the way Papa and I did with you girls—especially goodies like c-a-n-d-y and i-c-e c-r-e-a-m. Well, baby Matilda spends hours listening to her alphabet record, where a chorus sings out the A-B-C's over and over again. And yesterday, when they were out shopping, Matilda says, 'Mommy, let's buy some l-m-n-o-p'."

Nelly laughed at the memory of her granddaughter's clever remark. She licked her finger and continued, "And once when I told Junior he had mispronounced 'yelephant,' he said, 'No, I didn't, a yelephant is a yellow elephant'." She chuckled and glanced over at Roberta, who was staring at her as if she were deranged. Nelly relinquished the cute-kids theme and inquired, "Are you going to see your sisters?"

"No, I told you, I have a tight schedule. Besides, on my last call at Lucille's, I held her baby on my lap for ten minutes and what does he do but yank on my best pearls and break the gold chain. We spent an hour on our hands and knees hunting for pearls, and it cost me a bundle to have them restrung. That's fun? That's smile time? And listen to this—this is the part I couldn't believe—Lucille wasn't concerned about my jewelry; she kept worrying that one of the kids might find a pearl and swallow it. Not that she cared that it would be one less pearl on my necklace, she was afraid it might hurt the kid's stomach! He deserves indigestion if he's dining on fifty-dollar pearls! Lucille doesn't have a job, and she spends her days bringing up children—why doesn't she teach them not to pull ladies' chains off their necks?"

Nelly sighed again. "Lucille's son was five months old when that happened. You can't teach manners to an infant. Children at that age grab at anything that fascinates them. There would be something wrong with a baby that didn't tug on pretty objects."

"Then I wish they'd have babies that had something wrong with them," Roberta snapped. "I might have known you'd stick up for the kid. That's what I mean about this place—nobody has a realistic sense of values."

Shaking a bit as she poured Roberta a cup of coffee, Nelly switched the discourse to Roberta's friends from her school days. Ozzie Yitville, one of Bobbie's first suitors, was doing quite well; he had bought two cows recently. "I dare say you have lots more highbrow friends these days," Nelly commented as she set a tempting home-baked jelly roll on the table.

"Sam and I have no time for friends," answered Roberta. "We don't get a chance to clean the house and entertain people in it. Maybe some day we'll have couples over, and we'll drink liqueurs and eat truffles—provided they're served by a maid. But at present we don't want playmates." She took a long drag on her extra-thin cigarette in its sterling-silver holder. Seeing her mother's dazed expression, she attempted a further elucidation.

"We both work at least twelve hours a day, Mom. You can't imagine the competition I have to deal with. Computer companies are coming out of the woodwork. I wouldn't expect anybody in this one-horse town to understand. The local bank doesn't even have a computer system."

"The local bank is lucky to have a few depositors. Jobs aren't too plentiful in this area."

"I know! So why don't the residents move out and do something with their lives?"

Nelly thought of the small neat houses, lined up in rows on the tree-shaded streets, their yards framed with white picket fences. She pictured the children playing jackstones on the stoops, and hopscotch on the front walks. "Folks have different notions about what's 'something'," she answered, sitting down at the table to chat. "All some couples want is a clean little bungalow in a clean little town, a place where they can bring up their children in peace, with kindly neighbors to talk to and depend on when the going is rough."

"I know, the hayseeds around here don't have any ambition," Bobbie smirked.

"You don't understand, Bobbie—that *is* their ambition."

"How can that be an ambition—to stay in Clooney? That's impossible! I wanted to leave when I was nine. People here don't have any drive, and without drive they'll never get anywhere. And if they don't want to get anywhere except Clooney, they must be either lazy or crazy."

"Some people leave, and that's their privilege. I'm not saying there aren't any decent bigger cities. But some folks are partial to a village atmosphere where everyone knows each other, and people stop for a word with anyone they meet on the way to the grocery. When there's a birth or a death, neighbors come by with cupcakes and roasted turkeys. Your own sisters like it here.

"We have hoedowns and quilting bees, christenings and funerals. At the Ladies' Aid Sewing Circle, we knit or crochet, and we tear up our worn sheets into bandages for the city cancer center. The whole town celebrates when there's a wedding and grieves when there's an accident, like when little Kim Epson fell out of a second-story window."

"That's one of the things I can't stand," said Roberta. "Everybody knows everyone else's business. You can't blow your nose without somebody circulating a rumor that you have a cold."

"But if the cold turned into pneumonia, folks would be right there to help you out. Why, since Tootsie's baby was born three weeks ago, I'll bet twenty or thirty friends have stopped by to cook her supper, pick things up from the store, or take her other kids for a day. Money isn't everything, Bobbie."

"It's not the money alone, Mom, though that's part of it. It's the fame, the power, the glory. It's being introduced at a convention as the company's most outstanding manager. It's influential businessmen in custom-tailored suits jumping up when you walk into a room. Clooney is stagnant. The local yokels stand on street corners and talk about the weather. They even know the dogs by name. For me the utmost bore would be to stroll about with a carriage, listening to this meaningless prattle, and then to go home and shove gloppy goo into a baby's mouth. Where's the challenge?"

"It's in guiding those helpless creatures into becoming real people."

"Well, I think I guided myself, but at least you've got one out of three," said Roberta in a vainglorious tone.

Doing her own calculation, Nelly came up with two out of three. But she decided to end the debate by making no response. She saw that Roberta had not touched the jelly roll. Still trying to please, Nelly brought out a plate of fresh oatmeal cookies, which Roberta declined.

"I think you overwork yourself, Bobbie. How about an eggnog, or a vanilla milkshake? You look a whit peaked."

"In L.A. we call it slender, Mom." Roberta puffed on her fourth cigarette in an hour. "And no thanks, I don't want a milkshake. Do you have the makings of a Manhattan? Oh, never mind, I don't know why I'm bothering to ask that. Out here it's vanilla-milkshake country. Oh, I know Clooney has Frankenheimer's famous saloon, but the only customers are men in flannel shirts and dirty overalls. A big time on the town here is a pizza with pepperoni. That's what Ozzie and I had after the so-called Senior Prom—a pizza with pepperoni."

"Well, anyway, you used to come home from your dates with Ozzie laughing."

"Maybe I was laughing because the people here dote on such commonplace stuff."

Nelly said nothing. A visit from Bobbie was extraordinary, and Nelly was determined to keep this one cordial. She tried to disguise her feelings, and to feign a blase manner in keeping with her present company. She had not been invited to any one of Roberta's seven dwellings, and now she heard her daughter proclaim, "Some day Sam and I will own a stupendous mansion with indoor and outdoor swimming pools."

"Oh, I didn't know you liked to swim," said Nelly.

"Sam and I don't swim; that's not the point," stated Roberta, thoroughly confusing her mother. "Pools go along with the type of house we have in mind. It wouldn't make sense to buy a huge house without a swimming pool. But we're not buying any house until we can afford the help to go with it. I'm not a housekeeper, I'm a computer analyst. I have more valuable things to do with my life than swing dustcloths like Irma and Lucille."

Nelly said, "I see," even though she didn't. She scrutinized her daughter's pretty countenance and tried to make out how it would look without the layers of blush, powder, and foundation cream; and without the mascara, eyeliner, and blue eye shadow. She noticed that the corners of Roberta's mouth turned down.

When the talk shifted to clothes and furs that Bobbie had recently purchased, Nelly resolved to stick to non-controversial subjects for the rest of the visit, limiting her comments to 'That's grand,' or 'How lovely.'

———— ✠ ————

Roberta left. She did not kiss her mother good-bye. Her lips, impeccably brushed in the latest frosted shade, had not formed a single smile. Nelly waved at the door but Roberta did not turn around. She drove to the airport and flew back to Piglandia.

Nelly said aloud, "Well, she doesn't eat and she doesn't kiss—it's no wonder her lipstick is never smeared." She put away the cookies and the jelly roll, and sat down to think.

For years I've been feeling downhearted about all the good times Bobbie was missing, little things like taking a child to the playground. I see now that she would hate it. Today I'm going to stop praying for Bobbie to have a baby. The truth is, my Bobbie would be a terrible mother. Bobbie is sharp; she picked this up way ahead of me, and she made the proper choice. She's doing what she wants, she stays married to one man, and she has all those dandy things she likes. So why am I crying?

Well, it's taken me a long time to go along with what Bobbie does, so I can't complain if it takes Bobbie a while to respect what her sisters do. She's smarter than we are, and one of these days it will come out straight in her mind. Maybe she's right. Maybe she'll look happier when she gets her cook and her castle. She'll probably run the whole works pushing buttons on those newfangled computers. Anyhow, she's Bobbie, and I'm not going to try to make her somebody else.

Nelly wiped away a tear with the ruffle of her apron and started to hum.

Sam was no better than Roberta at fostering maternal and sibling relationships. On his last visit to his mother in Georgia—an uncommon event—he strode up and down the parlor like a caged panther. When his mother tried to start a conversation, he said, "I'm going to check out the construction in this burg." When he returned it was an hour before his flight take-off.

"Good seeing you, Ma," he said while putting on his coat. His mother watched him speed away in his rented Continental. She thought, his eyes were wide open, so I guess he *did* see me.

Several months after that, Sam stopped between flights at his brother's house in Minneapolis. In obvious distress, his brother asked Sam for a fifty-dollar loan, and he was about to explain the reason for it when Sam bellowed, "You haven't seen me for two years and as soon as I walk in the door you bleat out 'lend me fifty bucks'?" He was so irate that he gave no ear to the problems: his brother had no job, his wife was undergoing treatment for leukemia, and he had no cash to refill an urgent prescription.

Afterward, back home, Sam grumbled to Roberta, "My family thinks about nothing but money."

When mail came into the Norpeg household, it settled itself comfortably into its surroundings. Whoever came home from work first would bring in the envelopes and leave them in the least-littered niche available. The next night's batch would most likely be deposited in an unrelated spot. It might be left unopened for weeks. Perhaps the basis for this apathy was that the envelopes did not arouse curiosity. Office mail was stimulating, but home postal deliveries were prosaic: mainly bills, advertisements, and pleas for donations.

Roberta might browse through some of these items when her hair or nail-polish was drying, and then leave pieces here and there, on the radio, the dresser, or the toilet tank. Eventually many would be covered with coffee mugs and spoons, while others found their way down under the sofa cushions. The infrequent personal letters they received, mostly from Roberta's mother, were always misplaced without being answered.

In December, the Norpegs received the largest quantity of personal mail of the year—their Christmas cards. As with other mail, greeting cards were often brushed aside for many days. If the cards were covered up in the meantime by a blouse or a magazine, they might not see the light of day again.

Each holiday season Sam and Roberta received fewer Christmas cards, as their older relatives died, or failed to record constantly changing addresses. The decrease in card volume also confirmed that there was no room in the Norpegs' lives for the promotion of friendship.

Sam was out-of-town for a consultation when Roberta, coming home wearily at nine o'clock, brought in the mail that included Alex and Marcia Southerick's Christmas card. Since there were only two cards, Roberta decided to open them. She scanned Alex's note—'I'm going to ask you a tremendous favor...to lend me $1,000...' She thought little about it, but instead of dropping the card in the handiest open space, she put it on top of the other papers on Sam's desk.

When Sam returned the following day, Roberta was away at a seminar. He went directly from the front door to his desk to do some work before retiring. Thus he spotted the Southericks' card, which under other circumstances might have gone unread well past the stated deadline for a loan.

The four years Sam had spent in college comprised the longest period he had stayed in one place in his life; except for relatives, he had not been acquainted with anyone longer than he had known his classmates. Among those classmates, Alex Southerick had been his closest friend. Yet he skimmed over Alex's unique request with no change of expression, as if he were running his eyes over a dull news article. He tossed the card aside, lit a cigar, and started to read a book of building specifications.

Roberta was home for two days before she recalled the card. "Sam, did you see the note on a Christmas card from your friend Alex Southerick? I think I laid the card on your desk, or on the coffee table. I read it fast—I think it was about borrowing money."

It was midnight and Sam was pulling a pair of wrinkled pajamas out of the dryer. He reflected for a moment and then acknowledged, "Oh yeah, I saw it."

"Well, what about it?"

"Whatta ya mean, 'what about it'?"

"Are you sending him the money?"

"Nah."

"I haven't written our cards yet. He's your friend, do you want to answer the note on our card?"

"Don't send them a card, just omit them. Let them think we moved again."

Roberta scratched absent-mindedly at a cigarette hole on the lapel of her bathrobe. "What about next year?" she asked. "We'll probably be at this address for a couple more years."

Sincerely Yours

"Oh, cross them off the list altogether. I know we saw them when we lived in Boston, but we don't see them any more. Last time I saw Alex was at that class reunion four or five years ago."

"Isn't Alex the one who helped you with math? When I first met him in Boston, you told me that you and Alex were buddies in college."

"Sure, we were sports pals. We went to the football games together. And basketball. And yes, he came to my rescue in geometry and trigonometry. In fact he tutored me for six semesters. He was a whiz in math. So I passed the courses with flying colors. That was centuries ago. I don't need help now with math, or anything else. Forget it."

"All right." I have to admire Sam, thought Roberta. He's remarkably clear-sighted. He goes straight to the core of an issue and makes a split-second decision.

A few minutes later Sam's remarkable clear-sightedness inspired him to make a suggestion. "I've been thinking," he said. "You're up to your ears in work, but before the holidays you always go through your Christmas address book and write out card after card like an empty-headed robot. Why bother? They're no more than a bunch of names and addresses on a list. Who needs them? Are these people going to buy computer systems from you? Are they going to ask me to manage construction of a shopping mall? That's the question, and the answer is 'no'."

Roberta lit a cigarette and held it in her mouth while she rummaged through her desk drawers. She dug out her Christmas-card roster and started to read the names. "Mmmm, I guess you're right. I doubt if I'll ever see Tootsie again; she sends me a two-page photocopied newsletter every Christmas. She even puts in the earth-shattering news that her cat had kittens. Half the time I don't even read it. She has five or six children; I've lost track. Probably has a shape like a Tootsie-Roll to match her name. But

130

can you imagine a more tedious life? She must relate to her cat, they're both propagating the species. Here's another name, a woman in a nursing home. Why do I keep sending her cards? I don't even know if she's still alive. Habit, I suppose. Thanks for the idea, Sam. Not sending out cards will save me hours. But what about your mother?"

"Yeah, send one to my mother." His tone was conciliatory.

"I'll get two cards and you can write one out to your mother and I'll send one to Mom and that will be it. And speaking of class reunions, somewhere around here is a bulletin about your reunion coming up next spring. I can't plan that far ahead for a social affair, but I thought you might be interested."

"Nah, I passed my business cards out at the last reunion, and I didn't get a single job prospect. One of the guys was a lumber salesman, for Pete's sake. Jasper Zamp. He told me he used to sell shoes. What would *he* build? Nothing bigger than two feet, right? Jasper Zamp. A retail salesman with two kids. Probably has more by now, he seemed to be hung up on his kids."

"Well, if I come across the announcement again, I'll discard it. And now that we've decided not to send Christmas cards, I'll throw away this list of people we never see." The small address book with a faded poinsettia on the felt cover made a clunking noise in the metal trash container. It was followed later by Alex Southerick's Christmas-card request.

Mr. and Mrs. Luke Brend
649 Mandor Ave.
Gansville, Mass. *01443*

8

Luke drove slowly down Mandor Avenue. He looked
tired, and he sighed as he wondered what entries were listed on The Schedule for the evening. But as he approached
house number 649, his face changed, lighting up with a
wide grin. The reason was apparent in the form of three
boisterous young red-haired boys who came racing to meet
him, each striving to outdo the other in speed.

Luke parked in the driveway, and his sons clamored
inside the car to hug him and shriek and tug at his arms in
a frenzy that was cheeringly disproportionate to the fact
that he had been away from home but ten hours. The tempestuous greeting was swift, however. Father and sons wasted no time in entering the house, as all four of them knew
that supper would be served at exactly six o'clock, and not
a minute later.

The three boys had inherited their mother's brilliant
tresses; Luke was glad that they were not heir to his own
dull blondish-brown hair. So that his little redheads could
be ensured college educations, he had consented to divide
the home chores when Faye returned to her teaching pro-

fession a year ago. But he never referred to Faye's Daily Schedule, prominently thumbtacked in center position on the kitchen bulletin board; he depended on Faye to impart his duties. Because he did not want to accede to systemization, he did not even try to remember whether Monday was listed as Vacuum Night or Polish-the-Pots Night.

A conflict hung in his mind about The Schedule: he recoiled from the inflexible computation of every minute of every day, but on the other hand he had to admire his wife's ability to teach algebra, run a smooth household, and still give liberal attention to the children. Yet he could not comprehend why it was unthinkable to reverse the evenings once in a while, with no particular motive— sweep the walk on Tuesday instead of Thursday, for example. But this would be heresy, according to Faye, who upheld her position with a quote from her old friend Sheila, the uncontested Queen of Schedules: 'A slipshod schedule is a slipshod life.'

Luke had been enlightened about scheduling and Sheila many years before; in fact, on the day he and Faye got back from a two-week honeymoon. Faye announced that because they would be returning the next day to their jobs, she was going to coordinate an impartial division of housekeeping tasks; later they could discuss his assignments if he objected to them. She settled down at the kitchen table and worked out an agenda that covered, as Luke said afterward, everything except breathing.

Domestic burdens in a three-room apartment were moderate; Luke was not averse to watering plants or changing bed linens. The only notation he found intolerable— even abhorrent—was Scheduled Sex. He was dumfounded when Faye, working on her calendar, glanced up from the table and asked casually, "How much time should I allow for sex?"

It took Luke a moment to find his tongue. "I don't think sex is something that can be programmed," he finally said.

"I know from experience that what you don't schedule gets lost or forgotten, so it will be best if we list it."

A newlywed of two weeks, in love with his wife, Luke could not imagine sex being lost or forgotten just because it was not written down on a piece of paper. He told her this, but Faye responded, "Yes, it could happen. The chief reason I took up scheduling was that I had almost lost sight of my favorite hobby, embroidery."

What a comparison! thought Luke.

Faye went on, "When I was about twelve, I started to embroider a tablecloth. I loved doing it; I cherished every stitch. But then I began a paint-by-numbers picture, and I had disorderly leaf and shell collections lying around my room. Nothing was being actively pursued. Most of the time I couldn't even finish my homework.

"When I was fifteen, I met a girl named Sheila who was a cheerleader, a member of the Student Council, and president of the Science Club. She sewed her own clothes, cut and set her hair, completed all her schoolwork, and more than that, she cleaned her parents' house and started dinner while her mother worked. I asked her how she was able to accomplish so much. I'll never forget her answer—it was the turning point of my entire life—and I'm going to tell you what she said." Faye's eyes were shining, her voice reverent, as if she were about to reveal the Eleventh Commandment. Luke did not interrupt.

"We were walking home from school, and Sheila said, 'I don't have any surplus time this week, but if you want, I'll schedule an hour next Tuesday after school to guide you.' The following Tuesday I reached her house fifteen minutes late, and she said politely, 'Here's the primary rule. If you're going to do something at four o'clock, do it at four o'clock, not four-fifteen. You've already taken up one-quarter of our four-to-five-o'clock allowance. But anyhow, let's get going.' She sat down at her typewriter and inquired about my movements for one day, hour by hour, minute by minute; what things I did once or twice a week, and what I'd like to have done in six months.

"She explained that she allotted set periods for sewing, cooking, cleaning, and homework. Sheila pointed out how much time I frittered away by reading the funnies, or gabbing endlessly on the phone. Busy as she was, she squeezed in two more hours within a week to help me make up what she called a V.O.S.—my Very Own Schedule. And when I carried out my V.O.S., right to the minute, it worked like magic!"

Faye was exultant. "My mother and father couldn't get over it. I got everything done, including that huge table-cloth. My grades improved, and I found I had time to spare, so I joined the French Club and the girls' archery team. Ever since then I run on a schedule. In college I made top grades in my courses while taking part in seven extra-curricular activities. I've lost track of Sheila, but I'll be indebted to her for the rest of my days for showing me the light."

As she spoke, Luke studied Faye's facial expressions. He thought she had revealed a touching little story of high-school friendship; he did not regard the details as portents of things to come.

But during the ensuing weeks, as The Schedule became a major force in his life, Luke began to wish his wife had never seen either Sheila or the light. He felt cheated, because every moment of Faye's time was tied to a specific activity, right down to 'one minute to brush teeth.' If he said, "Hey, how about a break to snuggle on the sofa?", Faye sat down for a few moments but he could hear her mind clicking out an offsetting deletion from her thumbtacked slate. Even after he won a brief intermission, he was offended when Faye slipped away to do calisthenics or polish the faucets. Sure, everything gets done, he thought, but is it worth it?

Sometimes he had churlish reflections about Sheila: she must have scheduled three seconds to wave to Faye in the hall... I should meet the guy who married her; we'd have lots in common. But Sheila probably didn't schedule time to get married—or maybe she has a husband who's wild about scheduled sex. That way he can always be positive there will be no headaches on Wednesdays at nine-thirty.

Luke thought back to his boyhood home, which was normally strewn with mittens and jackets and sneakers, interspersed with collections of bottle-caps, comic books, and empty matchbook covers. He and his eight siblings brought home mud turtles and cans of worms and stray kittens and frogs in pails. His mother's only perceivable goal was to maintain her sanity. Luke had been catapulted from a home without any semblance of order into a temple of supreme organization.

He was quick to bring out the comical side of his plight. His sense of humor sustained him throughout the critical adjustment-to-marriage period, which in his case was complicated by adjustment to scheduling.

Faye decreed a fixed number of hours for work and a fixed number for sleep. "I'd better not have insomnia. I'll throw off the whole darn schedule," said Luke, chortling.

The Brends had 35 minutes for dinner. "Don't make anything too crunchy," Luke cautioned. "I might not be able to chew it in time."

Occasionally he paraphrased the classics and made quotation jokes. He had Horatio advising Hamlet, 'This above all: to thine own schedule be true.'

But after a few months of making light jests, inwardly hoping that The Schedule would go away, he resigned himself to the fact that it was going to stay, and keep on poking its thumbtacks into his wedded bliss.

It took a bit longer for penetration of the total concept: he would have to step aside and take second place, because the V.O.S. was Number One to his wife.

One Saturday morning in early fall, Luke looked out the window at the colorful foliage and bright sunshine. "What a beautiful day!" he exclaimed. "Let's go on a picnic."

"How can you say that when we're lined up to shampoo the rugs?" asked Faye, genuinely aghast. When she saw his face sag in disappointment, she added, "If you want to go on a picnic, I'll see if I can schedule one later in the month."

"That's not the same as going today—we might not have this splendid weather."

"Well, then, I'll arrange an alternate activity in case of rain."

Luke felt like a child at camp being placated by his counselor. He said coldly, "There *is* no alternate to a picnic in the woods on a sparkling autumn day."

But Faye hardly heard him. She was crouched down on the floor by the kitchen sink, reaching for the rug shampoo.

—— ⚜ ——

Luke resisted having his personal functions classified; he protested vigorously when Faye began to clock him with a watch while he was shaving, showering, and cutting his toenails. She also urged that he 'correct' a long-standing habit of reading in the bathroom, perhaps because it made methodical timing more precarious.

"You've missed your calling," Luke told his wife. "What a time-study engineer you'd make!"

He was staggered when Faye tearfully disclosed that she was making these calculations in order to give him his Very Own Schedule as an extra-special present on their first Christmas together.

"I wanted to give you the gift of light that Sheila gave me—your V.O.S., a whole new wonderful path," she sobbed.

His annoyance subsided. Until then he had regarded the scheduling as a personality quirk, but now he perceived that it was much more than that. Faye was taking her valuable scheduled time to compile notes for the most paradisiacal love-offering she could extend. He groped for gentle words to reject her Grand Prize. His voice was soft as he explained that hour-by-hour directives were not for everybody.

"You really choose to go on bumbling along in darkness?" Faye was incredulous.

He took her in his arms and held her close, to soften his refusal. Right then he would have liked to carry her into the bedroom, but it wasn't nine-thirty, and it wasn't even Wednesday.

After that, Faye and Luke each concluded that the other did not have an open mind on the subject of time regulation. There were not many uncommitted hours in Luke's life anyway; most of his time was taken up by his job as an accountant, and his commuting. In his limited leisure time, however, he was a pianist.

Luke had been captivated by music when he was four years old and had first heard the organ played at church. At nine, he earned the money for piano lessons by mowing lawns and delivering papers. His piano teacher, noting both his talent and his family's financial status, gave him an old, battered upright piano; Luke saved his money in dimes and quarters to have it tuned. When he was thirteen he refinished its splintery frame. Before reaching adulthood he was a versatile pianist who could play concertos as deftly as jazz beats; now he wanted to be free to play the piano when the mood struck him, not between seven and seven-thirty on Monday evenings. He pounded out turbulent themes when he was angry, and lighter melodies when he felt joyful. How could he know ahead of time when these emotions would surface?

He also liked to linger in the shower and think about warm raindrops. And he preferred to let nature designate the times of day that he would read magazines in the bathroom.

Whenever Luke thought about The Schedule, a perplexity kept recurring to him, and he finally expressed it one night when he and Faye were doing the dishes.

"Tell me something," he said. "During the year that we were dating, why didn't you mention that you lived rigidly by the clock?"

She wrinkled her brow as she tried to recall her rationale. "I suppose in the beginning it seemed rather private," she answered. "The amount of time I spent bathing and getting dressed and brushing my hair—I had those acts recorded, but that's not the kind of topic one discusses on a date. Then as we became more serious, I gathered that you weren't on any type of schedule, not even a rudimentary one, so I had in mind that when we were married I would surprise you."

You sure succeeded there, thought Luke, as Faye continued.

"Not many people know how to get things done, and they waste hours bewailing that they don't have enough time, the way I wailed when I was in high school. Thank

139

goodness I learned how to get organized when I was fifteen."

"Do you mean to tell me that you mapped out a distinct number of hours for our dates?"

"Of course."

Luke almost dropped a dish. Thinking over his courtship, he remembered that Faye was prompt for every date. Back then he had considered her punctuality to be laudable; his co-workers complained about having to wait while their girlfriends applied lipstick or took curlers out of their hair. He had also observed Faye glancing at her watch after a movie, and sometimes remarking that it had been a lengthy show, and she would like to go straight home instead of stopping for a snack. He assumed she was heeding her parents' curfew, and he thought that was praiseworthy too.

In his imagination Luke concocted 'Faye's Love Equations' as they might have been reckoned by his algebra-teacher wife:

x (dates) plus y (hand-holding hours) equals Infatuation

x (dates) plus y (kisses) equals True Love

x hours of sex equals one child

He ended his figmental equations to ask abruptly, "How come nothing was scheduled on our honeymoon?"

"Mostly because I didn't know what to expect—I was inexperienced, you know. Our honeymoon was my first unscheduled time since I was fifteen."

"Honey, you certainly deserved it!" said Luke with fervor.

"You're building up an antagonism about it," rejoined Faye. "Frankly, I missed my V.O.S. It was like not having a goal."

Thus, while Faye was proud that anyone could set a watch by her comings and goings, Luke chose to find out the hour from the radio. He did receive a fortuitous bonus because of his stance: a close rapport with Faye's mother, who had never been totally converted to the regimen either. Luke and his mother-in-law periodically shared covert winks when Luke made such remarks as, 'I know she loves me as long as she keeps me on her V.O.S.'

After two years of apartment living, Faye and Luke bought a conventional Cape Cod house, with a small back-yard, in the suburbs of Boston. A year later, Faye resigned her teaching post, just before her first son was born. The house, with its neat white clapboards and green shutters, was a dream house to both of them. Faye had a smack of New England thriftiness in her makeup; she budgeted carefully and postponed the purchase of new furnishings until savings accumulated. Since Luke had no predilections about decorating, Faye indulged her own bias for a colonial setting. She drew up a five-year outline for the gradual acquisition of Early American furniture throughout the house. Although a family of three children was created during the same time span, the furniture arrived according to plan and each piece was paid for in full with cash. As it turned out, Early American was a good choice, built sturdily of solid maple and appropriate for growing boys.

On the day that Faye quit her job to raise a family, she cut Luke's home labors down to almost nothing. Even when the second and third boys were born, she handled everything except the lawn. Luke marveled at how she stretched her hours to fit in the extra work that more children entailed.

"With Ethan, I eliminated canning and freezing from the vegetable garden," she said blithely, "and with Joel, I eliminated the whole garden."

141

Faye's system revolved around seven lists that embraced every conceivable action needed to maintain a house and yard and a family of five. 'The Big Seven,' Luke called them: Daily (make beds, cook meals, take shower); Twice-a-Week (vacuum, do laundry, dust furniture); Weekly (scrub floors, iron clothes, buy groceries); Twice-a-Month (clean cellar, bake cookies, wipe cabinets); Monthly (pay bills, polish furniture, defrost refrigerator); Twice-a-Year (wash windows, change curtains, tidy closets); Yearly (shampoo rugs, have family party, decorate for Christmas). Because 'clean up cellar' was scheduled twice a month, Luke swore he owned the most sanitary basement in Massachusetts.

The most destructive bombs that were ever dropped on The Schedule were sicknesses in the family. When any of the boys became ill, Faye almost made herself sick too by taking care of the ailing child and then staying up late to carry out her day's program, reducing her normal span for sleep.

Luke had never been so sick as to disorganize The Schedule. Thank God for that! he thought one day when a severe backache kept him home from work. I can foresee the calendar entries when I die:

'Funeral for Luke - 4 hrs.'

'Clean out Luke's bedroom closet - 2 hrs.'

This amused him to such a degree that he laughed out loud, but when Faye asked him "What's the joke?", he could hardly tell her that he was chuckling over the schedule he predicted she would write for his funeral day.

Faye herself did not swerve from her plotted course because of minor ailments such as colds and headaches; pain and suffering were not nearly as oppressive to her as an unfinished agenda. Once she was gravely ill with pneumonia, and had a fever high enough to make her forget her schedule for two full days. On the third morning when

Luke asked her solicitously if she wanted anything, she whispered weakly, "Please bring me my calendar so I can see what isn't getting done." She propped herself up on pillows and inserted the foremost neglected entries into the following week's chart.

Luke deplored her putting this unnecessary strain on herself; nevertheless, her pneumonia left him with a side effect: a grudging appreciation of The Schedule. He had taken time off from work to nurse his sick wife and to oversee his three preschool sons. During this stint he had discovered that the everyday needs of children six months old, two-and-a-half, and four-and-a-half were so multifarious that he had little chance to cook or clean or even eat. When he returned to the office after a week, he was thoroughly fatigued, despite having left dirty dishes in the sink and overflowing hampers in the bedrooms.

He was forced to concede that The Schedule enabled Faye to take care of a house and three youngsters, and somehow keep all of them clean. It seemed to him like a miracle that she could also prepare flavorful meals, in contrast to his dried-out hamburgers with canned beans.

In a few weeks Faye had everything humming again, although Luke thought she would have a relapse when she had to omit an entire semi-annual ritual, the Changing of the Curtains.

◆━◆

After ten years at home with the children, Faye returned to her teaching career. The boys were ages six, eight, and ten. ("The Schedule told us to produce a boy every two years," said Luke with mock solemnity.) Luke agreed to share housekeeping duties when Faye went back to her job, and Faye made up a revised schedule to accommodate her new hours. Luke's workload burgeoned overnight from nothing to plenty.

At this stage, all of the children were able to read, and each child had a schedule written in words at his individual reading level. Douglas was given the privilege of running the vacuum cleaner, almost like an award, on his tenth birthday. Eight-year-old Ethan did a creditable job of dusting the furniture twice a week. After school, Joel, six, took the clean dishes out of the dishwasher and set the dining-room table.

A child who executed every item of his daily rota, with no verbal reminders, earned a gold star on his calendar; twenty gold stars in a month merited an ice-cream sundae, while a perfect record reaped a surprise present in addition to the sundae.

How the boys scrambled for sundaes and surprises! Luke recollected his own childhood, when he and his sisters and brothers sought to avoid toothbrushes at any cost. His sons wrestled with each other for first rights to the bath- room sink: toothbrushing earned one more notch toward a gold star.

With this background, Luke wondered if the boys would grow up to find scheduling a comfort or a curse. Would it be their pathway to light, or blight? He hoped they would take a middle road, tempering systemization with a high degree of flexibility.

As for himself, after years of exposure to Faye's monomania, he mostly took it in stride. He was not by any means a devotee of scheduling, but he had come a long way since stating that V.O.S. was the acronym for Very Obnoxious Servitude. At work he even boasted about Faye's efficiency, mainly when other accountants grumbled about their wives' incompetence: 'Cora lost the medical receipts for our income-tax return.' 'Rachel couldn't balance a checkbook if her life depended on it.'

Filing essential records was incorporated in Faye's 'Household Papers Hour.' "I've got to hand it to my wife," Luke would brag. "I can ask her for a car-repair bill dated three years ago, and she'll come up with it in a jiffy." He basked in the envious glances of his co-workers as he mused, now you know the conveniences—I won't cite the drawbacks.

Luke still resented that sex was part of a timetable instead of a spontaneous affirmation of love, but no amount of pleading had converted Faye. This subject had kindled their first argument, shortly after their honeymoon, when Faye had insisted on slating sex for Sundays and Wednesdays at nine-thirty. Luke had reiterated again and again that sex at an unplanned hour would be less mechanical and more elevating for them both. But Faye remained adamant and Luke found out very early in his marriage that there was no use in feeling passionate on a Tuesday at midnight or Saturday at noon. Only once did Faye assent to nonscheduled sex, and the attempt turned out to be joyless.

The situation seemed all the more anomalous to Luke because he knew that Faye enjoyed sex as much as he did. It took him years to understand that Faye's obstinacy had nothing to do with his personal appeal—that Faye simply could not relish sex if in the back of her head she thought she really ought to be doing the laundry. But if she indulged in sex at the proper, scheduled time, she could relax and savor it with no guilt feelings to bother her.

To Luke's constant amazement, Faye could swing right into the mood of whatever action her schedule dictated at any given moment, whether it was sex, scrubbing walls, or cooking spaghetti. Was it a conscious eye on the waterproof watch that never left her arm, or the preconditioning of her psyche? Contrary to sex-manual women Luke had read about, who were supposed to like prolonged cuddling after sex, Faye liked to jump out of bed and do the ironing.

145

When Luke noted this phenomenon, he nicknamed The Schedule 'Simon,' after the traditional childhood game in which the participants must do as 'Simon Says.' Simon says 'Sex,' so Faye is ready, even eager. Now Simon says 'Iron blouses!'

He confided the name to his mother-in-law. "Faye will never go hungry," he declared with a grin, "because three times a day Simon says 'Eat'."

Though Luke did not want to join the game, he allowed that Simon was an integral part of his marriage. He had a solitary laugh when he thought of himself as one character in a ménage-a-trois. He was still unnerved by the limitations that Simon imposed on sex, but he could identify his advantages. Above all, he believed the boys received more care and supervision than they would have without Simon's watchful eye. Time reserved for the children, like everything else, was inviolate, and Faye could not be accused of employing it to gossip on the phone or to engage in any other unrelated pastime.

Luke found it less easy to be dispassionate about the side of his wife's temperament that he summarized as 'Faye Is Always Right.' Not only did Faye claim that scheduling could produce Utopia for every man, woman, and child, but she deemed her assessment of other matters to be indisputable as well. In discussions, she could come up with sure-fire solutions for global problems that baffled the world's most renowned statesmen.

Faye's viewpoints were not prefaced with 'I think' or 'I believe'; they were dictums of unqualified fact. Words such as 'possibly' and 'probably' were not included in her vocabulary. All things fit together like algebraic equations, and x plus y must eternally equal z.

The always-right idiosyncrasy was not reserved for Luke. Faye's sagacity was unequalled by any friend, relative, or neighbor.

If Faye and Luke went to see a play or movie with a group of friends, Faye's review of the show—uttered with an air of advanced enlightenment—was plainly the only one to be seriously considered.

At home later, Luke would dwell on questions that had no answers.

Is this facet of her nature related in some way to her success in time management? Does she feel superior because she accomplishes more than any three other people combined? Or is this trait entirely coincidental?

———— ⚎ ————

Though a dichotomy of mankind would have placed Faye and Luke in opposite corners, neither one had ever considered separation from the other. The Brends' religion stressed the doctrine 'till death do us part'; moreover, Faye and Luke held a joint conviction that children should have both their parents with them. Luke was devoted to his boys, and he believed Faye to be a superlative mother. Though none of his sons seemed destined for academic honor rolls, they all had satisfactory grades, and merry, outgoing dispositions.

Luke had the uncommon faculty of being able to judge family members objectively. He lauded Faye's virtues: she was steadfast, persevering, and industrious. Luke said she would not know how to be lazy. She works like a beaver, she gets results—who am I to decry her methods? he asked himself. He understood that she disliked his non-schedule as much as he disliked her schedule.

Open-minded evaluations could be swept aside, however, by the prime essential: Luke loved Faye very much. He watched her dashing from chore to chore so she could plot twenty minutes of embroidery once a month—he shook his head, but he loved her. There was something both appeal-

ing and repelling about her certainty, accented by a jaunty
flip of her long red hair as she spoke.

It enchanted Luke further that his beautiful wife did
not possess an iota of vanity. He did not know if she was
unaware of her beauty, or merely disregardful of it; at any
rate, primping was too time-consuming for Faye, who
would usually forgo even a three-second application of
powder on her upturned nose.

For her part, Faye was contented, especially on the days
that her V.O.S. worked without a hitch. The biggest disillusionment of her life was that Luke had not become an afi-
cionado of scheduling. He performed most of his chores on
her designated days, but he did not adhere to The Schedule
hour by hour. He might be playing the piano at seven
o'clock, instead of taking the garbage out, but the garbage
would generally be disposed of by evening's end. He was
the only member of the family who did not have his V.O.S.
Although Faye would have liked him to have his Very Own
Schedule to fulfill her own expectations, she nevertheless
believed that it would be best for him also. What she
regarded as a regrettable deprivation, he regarded as a nar-
row escape.

----×◆×----

Fifteen minutes, immediately following dinner, were
allotted for opening and sorting the mail, at the same time
that Ethan and Joel noisily cleared the table, and Douglas
rinsed the dishes for the dishwasher. Joel was appointed to
fetch the mail from the mailbox after school, and deposit it
in a basket near the dining-room table, where Faye could
attack it the second she swallowed her last spoonful of
dessert. Bills were quickly scuttled into the 'Pay Bills' fold-
er. Personal letters were read hurriedly by Faye and more
relaxedly by Luke, then filed under 'Write Letters,' and

bank statements were separated for 'Money Management' hour.

Faye's magazines were set aside for Reading Period, one-half hour prior to sleep, on non-sex nights only. But when Luke's *Music World Bulletin* came in, he read it instantly, before embarking on any tasks for the evening. Faye protested mildly once or twice on the theory that this was a poor example for the children. But Luke kept on reading, saying that it was healthy for the boys to see a balance, and learn early that growth presented options.

＊＊＊

As in most households, every aspect of the Brends' lives was faster-paced in December. Christmas cards arrived in profusion, and Faye enlisted the children's help in slitting open the envelopes so that she could finish scanning the cards within her mail time-slot.

It was in this climate that Alex and Marcia Southerick's Christmas card arrived on December 14th. It happened to be at the very bottom of the basket, and Faye snatched it up hastily at the end of mail-time.

There were few things in life that had the potential of throwing Faye off schedule, and Luke had infinite respect for anything that could do it. When he saw her intently studying a Christmas card, even though mail-time was over, he knew it had to say something besides 'Merry Christmas.' Though wildly curious about any great matter that had the power to keep Faye at the table for eighteen minutes instead of fifteen, he said nothing.

"Here's a peculiar note from Alex Southerick," Faye said at length.

"Oh, how is he?" asked Luke nonchalantly. "I hope his family's all right."

"We used to see the Southericks on the second and fourth Saturdays," mused Faye, bypassing the question. "To play pinochle, remember?"

"Yes, and Michigan Rummy," Luke recalled. "It was fun, wasn't it? I still miss them, especially Alex at work. He was one boss in a million."

"Marcia was a cordial hostess; what a shame she didn't know how to regulate her time," said Faye. "Remember when we went to their house for a Valentine party? Alex told us Marcia was running slightly late; she was just getting out of the *shower!*"

"Yeah, that was funny." Luke grinned. "She came into the living room with apologies and her head in a big checkered towel."

"Funny! I thought it was a disaster. I don't know how she was able to laugh at her embarrassment. I felt so sorry for her, I wanted to give her lessons in scheduling then and there, as a gift."

Luke shuddered. Who is better off, he theorized, Marcia giving parties with her wet head in a towel, or Faye washing and drying her hair next to a chronometer? Or is one person as happy as another as long as he is true to himself? Aloud he said, "Let me see the Southericks' card."

Faye sprang up briskly, handing him the card as she said, "Listen, this is Thursday. Let's discuss it while I'm wrapping Christmas presents and you're washing the floor."

Luke read Alex Southerick's note and felt as if he had been punched in the chest. '*...If you can possibly see your way clear to sending me $1,000 within the next two or three days...*' He decided that this was one of those rare instances when he would give First Opinion.

"I think we should send Alex a check tomorrow morning," he said. He turned his back, ostensibly to take the mop and bucket out of the closet, but primarily to conceal his emotions. "He was a darn good boss when I started in the Accounting Department. I panicked when I found out they used a different system from the one I was accustomed to, but Alex helped me and molded me when I was as green and shaky as lime Jello. And he supported me when the inner office wanted to crucify me for somebody else's mistakes. I owe a great deal to Alex. Besides, it sounds as if he needs the money badly."

There was an interval of silence before Faye responded, and when she did, her words were measured. "You are reacting emotionally, and because of that you are ready to move on impulse. But you are not using your head, or any prudence whatsoever." As she spoke she was stacking an assortment of gifts to be wrapped.

Luke swished the mop and waited for her to resume. "You said it sounds as if he needs the money badly," she said. "That's true, but why? Why doesn't he have at least $10,000 in the bank? Alex is older than you, and when he lived here he had a better position. We weren't nearly as well off as they were. We're raising three children; the Southericks have two. But *we* have $10,000 in the bank in the boys' college fund. Why don't they have any savings?"

Luke tried to think of an acceptable defense. "You're right, Alex is older—his son and daughter would be in college now. That's a lot more expensive than grade school. And Alex might have invested in assets that can't be liquidated fast—real estate, for example. Or holdings that he doesn't want to sell—stocks that are low, or gold and silver. Or he might have put his money in a Certificate of Deposit, and he doesn't want to pay a penalty for cashing it in early."

"But he says he's paying the Treasury Department rate on this money for a month."

"That's cheaper than losing several months' interest. And it's possible that he has his money invested at a higher percentage. Alex is sharp in math. He was a wizard on the job, and he was valedictorian of his college class. Alex is no dummy."

"Smarties can make flimsy investments too. Intelligence doesn't make him infallible. Except for Christmas cards and incidental birthday cards, we're out of touch. We don't even know what his current job is."

"Yes we do. He enclosed his card." Luke walked over to the dining-room table, picked up Alex's business card, and read, "Vice-President in Charge of Marketing, Kinnelac Corporation. There, Faye, you've heard of Kinnelac. And don't say the card might not be valid—it has to be, if that's where we're sending the money."

"Or where we're *not* sending the money. Actually his title is neither here nor there. We don't know when he started in that capacity, what he owes, or what he has. All we know is what he doesn't have—he doesn't have $10,000—and if he's that insolvent at this stage in his career, that's a danger signal. So you'd be mailing off $1,000 to a man in his forties who is in dubious shape financially, making him a bad risk. I'd say our chances of getting the money back are slim, one in a hundred. And our chances of ever seeing them again are nil also, so it doesn't make much difference whether or not we send it."

"What does that mean—we're friends, folks, but not if you move away?"

"I simply meant that the subject is not apt to come up again. Let's examine Alex's note more carefully. Why no banks or lending institutions? Does he have a poor credit rating? Or too many loans out already? If we were in a predicament and we had to get $10,000 in a hurry, we'd borrow it from a bank, wouldn't we? A person would have to be in pretty sad straits to write ten friends for a $1,000 loan each. You have to admit it's a farfetched way to borrow money."

"Maybe he would like to keep this emergency undercover. There could be excellent reasons why he doesn't want his banker or his company to know about it."

"In any case, if he's as brilliant as you say, he should have $10,000 or more that's accessible for emergencies. The note doesn't specify if the money is for business or personal use, yet he wants it sent to his office. And in such a big rush that there's no time for a loan contract! And he says he can't disclose any information about the loan. Why not? It's possible he's involved in a 'get rich quick' scheme, like those pyramids that don't materialize."

"Alex is much too brainy to fall for any plan that isn't stable. And this loan doesn't necessarily mean that he doesn't have $10,000—maybe he has $40,000 in the bank, but he needs fifty. And Alex is a man of principle; he'll make certain that his friends get their money back."

"That would be his intention, I grant you that. But if he loses all the money, it's gone. And if he can't borrow money from a bank now, how could he borrow it to pay us back?"

Faye rose from her stool with a gesture of impatience, leaving tags, seals, and presents in disarray. Since her standard policy was to finish a job before moving on to the next, Luke knew that the issue of Alex's loan had been relegated to the Important Decision category.

"I think we should write down the pros and cons of making this loan," said Faye. "You list the pros."

Luke appeared stricken. This is the death blow, he thought, this will kill the loan for sure. Though he could win at checkers and scrabble, Faye invariably won at Pro-and-Con.

"I don't have anything against Alex and Marcia Southerick; I've always liked them both," Faye contended, putting a pad and pen near Luke. "But we can't afford to lose $1,000 out of our sons' Education Fund just because we're fond of someone. We have to figure out our answer sensibly."

Luke stared at Faye's paper as she headed the con list with 'Money not likely to be returned.' The next time he looked up she had fourteen cons and was still scribbling.

Racking his brain, Luke had been able to produce only a short list: Alex and Marcia Southerick are old friends; it would be nice to give Alex a vote of confidence when he needs it; and Alex was extremely helpful to me when I started in Accounting.

Faye surveyed his meager offering and scoffed, "What sort of reasoning is that?" She shoved her tabulation in front of him and said, "Here are the cons. I guess it's hard for you to accept that your former boss is now in a financial bind. But when you go over my list you'll see that this loan to Alex would be irresponsible."

Luke felt like one of Faye's students who had not been able to grasp an arithmetic formula, so Teacher was clarifying it on the blackboard. When he read the list it was obvious that Faye had not once considered the loan from the Southericks' standpoint, unless one counted the backhanded assistance conferred in entry #11, where Faye had written: 'This refusal could be for Alex's benefit—he may learn to handle money better if his friends don't bail him out.' A teacher through and through, thought Luke.

He stiffened in disbelief at the next notation: 'Could not sue on the strength of this note.' Sue our old friend Alex? He thought, I'd rather not lend him the money in the first place than sue him for recovery, if it ever came to that. His muffled groan expressed capitulation in the battle of Prudence vs. Impetuosity.

After a while he asked, "What will you write on our Christmas card to them?"

"Oh, that's taken care of. I'm sure they already have our card, crossed in the mail. I wrote a short note on it about the children. You know our cards are always mailed on the first Tuesday in December."

With the bearing of a person who has put affairs in order, Faye went back to wrapping Christmas presents. A music-box that she pulled out of a container started to tinkle *I'm Dreaming of a White Christmas*, but Faye had no time to dream. She snapped the lid closed—deactivating the music—and taped gift paper around the box in a flash. She was one-half hour behind schedule and she intended to correct the deficiency by skipping her Reading Period that night.

Leaving the rest of the unmopped floor to do later, Luke retreated to the piano room and played his own interpretation of Sibelius' pensive *Valse Triste*. Afterward he remained seated, motionless, at the piano. He found himself speculating about how things might have turned out if Faye had never met Sheila. Maybe Faye's tablecloth would still be lying unfinished at the bottom of a dresser drawer. He chuckled as he envisioned Faye running into class late with her hair wrapped in a big damp checkered towel. Then the smile was suddenly replaced by a look of sadness as his thoughts turned again to Alex Southerick.

Hope it's nothing serious, old friend.

Precisely at that moment three clamorous boys came racing downstairs, defying logic by landing safely at the bottom, tumbled one on top of the other. Luke surveyed the squirming arms and legs of his laughing sons, and he laughed along with them. Then he pounded out a peppy, honky-tonk-style rendition of *Yes, We Have No Bananas*.

As the musical catharsis worked its magic, his facial lines relaxed and his frown disappeared. He looked almost as exuberant as the children.

Mr. and Mrs. Gilbert Desston
55 Nancilly Court
Ranchbuck, Colo.
   81644

9

Steering fast around the long circular driveway, Isabel braked her coupe so abruptly that its tires squealed a shrill protest before the car jerked to a halt at the door of her home.

'Home' was an opulent two-story mansion that burst into view at the last turn of a winding half-mile driveway. Eight fluted Corinthian columns lined the veranda like tall white exclamation points. Beyond the porch the massive double doors, illuminated by gargoyles, looked too ornate and heavy to be opened by human hands.

No observer of this majestic showplace would have guessed that the financial affairs of its occupants were as precarious as they were lavish. Isabel's genuine alligator purse held twelve department-store charge cards and nineteen overused credit cards.

But practical matters did not worry Isabel. She dashed into the house, the high heels of her matching alligator shoes clicking in staccato rhythm as she hurried through the marble foyer. She paid the baby-sitter and started mixing a martini without a word to her four-year-old daughter, who was sitting quietly at the kitchen table crayoning a page in her coloring book.

It was the child who initiated the conversation. "Hello, mother," she said without enthusiasm.

"Did you have a nice day, Phoebe?" asked Isabel.

"Yes," said the child in the same dull voice.

"Good." Isabel smiled fleetingly and inhaled a cigarette slowly. Her mind was on a hundred things, and not one of them was Phoebe.

"Do you want to see my picture?"

"Not now, Phoebe, later. After dinner. Right now I have to shred lettuce, and put salmon steaks on the broiler. This is cook's day off."

Phoebe sighed and went on coloring. Young as she was, she knew that 'later' would never come. Her father would appear, practice a speech, and pat her on the head. Her older brother—her idol—would come in and pick her up and carry her on his shoulders. He would talk to her and examine all her pictures. Then everyone would eat, and her mother would rush off to a meeting somewhere as yet another baby-sitter arrived at the door.

More or less, this was the daily pattern in the lives of the Desston family. Gilbert Desston was part owner of a distinguished brokerage firm. Isabel was circulation manager of the newsmagazine *Today's World*, where she had worked since her first child, Owen, was five years old. Owen Desston was now a senior at nearby Vanderhoff Private High School. And his sister Phoebe was a small child who lived on the fringes of a frenetic household.

When Phoebe was born, Isabel allocated three weeks to stay at home before returning to the office. At the time she was advancing rapidly in the magazine circulation field. She was also president of Business and Professional

Sincerely Yours

Women, chairperson of the Hospital Auxiliary, director of
planning for the Suburban League, and corresponding secretary of the Ranchbuck Women's Club. Thus, Phoebe had
been attended by nurses and sitters from infancy.

Gilbert was the masculine counterpart of 'pillar of the
community.' He was described as 'refined' and 'cultured.'
He interacted well with others, and he charmed everyone.
At the time of his daughter's birth, he was a hospital
trustee, president of the Kiwanis Club, assistant treasurer of
the Elks lodge, and chairman of the Fresh Air Fund for
underprivileged children. Isabel had taken advantage of his
amenable nature many years before, prodding him to join
civic associations and to accept nominations for office.

Now and then Gilbert found his wife's obsession with
public image a bit tiresome; nevertheless, he had been
shaped rather easily into Isabel's 'ideal husband' mold. He
was in demand as a witty speaker, and every pre-speech
introduction reiterated his own firm belief that he was
making a substantial contribution to society. If he was
selected for a new appointment, Isabel's enthusiasm added
to his complacency. And so, ego-driven and wife-driven,
Gilbert went on speaking at more engagements and undertaking more chairmanships each year.

Isabel gloried in the local newspaper headlines:
'Desston Honored at State Dinner'; 'Gilbert Desston Voted
Outstanding Citizen of the Year.'

"Wait till the neighbors see that," she would gloat. She
was not envious of her husband's headlines. She reaped
plenty of her own, but she also felt that she shared in whatever prominence Gilbert attained.

But in spite of the testimonials, Gilbert Desston, the
Outstanding Citizen, had the same allotment of 24 hours a
day as less exemplary mortals. He had been left with little
time for his son Owen when he was growing up, and now
had even less time for his daughter Phoebe. Whenever
Gilbert had inquired about Owen, Isabel had assured him

158

with her own perception of the truth: Owen was doing fine—he had auspicious grades in school and first-rate sitters at home. Now Isabel was still acclaiming the household help when Gilbert asked about Phoebe, who had a closer relationship with the housekeeper and six or seven baby-sitters than she had with either her mother or her father.

If Isabel had believed that Phoebe needed more fatherly care, she probably could have arranged it. Gilbert would have given up some of his activities to oblige his wife, but such drastic measures never occurred to Isabel. Anyone could see that Phoebe had everything. Besides, whoever saw a headline, 'So-and-so Played Games with His Children Tonight'? Hence, Gilbert's attention to his daughter consisted of a few observations at the dinner table and hasty good-byes as he rushed out to a committee discussion about disadvantaged youngsters in Colorado.

Isabel and Gilbert Desston belonged to so many clubs, and had so many charge accounts, that their daily mail was voluminous. Since most of the mail had no intrinsic value, Gilbert could not comprehend why Isabel was so proud of its bulk. He once overheard her asking the postman if they had more mail than others on his route, and she was jubilant when he replied in a weary voice that the Desstons were by far his 'heaviest' patrons.

Isabel always sifted through the mail impatiently, thirsting for select invitations. After comparing these with club affairs, and marking her calendar accordingly, she scanned the personal letters and dispatched them at once to Gilbert's desk along with the bills and bank statements. Sweepstakes entry forms that told her she might already be a millionaire were stuffed into her briefcase for her secretary to complete at the office.

Sincerely Yours

Her busy schedule then held sway; she left a big batch of junk mail to examine later. As with Phoebe, however, 'later' never came, and the mail stacked up day after day to tottering proportions on desks and tables. When the time came to dispose of the heaps—usually in preparation for guests—the housekeeper was instructed to put the mail in a cardboard box labeled with the month and year; Isabel was going to leaf through it in her fantasy future.

In the spacious basement there were over seventy cartons of unopened mail, all neatly sealed and tagged. Although Isabel knew that most of this accumulation consisted of outdated material that would have no significance if and when she inspected it, she was still reluctant to discard it without a cursory examination, 'some rainy Saturday when I'm not doing anything.' Mail addressed to her had a nebulous value which she herself could not define.

Gilbert said that hell would freeze over before there was a rainy Saturday when Isabel was not doing anything. And the store of boxes in the cellar kept amassing. With the sense of humor that seasoned his popular after-dinner speeches, Gilbert called this hoard the Procrastination Mountains, which he hoped some day would become part of the Great Smokies.

On his seventeenth birthday, Owen received from his parents a brand-new, creamy-white Corvette, and for the next several weeks he spent most of his after-school time gazing at it, polishing it, and taking Phoebe for rides in it.

One evening when Isabel had car trouble, she phoned and asked Owen to pick her up at a meeting. She was glad he had the glossy new sports car, and she meant to make a dramatic show of entering it—with a trill of laughter or some other device to make heads turn—so that not a single woman would miss seeing it.

Arriving early, Owen sat quietly in the back of the room and watched his effusive mother moving gaily from one group to another. She smiled at Ursula Ackerman, the neighbor he knew she despised. She smiled at Mrs. Ritchey, whom she called Ritchey-Bitchey at home. She beamed at Mrs. Bellton, whom he had heard Isabel ridicule again and again, because her slip showed, or because she wore the same dress to two successive dances. Owen thought, now I know why there are so few smiles left for Phoebe and me. Her smile machine gets tired.

Not that Isabel was nasty or even irritable with her children. It was more as if she were drained to the point of detachment when it came to her children's accomplishments in their smaller orbits. When Owen burst into her bedroom one summer afternoon, dripping wet, to shout that Phoebe had just swum her first real strokes in the pool, the news held no excitement for Isabel, though she smiled and said "Marvelous!" while continuing to look through her closet for a ballgown. Owen had the feeling she would have smiled and said "Marvelous" with exactly the same inflection if he had reported that Phoebe had just been eaten by an alligator. She does smile at us, Owen granted, but her mind isn't on it.

Sitting there in the back of the meeting room, Owen thought about his childhood.

I wish that Mother and Dad had yelled at me when I was a kid. And I wish they would holler at Phoebe once in a while. It would prove that they know she's there.

— ≍✧≍ —

Owen was the only person who was sensitive to the fact that his leaving for college in less than a year would be a harsh jolt to his little sister. He had grown up in a world of baby-sitters himself, and now Phoebe's dejection and lone-liness haunted him like familiar ghosts. His mother was

161

long away from cribs and diapers when he was thirteen and his sister was born; he had become Phoebe's substitute parent as well as her favorite pal. He even took the tot on daytime dates with his girlfriends, because he could not bear to see sadness in her soft brown eyes. He would literally stand on his head to make those doleful eyes sparkle. He tailored his date activities to accommodate a toddler, choosing picnics or zoo visits instead of sports like tennis. And he was not a bit perturbed when his female classmates joked about his diminutive chaperone.

When the matter of colleges came up, for Phoebe's sake Owen beseeched his mother to allow him to commute to the local community college.

"It has the major courses I need for the first two years," he reasoned. "I'll come out with an Associate Degree in Education, and transfer to a four-year college when Phoebe is a little older. I know two guys who go to Community, and they rave about it. I could learn there as well as anywhere else."

"It's not a question of what you'd learn, or how well," replied Isabel. "Community College has no status whatsoever. Some day you'll be grateful that we insisted you attend a prestigious college. We'll have to take out a loan for it, while we're still paying off the swimming pool and your new car—that's how much it means to us. And why do you want a degree in education?"

"Because I want to be an elementary-school teacher. I've enjoyed teaching Phoebe how to read, print her name, add and subtract—that's what helped me decide on my calling." Isabel looked up in surprise. She had not been aware that Phoebe had achieved any of those skills.

Owen went on, "I can start out teaching normal children, like Phoebe. Giving her lessons has been a snap; she's really bright. But I think I have the patience to tutor mentally handicapped children—and I know I'd like the challenge. The county has special programs for juveniles with serious learning difficulties."

"And where do you hope to go after that?"

"That's it, that's what I want to do."

"Good Heavens!" Her voice couldn't have sounded more tragic if he had proposed holding up banks for a living. "You'll never get anyplace in a dead-end job like that!"

"I think it's a pretty worthy objective," said Owen staunchly. Then, believing it would strengthen his cause, he added, "I've already discussed it with Mr. Stefkins—he's a great guy who teaches the special-education class at Ranchbuck Elementary."

Isabel's stony silence told Owen that he was not gaining any ground. He finished weakly, "I want something that seems worth doing."

"Worthiness is not what we're talking about," said Isabel. "Many things are worth doing. Why isn't it just as worthy to be an engineer, for example, and design bridges for people to cross over? Or a lawyer, and defend innocent people in court? You don't have to teach idiots to be worthy! Your great Mr. Stefkins—where does he live? What kind of a car does he drive? Is it as high-priced as your new Corvette? Those are your standards, Owen. You may think they're unimportant now, but that's because you're young and have a sophomoric outlook. With that kind of occupation you'd have to drive ten-year-old cars and live in low-class neighborhoods like your aunts and uncles." Her tone implied that he might as well live in a foxhole.

But Owen had taken to visiting his aunts and uncles, without his parents' knowledge, shortly after receiving the new car for his birthday. His mind flashed back to scenes from the foxholes.

Sincerely Yours

Isabel's four sisters and their large families lived near each other in the same section of Ranchbuck where they had been raised. Undersized dwellings were arranged in rows on undersized lots. Each house was identical to all the others on the block, differing only in color. The first time Owen had visited in this area, after finding the house number in a telephone book, he had rung the doorbell apprehensively, not knowing what kind of reception he would receive. He had seen his relatives only sporadically through the years, and he was not sure that he would recognize most of them, or that they would know who he was.

He was taken aback when his aunt and uncle seemed happier to see him than his own parents ever did. Uncle Hector slapped him on the back and shook his hand with gusto. Three aunts took turns in hugging him hard. Owen was exhilarated by the hearty welcome.

He began to visit one house or another regularly. He discovered that numerous cousins were as likely to be congregated in one house as another—the four houses were 'home' to all.

His cousins included him in anything they were doing, whether shooting baskets or 'shooting the breeze,' their term for idle talk. When they went to a movie with boyfriends and girlfriends, they found a last-minute date for him rather than leave him behind.

On almost every visit, aunts and uncles begged Owen to bring his little sister with him. Two of them had children her age, but none of the relatives had ever seen Phoebe. Owen fabricated alibis; he could not bear to hurt them with the real reason he didn't bring his sister: he was afraid Phoebe would mention the visit at home. His mother would be furious with him for hobnobbing with relatives in the least affluent part of town. Though Owen could have tolerated his mother's pique, he did not want Phoebe to be exposed to the deprecation of relatives he hoped she could meet open-mindedly when she was older.

Sometimes Owen felt ill-at-ease driving to his aunts' houses with his sleek new Corvette, especially when he found out that his cousin Ferdie had two jobs after school to earn money for a secondhand car, 'anything that runs.' Often Owen would leave the car home and ride crosstown on his imported ten-speed bicycle, still conspicuously superior to his relatives' run-down bikes.

Owen yearned to be part of his cousins' noisy, laughing groups. He marvelled at how they could call one another 'creep' or 'dummy' or 'klutz,' yet beneath the banter, the love came through. They had all treated him cordially, but they had never teased him about anything. Owen ached to be one of them, to truly belong. But there was no way to impart this feeling to his mother.

———— ◆ ————

After Isabel's remark about 'living in low-class neighborhoods like your aunts and uncles,' Owen paused for a moment, and then he said soberly, "I wouldn't really mind that, Mother."

"That's easy for you to say while you ride around town in your brand-new sports car, or listen to your tapes on a $1,500 stereo system. You don't know any other lifestyle than the one you have here. You have a lot to learn."

"I'm crazy about my car, and I'm not going to pretend that I'm not. But I think I could change my lifestyle if my job required it."

Isabel attempted another approach: "You're graduating from a top-ranked school, and you have the fourth highest grades in your class. Teaching half-wits who can learn at a minimum level would be a waste of your intelligence."

"A person with true intelligence wouldn't waste it under any circumstances," Owen responded. He had a sensation of sinking, and a fierce desire to stay afloat. "We could try Community for a year, and then you and Dad could evaluate my studies and see what you think."

"I already know what I think. I also know what our friends and neighbors would think—they'd think that was the only place we could afford to send you. Don't you realize that this would fill us with shame? How could we face our colleagues? You should be glad your parents are willing to borrow the money to send you to an Ivy League college."

"But what about Phoebe? If I were at Community, I could study here at night and watch Phoebe for you. And I could take her out on weekends. She's going to be really upset and lonesome if I leave home."

"The fact that your sister will be upset is not one of the criteria to use when selecting a college. If I thought for one minute that Phoebe was going to be responsible for destroying your life, I would not have permitted you two to become so close. Can't you understand? This is a matter of image. It's a matter of our standing in the community."

Isabel crushed out her diminishing cigarette and lit another. Her voice, which had become intense, was back under control. "Anyway, Phoebe will be in kindergarten next year when you leave. I can't see why you're worried about her. Doesn't she have everything? Look at her toys. I order the entire list recommended for her age group by the Toy Counselors of America. Her clothes all have designer labels. She has far more than you did when you were her age. That's why I started working. Your sister isn't lacking one solitary thing."

Owen felt as if his heart and stomach were having a fist-fight, but he had neither the courage nor the command of words to defy his mother's smug assertions.

Never before had Owen heard his mother concede that she had a practical purpose in taking employment. She had trumpeted to the world at large that she did not work for the money, but rather for the inner fulfillment that only a career could provide.

Shortly after Isabel's accounting of Phoebe's matchless possessions, Owen was buoyed when his easygoing father entered the room. Isabel's unyielding view had bolstered Owen's conviction that commuting to college was imperative. But he still felt like a struggling swimmer in need of a life-preserver as he repeated his stance to Gilbert. His eloquent appeal failed. To his consternation, his father agreed wholeheartedly with his mother.

"Your choice of college will be on your resume for the rest of your life," said Gilbert kindly. "I'm pleased that your grades are excellent, and that you qualify for the very best."

"But Dad, I won't need a long resume. Can't you see how rough it will be on Phoebe to be here alone? That's the most important thing," implored Owen. "As for me, I just need the basic courses to earn a degree. When I get a job teaching, I can take more courses at night, and work my way into teaching special-education classes—it's not a crowded field."

"Small wonder!" shot back Isabel. "What does it pay? Peanuts, that's what! And where is the prestige?" She blew out rapid little puffs of cigarette smoke. "But I'm not worried. You'll change your mind when you're at a top-notch college where other students are aspiring to make big money as doctors or lawyers."

A familiar sense of rejection welled up and engulfed Owen's mind. He thought back to fourth grade, when his parents did not come to his class pageant—in which he played the bottom half of a dragon—because the performance took place on the same night as a country-club gala. A sitter with orange hair and three rings on one finger had escorted him. Later, he watched the swarm of parents hugging and congratulating their children as he stood alone. Then the mother of the top half of the dragon invited him to come to a 'cast party' at her house. He longed to go, but the orange sitter said 'no.' And the mother with big round eyes said in a sorrowful voice, "But he will be the only one not included!" He was glad the mother gave him a great big hug before the sitter dragged him away.

"Now, these are the colleges where you should apply," said Isabel, handing her son a list which had been typed by her secretary. Owen regretted his scholastic achievement. He read the names of the schools despondently, clinging to the foolish hope that he would not be accepted at any of them.

Owen could think of no way out of the quagmire. He followed orders, but he had none of the normal feelings of anticipation as he applied to the listed universities. Eventually he was accepted at several of the best-known colleges, and since he had no preference, he decided he might as well yield to his parents on one point and go to their first choice, which was Harvard. He thought, I guess that will sound laudable enough to their friends; his parents thought, thank goodness, Owen has finally come to his senses.

⚊ ▣ ⚊

It was almost the middle of December. Owen had left for college four months earlier. Phoebe had been withdrawn ever since, but no one seemed to notice. She faded away into corners, clutching the Lhasa Apso puppy that her brother had bought for her before leaving. The only times her face brightened were when Owen telephoned, or when she received a card or letter from him in the mail. Though she never cried at Maple Tree Private Academy, her woebegone look caused the kindergarten teacher to assume, mistakenly, that she was heartsick about leaving Mommy to go to school.

Owen had departed with both sadness and elation. He was sad because he knew his absence would depress his adored sister. But he was elated when he went to say goodbye to his wrong-side-of-town relatives. His cousin Ferdie had shaken his hand and said gravely, "Now listen, creep,

168

don't come back to see us on your breaks until you at least get a decent car." Everyone had roared with laughter, and his aunts had tears rolling down their cheeks when they kissed and hugged him good-bye, as if he were one of their own sons. Uncle Hector had thrown his heavy muscular arms around him and said "God bless you!" And Aunt Lena had presented Owen with a handmade, mono-grammed bookmark that he knew he would cherish forever when she said softly, "A little part of us will be with you always."

Although Owen appreciated the matched luggage given to him by his parents, with a reminder from Isabel to take good care of it because it was very expensive, the sight of the five trim leather suitcases did not stir his emotions as the little felt bookmark did.

Owen was looking forward to flying home for Christ-mas; Phoebe was more anxious for Owen to arrive than Santa Claus. The Desstons were giving an extravagant cocktail party on the Sunday before Christmas, and Isabel had ordered five gigantic Christmas trees and 150 red and white poinsettia plants. The housekeeper had agreed to decorate the trees, each in a different mode, and the florist would arrange poinsettias in every room of the house, including the bathrooms.

At this time of year the Desstons were deluged with both mail and parties. On a crisp Saturday morning, less than two weeks before Christmas, Isabel entered the den with the careful steps of a tightrope walker, balancing a heavy pile of mail on her left arm, while carrying a tall glass of orange juice and vodka in her right hand. Gilbert was seated at his desk with a cup of black coffee, figuring out which bills would take precedence that week. Phoebe fol-lowed her mother and sat cross-legged on the floor, her dog nestled in her lap, patiently awaiting any word from Owen.

Isabel took a cigarette from a jade holder on her desk, sipped her drink, and started to divide the mail into piles.

Sincerely Yours

There were dozens of Christmas cards—these were opened immediately, because they frequently enclosed invitations to holiday functions. Isabel opened the cards with her calendar propped up in front of her, as numerous dates had to be arranged.

Suddenly she squalled, "Oh no, another $1,000! Gilbert, look at this!" She handed her husband the handwritten loan request from Alex Southerick. As Gilbert read it, she kept on jabbering. "Well, like it or not, we'll have to send the money. We don't want them to think we can't spare it. It makes no difference what we say, if we don't do it they'll have it in their heads that we couldn't produce the cash. Then how could we cope with meeting them at your class reunion next spring? Alex would be saying, 'Hello, how are you?' and thinking how badly we must be doing."

Gilbert nodded his compliance but showed little verve. "The fact is, business has been slow for months. Besides that, we have more household debts right now than we've ever had."

"I know, but we don't have to advertise it in the *Alumni News*. I'm sure Alex's other nine friends will dash off a check without a quibble. We can't be the only ones not to send it!" Isabel sounded stricken.

She lit her third cigarette in succession and began to reminisce. "How long has it been since the Southericks moved from Colorado? About nine or ten years? That was the winter that you and Alex worked together on the Community Fund drive. Alex and Marcia lived here a couple of years, and then Alex took a fabulous new position. He was heading upward in the corporate world, or that's what we surmised. Doesn't sound that way on this Christmas card, does it? Just the same, I'd never be able to look Marcia in the eye again if she thought we couldn't accommodate them with $1,000."

Gilbert was glum. "I don't mind lending the Southericks the money," he said, "but December's a terrible month. It would help if we didn't have these high payments on the swimming pool."

"Why, oh why, did the Nigbees and the Thallens have to put in swimming pools on our block?" wailed Isabel. "If it weren't for them, we wouldn't be footing these astronomical payments. I can't see why the country club pool didn't suffice; I thought it was quite adequate. I guess I'm easily satisfied."

Gilbert raised his eyebrows in mute disagreement, while Isabel went on. "And the pool has been useless! You and I haven't wet our feet in those gallons and gallons of chlorinated water. But I think Owen swam in it, and he put Phoebe in the shallow end last summer. I suppose I should plan a pool party next year to merit the investment, and to show our pool off—it's a much larger pool than the Thallens', and the Nigbees don't even have a diving board."

Isabel continued prattling while Gilbert stared at Alex Southerick's Christmas card. "Another thing," she said, "I neglected to tell you—I have heard no fewer than four people announce that they are buying home computers. Whatever will we do with one, and where will we put it?"

Gilbert did not have time to solve this new dilemma, because Isabel rambled on, "And let me repeat, dear, your class reunion is this spring, and...."

"I didn't know we'd decided to go to that," Gilbert interrupted.

"Of course! It's marked on your calendar so you don't make any other commitments. Everybody will be there! The Jackleys—he's president of International Beans, you know; and the Darthrups, he's in the state Senate and she writes romance novels. And Patrick Eggleson is getting to be a famous trial attorney. I see his name in the papers more and more. No, we simply cannot miss the reunion.

"By the way, let's not sit at the Southericks' table this year. We sat with them at the last reunion, remember? But now he's clearly on the way down. I must say Alex doesn't have much pride. Heaven knows there were low periods when an extra $10,000 would have come in handy for us, but I'd die before I'd write ten friends for it. Seems degrading, doesn't it? Anyhow, let's try to be seated with the Egglesons, or at least the state Senator."

"I'm sure you can lead us to sit with whomever you wish," said Gilbert, basing his judgment on past experience.

"And for goodness sake, let's steer clear of that lumber salesman—what's his name again?—Jasper Zamp. His wife looks as if she orders her clothes from a mail-order catalog. We don't want to land at *their* table. Why did he go to college to sell lumber? Anyway, I cut the Zamps off our Christmas-card list years ago. I'll keep Alex and Marcia Southerick on for a while, but frankly, I'm shocked about Alex and this loan. You told me he was voted 'Most Likely to Succeed' in your class, so I've thought all along that our friendship with the Southericks was worth fostering. Do you recall when your college had that special Alumni Weekend Outing? Marcia's outfits were almost as stylish as mine. We spent a great deal of time with the Southericks that weekend, and now it seems like a pure waste. Proves how wrong you can be about people."

"Maybe this is a minor temporary setback," said Gilbert charitably. "He only wants to borrow the money for a month."

"Well, when he returns it, I have a good use for it," replied Isabel. "What I started to say a while ago was that I would love to have a mink stole for the reunion. You know how the women always show up with new furs, or gold bracelets, or diamond earrings dangling to their shoulders. I know I have my full-length sable, but the reunion is in April, ideal mink-stole weather. Nine more wives had new ones last time—I counted them; Hazel and Naomi wore their old ones they've had for ages."

Gilbert was amazed at his wife's ability to retain such details. How curious, he thought, that she completely forgot both my birthday and Phoebe's birthday this year. Aloud he said, not argumentatively, but gently, "You could have had the mink stole before this if you hadn't wanted to spend $500 on a custom-designed mailbox."

The Desstons' recently acquired mailbox was a small replica of their home, built to scale with tiny doors, windows, and white columns; and minute shingles on a roof that hinged open for the mail.

"But you know that was only because the Inkdalls put up that mailbox with the gold-plated numbers on it, and bragged that their numbers weren't brass. Anyway, ours is better, more costly. Besides, $500 is a drop in the bucket toward the mink stole I have in mind."

"A drop is better than dry, my dear," said Gilbert pleasantly. "It could have been the down payment. But getting back to Alex Southerick—if we charge our Christmas presents and delay a car payment, I can send him a check for $1,000. And when the pool is paid off in March, you just go ahead and pick out your mink stole."

Mr. and Mrs. Jasper Zamp
992 Ullstra Road
Frankston, N.J. 07415

10

Tara smiled as she took the heavy batch of mail out of the mailbox. She poured herself a cup of steaming coffee, selected a caramel-nut doughnut from a boxed assortment, and curled her feet up under her in a comfortable but misshapen loveseat. These acts began the late-morning ritual she called 'snugglin' up with the mail.'

Jasper often said that no one could squeeze more pleasure out of the daily mail than Tara. And he was probably right. Tara had devised her ritual after leaving an office position and discovering that a homemaker's working hours never ended. The incoming mail provided the excuse for a short respite.

Tara did not screen mail hurriedly, like most people. Without sorting, she examined each piece of mail in the chance order relegated by the mailman. She even read the sales and donation appeals, treating all items as if they were of equal urgency. As she went along, she separated everything into neat piles: bills, personal letters, papers to be thrown away, and now, in the month of December, Christmas cards.

About twice a year she repeated the same joke that at least it wasn't a *male* she snuggled up with, sounding so ingenuous that everyone laughed at each repetition. She liked the phrase 'mail superiority' too, and used it freely when the mail warranted it, being careful to clarify it by spelling 'mail.'

She made other word plays as well, her favorite being, 'I'll pare a pair of pears for us.' Jasper swore she bought pears for the sole purpose of saying it. Still, despite her accuracy with homonyms, Tara was more often a Mrs. Malaprop. She would say 'A stitch in time saves mine,' or, 'You have to make your bed if you lie in it.'

She sang songs with a similar lack of precision. From the shower Jasper would hear familiar melodies: *My Mild Irish Rose*, *Down by the Old Millstone*, and *Take Me Out to the Ballroom*. Currently, she was verifying the Three Kings' ancestry in *We Three Kings Are Orient-al*. She also liked *The First No-Hell*, but the hymn she warbled and garbled most frequently was *Good King When His Lens Looked Out*.

In the early months of marriage, Jasper had tactfully disentangled Tara's slip of the tongue when she admonished, 'Don't stir up a hermit's nest.' Subsequently he had corrected her when she was singing to a neighbor's toddler and she came to the line, 'Sing a song of six pants, a bottle full of rye.'

When Jasper intervened, she balked at 'sixpence.' "Where do you think we are—England? We don't have pence in America," she said defensively. Jasper doubted that she had knowingly Americanized the nursery rhyme, but he said no more; he had a sudden revelation that it would be infinitely more fun in future to listen quietly and resist logomachies. Would his children teach their children, *Trickle, Trickle, Little Star*? Could a star trickle?

Notwithstanding Tara's tendency to mix up words and titles, Jasper never lost sight of the fact that his wife was endowed with a plentiful supply of common sense. And somewhere in the house, in a hinged box lined with purple velvet, was a medal she had earned in high school for consistent inclusion on the honor roll. Jasper acknowledged these particulars, but once in a while he would smile and think that it was a good thing her teachers didn't test her on songs and proverbs.

—·—··—·—

When Tara opened the Southericks' Christmas card—expecting nothing more than a signature—and read Alex's request for a $1,000 loan, her eyes widened. '...*Please do not telephone me for additional details as I cannot disclose any other information...*' What a captivating message! After Tara finished examining the rest of the mail, she picked up the note and read it a second time, savoring its element of mystery.

Just then, Sally, her three-year-old who was recuperating from chicken pox, woke up with a whiny cry, and Tara put mystery aside to take care of her. Before illness intervened, Sally had jabbered incessantly about Santa Claus, and Tara was thankful that Sally's recovery period would be over before Christmas, so that her little girl could take full delight in Santa's visit. Last year, when Sally was only two, she had been confused by the holiday turmoil, but this season she was at the optimal age for enchantment. Tara was promoting the Santa myth for all it was worth. At 37, she assumed that Sally would be her last child, and therefore her last excuse for annual encounters with the jolly legendary figure.

Holding Sally on her left arm, Tara made peanut-butter and jelly sandwiches with her right hand for her sons, Drew and Leonard, who would be home for lunch any minute. She could hear blustery winds blowing outside, and decided to open a can of vegetable soup for a starter.

The boys came wrestling noisily into the house, yanking off jackets and woolen hats while scuffling their way into the kitchen. Lenny threw Drew's mittens under the table, and Drew ran into the hall and flung Lenny's coat behind the living-room sofa. At the sight of food the boys quieted down, running and landing at their places, which were set strategically at opposite ends of the table. As a rule the boys clowned for Sally, but having been cautioned not to stimulate her because she was sick, they had only each other for lunchtime antics.

It seemed to Tara that these two wrestled from the moment they awoke until they closed their eyes at night. Leonard, the eight-year-old, had bigger bones than his medium-framed brother Drew. Although Drew was two years older, the boys behaved like peers.

After lunch, the boys tumbled out the door and Tara started on her busy afternoon schedule. There were torn dungarees to mend, Christmas cards to address, and kitchen curtains to stitch; and all the while, Sally had to be kept in bed and entertained. Because Sally's chicken pox had struck during a week of hectic Christmas preparations, Tara had given up on reupholstering the worst of the stuffed chairs before her annual holiday party.

Since buying a home fourteen years ago, the Zamps had never had the funds to decorate it as Tara would have liked. She was constantly modifying her projects to fit a strict budget, yet she managed to bring professional touches to her rooms. She had taken an adult-school course in upholstery and had re-covered the dining-room chair-seats. For the coming holiday she planned to sew place mats with the remnants of striped fabric from the seats, and then buy napkins in a matching solid color.

She was so occupied for the remainder of the afternoon that she forgot about Alex Southerick's unconventional Christmas greeting until Jasper came home. He gave her a hug, and asked the usual questions.

"How's Sally?"

"She's less cranky today. Her fever's down."

"Good. What's for supper?"

"Hamburgers on buns. I've been snowed under."

"I love hamburgers. What kind of mail?"

"Super! A New Year's Eve party invitation and a Christmas-card note from your old college friend Alex Southerick that really had me buffled. I left it on top of the other cards, on the coffee table."

Jasper knew that 'buffled' was a cross between 'baffled' and 'buffaloed'; he thought it was a rather witty hybrid. As he left the kitchen he heard Tara regaling Sally with a lively rendition of *Pop Goes the Measles*. He just grinned.

— ✦ —

Jasper had blue eyes, a short dark-brown beard, and an ingratiating smile. His benign appearance was rakishly altered by a jagged dog-bite scar that showed above the left side of his eyeglasses. He was the assistant manager of a small restaurant. As he frequently remarked, the title sounded impressive on resumes, but did not convey the harsh reality of a job that encompassed everything from bookkeeping to floor-mopping. Nor was his salary commensurate with his duties. Jasper was unhappy with his position; in fact, he had been disillusioned by every career choice he had made since graduating from college 24 years before. He had decided that providence was a more important factor in achieving financial success than brains or diligence.

When he started out as an energetic restaurant-management graduate at 21, Jasper had resolved to work his way up from the bottom in a fast-food eatery. He was the most industrious person employed there. Over and above performing his routine chores, he contributed many cost-effective suggestions. Finally, after two years, the night manager resigned, and the entire staff assumed that Jasper would be given the promotion. For three weeks he served as acting night manager. Then the blow came. The boss brought in his nephew, who had never seen the back end of a restaurant before, and introduced him to the crew as the new night manager. Jasper quit the next day.

Three or four jobs later he met Tara. Though he was working as a shoe salesman at the time, he was making a survey, in the evenings, of the area restaurants. He wrote copious notes about their merits and deficiencies for future reference when he opened 'his own little place.' Tara was a winsome hostess in a popular suburban cafe. She had a perky, wholesome look, a pixie haircut, and a freckled pug nose. She was accustomed to patrons asking her for dates, which were mostly declined. Week after week she refused Jasper's bids, but Jasper persisted and eventually triumphed. She had dinner with him in a competing steakhouse on her day off.

After a five-course meal, Tara and Jasper sat in their secluded booth, talking for hours. They discovered that they were both born in October, and that each was the oldest in a family of three, remarkable coincidences that provided an instant affinity. By midnight, when the dining room closed, Tara knew every aspiration that Jasper held dear. She had also discerned that he was professionally frustrated and scrupulously honest.

"When I was eight," Jasper told her, "I found a nickel in the return-slot of a pay phone. My mother—who had taught me the rules of moral conduct to begin with—tried

179

to persuade me that uprightness did not demand my sending that nickel to the phone company."

Tara laughed. "Naturally; it wasn't theirs."

"I know. That's what my mother said. But I couldn't see how it was mine either. My mother told me I could keep it, but I raced back to the phone and put the nickel back in the slot. I reckoned that the person who made the call might come back for his money."

Jasper gazed into Tara's eyes. "I've never told anyone half the stuff I've told you tonight," he said. "I was afraid people would think I was odd."

When he returned home late that evening, he thought a great deal about Tara. Although Tara had sided with most of his convictions about restaurants, she had also expressed perceptive observations of her own. She was candid; if she had contradictory views, she disclosed them without qualms. Her practicality came through, but it seemed like a good balance for his idealism.

As for Tara, she was madly attracted to Jasper for reasons she could not define. Was she enthralled because his personality contrasted so sharply with her own? Or was it be- cause he was so unlike any man she had dated before? Maybe it was simple body chemistry—she did not know.

A whirlwind courtship followed. Tara took a daytime position in an insurance office because hostessing was a late-evening occupation not conducive to weekend dating. During this period it became apparent that Jasper was inclined to be short-tempered when trifling matters did not meet his perfectionist standards. Well, nobody's perfect, thought Tara, laughing at her word choice.

Within six months, Tara and Jasper were married. The first weeks of marriage were so rhapsodic that Jasper whistled even while he was selling shoes, a job he actively disliked. But after a few more months of catering to women who had giant feet but wanted midget shoes, Jasper came home roaring louder each night about feet, vanity, and a number of irrelevant grievances.

"Hide in the closet when you put on your shoes," he said to Tara. "The next woman I see putting on shoes is liable to get clobbered."

The following day a buxom woman with size ten feet complained to the store owner because Jasper would not squeeze her heels into a size seven sandal after her wide toes had broken the stitching on the front part of the shoe.

Later Jasper gave his notice, and in two weeks he was working as a waiter in a country restaurant called The Friendly Nook. He found waiting on tables to be relaxing. He was a superb public relations man; the customers invariably liked him. But the restaurant was not doing well, and a year later it was advertised for sale.

This development gave Jasper a sudden inspiration. To own a restaurant had always been his ultimate goal. Was it within reach?

"It has vast possibilities," he told Tara. "We can refine the ambience with candles, flowers, and tablecloths instead of plastic place mats. Put beautiful prints or paintings on the walls. You know how much I've dreamed of having my own place; I've hung on to those notebooks I filled before we were married, about the weak and strong points of forty restaurants in this county. And you have restaurant training too. When we get big you can say good-bye to offices for the rest of your life. How can we go wrong? Let's take out a loan and give it a try."

"Well—we'd be starting out on a shoelace," said Tara.

Though she sounded dubious, Jasper could tell she was wavering. "Maybe it was fate that I took this particular opening when I had my pick of three waiter's jobs," he said. He tended to view events in his life as prophetic. "We were meant to buy this business, see?"

When Tara eventually caught his enthusiasm, he was jubilant. He went through a series of impassioned highs and lows. He was tense and anxious while waiting for the loan to be considered, ecstatic when it was approved, and spellbound when he finally turned the key in the lock.

"Down to the last floorboard, these premises belong to Mr. and Mrs. Jasper Zamp," he said in a hushed voice.

"And the bank," said Tara, ever practical.

Next came a prodigious amount of hard labor. Tara's employment provided a paycheck for living expenses, but the Zamps were frugal and saved every possible penny for use in the business. Tara drove directly from the insurance office where she worked to The Friendly Nook in the neighboring countryside. She and Jasper ate hurried snack-dinners while they plotted their spectacular Grand Opening 'Under New Management.'

They talked about changing the name of the restaurant to Wander Inn or Ramble Inn or Fellowship Corner. Tara suggested Zamp Inn, and even designed a newspaper advertisement:

Let's go, everyone!
STAMP IN
to the
ZAMP INN

But Jasper said people don't stamp into restaurants, they walk in. Tara said she couldn't make a rhyme out of that. Then the budding restaurateurs considered that the large outdoor sign was one of the few items in excellent condition, and this was the deciding factor in retaining the name of The Friendly Nook.

Jasper believed that the dingy atmosphere was one reason that The Nook had fared poorly. He removed the furniture, the pictures, the draperies, and the worn carpeting;

then he painted every inch of every room. To make maximum use of their limited space, he and Tara rearranged tiny cardboard tables and chairs on a scaled drawing until they came up with a floor plan that seated more diners without crowding. They installed recessed lighting, and hung interesting artwork on the walls. Their bones and brains were weary when they retired late, night after night.

Next they hired a chef with estimable references, and they sampled and approved his delicacies. Finally, they advertised Opening Week discounts to lure the public to come and see the improvements.

Tara scheduled new hours at her insurance job, starting earlier and leaving at four so she could be The Nook's hostess-cashier while dinner was being served. Jasper handled ordering, marketing, bookkeeping, menu-planning, and general management; in rush periods he helped the chef. Jasper's younger brother came to work as a busboy part-time, and Tara's sister waited on tables.

Diners came and went, looked pleased, and came back. Any complimentary comment caused giddy rejoicing in the back room.

"The finest sherried flounder in the state," declared one patron, and later Tara and Jasper skipped around the kitchen and clapped their hands. Then Tara pursed her face into a stern scowl and said, "This lack of decorum will never do for the proprietors of The Friendly Nook." Worn out to the point of silliness, they roared hilariously.

For months the dining room was filled to capacity daily, with waiting lines outdoors and through the lobby. Then business started dwindling. The Zamps—too preoccupied to watch television or pay attention to local news—were 'buffled' for several days by the decreasing number of customers. The reason became clear late one afternoon when Tara was not able to get to the restaurant after work because she could not buy gasoline. Her sister and Jasper's brother did not arrive either. A severe gasoline shortage had jolted the region.

The Nook was located fifteen miles from town. As much as habitués might relish the chef's veal and seafood specialties, they could not walk to obtain them. Even Tara's and Jasper's families, loyal supporters from the outset, were not able to burn precious fuel for such luxuries as out-of-town dining. Eateries with dirty floors and second-rate food were thriving in business districts, while The Friendly Nook stayed empty.

The news media predicted long-term woes: after the crisis was over, the cost of gasoline would double or triple. Tara wanted to sell without delay. "We're losing money every day we stay open," she said. "No gas, no customers. You have to let sleeping dogs die."

Jasper had to smile at the fate of Tara's poor slumbering canines. But losing his 'own little place' was intolerable to him, and with blind faith he insisted on keeping it open. He laid off all the staff, including the chef, and did the cooking and cleanup himself. "If only we had enough money to wait until this blows over," he lamented.

He appeared beyond solace, and Tara tried to cheer him by thinking of the benefits to be gained by selling the restaurant. One of the casualties of the business had been their sex life, which in less than a year had gone from rapturous to adequate to almost nonexistent.

"At least we'd have more time for sex," she said. "I know they say abstinence makes the heart grow fonder, but I can't say I agree."

This misquotation was delivered by Tara with what Jasper called her satisfied-cat look, which Tara had whenever she fit a proverb, however inexactly, to a specific situation. The sentiment, together with the look, wrested a smile from Jasper, but not an acquiescence to close The Nook's doors. The Zamps struggled with the unprofitable restaurant for another month, when the decision was made for them: Tara became pregnant. The joy of the coming baby softened the heartache over the demise of The Nook. Jasper put the restaurant on the market, but kept running it for four more months because there were no prospective buyers. True to forecasts, gasoline prices soared as the lines at the pumps shrank. The high cost was crippling to a remote establishment that was not located near any other business. Some patrons returned when the over-priced gas became accessible, but many did not. Tara would have to be leaving her job soon, and The Friendly Nook was still producing a negative net income. Finally, Tara and Jasper were forced to sell the restaurant for a fifth of what they had paid for it, leaving them with loan payments for the next eighteen years. They were glad that they managed to pay their creditors, many of whom had been exceptionally patient. After the legal closing on the Nook sale, Jasper went home to his bedroom, locked the door, and turned the radio on at full volume. Then the tears came, the tears that Tara was not supposed to hear. What she heard later was the outrage, released in bursts of wrath over petty irritations.

When Jasper was in a testy frame of mind, he could bark about anything, even the absence of a salt shaker on the dinner table. Tara, calmer by nature than Jasper, was rarely the instigator of a quarrel, but she defended herself staunchly from unjust attacks; when shouted at, she shouted back.

"Where is it written in the marriage contract that the wife must put the salt on the table?" she screeched one night.

"You want me to write out a contract? I'll write it, and I'll put in other commodities, like napkins."

"Haven't you ever noticed that I have two hands, not ten?" Tara had worked late at the office, and she was concerned with making a fast supper, not with fussy table-setting.

"I noticed that, but not the two heads," Jasper countered.

It didn't take long to proceed to more abusive epithets, none of which either Tara or Jasper believed. Soon they were both contrite, thus rounding out their habitual cycle. In their marriage of extremes, sharp moments were followed quickly by tender ones, and despondency could be replaced by elation within an hour.

In a sunny humor, Tara once called Jasper her 'uncut diamond—rough on the outside but beautiful inside.' After their next tiff Jasper said, "Three days ago you described me as a priceless diamond."

"Diamonds have the same composition as coal," she stated curtly. "Today you're coal."

Tara was eight and one-half months pregnant when she gave up her job. Jasper was at the lowest financial point of his life; he filled the first vacancy he could find, selling lumber for a small salary plus commission. To boost his pay he worked sixty hours a week.

Two weeks later, their son, Drew, was born. Though nearly bankrupt, Tara and Jasper—who fought over minutiae such as salt and napkins—agreed without question that Tara would stay home and take care of their son.

Drew was almost two when a second son, Leonard, was born. Jasper was still putting in long hours selling lumber. Tara's well-meant suggestion that she find a hostessing job at night, when the children were asleep, met with a booming 'no' from Jasper, who interpreted it as a thrust at his own inadequacy.

Jasper remained a perfectionist in an imperfect world. He yearned to be a perfect father, a perfect husband, a perfect breadwinner. When he violated one of his self-imposed standards, he went into a rage that was far more damaging than the original infraction. After he composed himself, he was so disturbed by his behavior that he became cross and oversensitive, thus diminishing even further the perfectness that was his chimerical dream.

Although The Friendly Nook had closed through no fault of his own, he regarded the venture as another entry in his failure file. He did not discern that business failures were not failures at living; nor did he have the overview to perceive that a failure could be an advancement in the long run. His reverses lay in his mind like smoldering ashes in a dormant volcano that might erupt at any moment for no predictable reason.

One evening Jasper tripped and sprawled over a small toy. It was a soft tumble, on a thick carpet, and Tara chuckled and said he looked like a stunt man in a slapstick movie. Tara's lighthearted observation, plus the fall, made two sparks—all Jasper needed to kindle a fire. He launched a diatribe about toys not being put away, and about the impropriety and heartlessness of laughing at people who fall.

"If I fell down the stairs and killed myself, would that be funnier?"

"I wouldn't laugh unless I saw the person wasn't hurt, you idiot!"

"Oh, now I'm an idiot! Am I an idiot to be out there making a living for us? You're the champion idiot for snickering when there is no joke. And a double dumbbell for not putting the toys where they belong."

Tara snatched up baby Leonard, who was creeping across the floor, and carried him into the children's room, where Drew was asleep. She hated to wrangle in front of the children.

After depositing the infant in his playpen, she was back at the scene in a flash with her defense: "If I picked up every toy that was out of place, I'd have a broken back."

"Oh, is this my cue where I'm supposed to laugh? A broken back? Ha-ha-ha!"

Such was the caliber of many disputes that had no connection to the root causes of Jasper's anger. Afterward, Tara and Jasper always 'made up' when the children were present. Tara said, "They have to see that we really love each other, because sometimes it might not seem like it."

This time Jasper was thoughtful. "Earlier tonight," he said, "before we had this senseless fight, you skipped out to the backyard with Drew to watch lightning bugs. You got as big a charge out of chasing those fireflies as Drew did. I love you, Tara, for being that kind of person—and a whole lot more."

———————

Sally was born when Drew was entering second grade, and Leonard was ready for kindergarten.

Like all mothers, Tara inspected Sally at birth to see that exterior parts were accounted for, and that the proper number of toes and fingers were in place. It wasn't until Sally was eight months old that Tara noticed with some alarm that the little girl did not respond if she spoke to her from the right side.

Tara's pediatrician advised waiting until Sally was two years old for audiology tests. On her second birthday an otologist diagnosed her as totally deaf in the right ear, with a moderate hearing loss in the left. She was fitted with a hearing aid for her left ear, but according to the doctor, her limited left-ear hearing would gradually deteriorate, leaving her deaf. Sally was a bright child, but because of her hearing loss she did not talk at the two-year-old level, and the otologist advised immediate speech therapy, together with lessons in sign language.

Tara's ensuing doldrums were lightened considerably by Jasper's outlook. Tara had expected Jasper to thrash through the house raving, "Why us? Why Sally?" But instead he said gently, "This is a privilege—it shows that God trusts us to bring up a child with a deficiency. You know, throughout each pregnancy you said, 'We don't care if it's a boy or a girl, as long as it's healthy.' To me that sounded callous, as if we'd be dissatisfied with the merchandise if it were defective. I used to think, yes, I want our baby to be healthy, for its own sake. But I won't mind if God chooses us to be the parents of a child with a disability, and I know we'd love it just as much."

Tara was uplifted by this surprising tolerance from a man who demanded perfection in so many other ways.

That night Jasper urged Tara to search out the best ear specialists in the world, vowing, "We'll do everything for her that's available, anywhere."

When Tara learned that the nation's best otology center was 3,000 miles away, she said, "We can't afford it. The traveling expense alone would be more than we could handle. We're down the river with no oars."

But Jasper reached for a paddle: he took on small carpentry jobs during evenings and weekends. Such contracts had been offered to him before, through his lumberyard connections, but he had rejected them because he already worked long hours and wanted to spend the remaining time with his family. In estimating lumber quantities, he had studied blueprints for everything from miniature patios to tall condominiums, and he had often wondered how well

189

he could put that paper knowledge to work if he had real tools and materials at hand. Now the need for extra income compelled him to find out.

He started with minor jobs, installing shelves and planing doors; then, reassured by his success, he forged ahead to more complex projects. His chief hindrance was his inborn trait of perfectionism, which kept him working long after a job was well done. One customer was put in the implausible position of begging him to leave a job done to imperfection.

"I like it, I love it, go home!" entreated the woman, when, at midnight, Jasper was still rankled by a kitchen cabinet that was three-sixteenths of an inch out of plumb.

Finally the day came when Jasper announced to Tara, "Make an appointment for Sally at the ontology center. We're flying her out there."

A month later they were on the plane. Drew and Leonard went along, even though willing grandparents were close by, and baby-sitting would have cost nothing.

What confounded Tara the most was that Jasper had not rampaged about anything for five months, despite having worked sixteen hours a day without adequate rest. This record was phenomenal for a man who was given to exploding at frequent intervals, even when he was under less strain and had slim cause. Tara had basked in the tranquillity. It seemed as if Jasper was at his best when faced with an extraordinary challenge. Or perhaps he was sustained by the prospect of helping his daughter, a gratifying substitute for the career fulfillment that eluded him.

The trip came to naught medically. The specialists concurred that Sally had an incurable congenital defect that might eventually result in total deafness in both ears. There was no medical treatment, no projected surgery.

Yet the journey was the first vacation the Zamps had ever had, and they were able to enhance it with sightseeing

190

and fun. Tara observed, "Every lining has some silver in it," and Jasper looked impish and said, "In that case, I think I'll search my jacket pockets."

Nevertheless, correcting Sally's deafness now appeared impossible, and after they returned home Jasper succumbed to fury, the reaction Tara had envisioned from the beginning.

"Medical technology! Great advances! Baloney!" he stormed. "Why can't they fix something easy, like a deaf ear!" He yanked off his eyeglasses, threw them on the floor, and stomped on them. "Why should I see, if Sally can't hear?" he shouted.

Tara did not feel like shouting back. She gazed dispiritedly at the bits of glass and broken frames, and thought of the money it would cost to buy new glasses.

"I thought you weren't angry about Sally," she said in a low voice.

"I'm not angry because we have a daughter with a handicap," he thundered. "I'm angry because there's nothing we can *do*. I want to help her! And all my hopes have disappeared, zoom!"

Tara wiped away a tear with a quick jerky movement, as if annoyed by the intrusion. She had been heartened by Jasper's initial attitude about Sally's impairment; in fact, his placidity had carried her over the hurdle of that first diagnosis. Now she was discouraged to see his anger. "Do you think you're helping Sally by fuming because God hasn't provided a remedy for her?" she asked.

Jasper swung around, his mouth open, ready to countercharge. Then he turned abruptly and left the house without a word, slamming the door behind him. Tara stood by the window and watched him walking briskly up the street. The weather was dim and drizzly. I hope he doesn't get hit by a truck without his glasses, she thought.

191

Meanwhile, Drew, Leonard, and Sally—the three of them calm and unperturbed—had left the room on tiptoe at the first sign of their father's rising voice. Tara had made a habit of shooing the children into other rooms at the start of any quarrel with Jasper. By now the youngsters were accustomed to parental clashes; they had made the gleeful discovery that they could take advantage of such opportunities to watch television programs ordinarily forbidden them. Their muffled snickers would go undetected while their mother and father were immersed in a rousing squabble in another room.

This time, however, they were thwarted, because their parents' discussion had not developed into the usual prolonged conflict. When Jasper left the house, Tara marched into the family room, snapped the television off, handed Sally a toy, and steered the boys to their most avoided activity, homework.

Within two hours Jasper reappeared, his beard dripping, his jacket soaked from the rain. "Thanks," he said, shivering in his wet clothes. "I have a better insight now. And I suppose Sally could have construed my hollering to mean I'm discontented to have her exactly as she is, which you know isn't true. But I don't want our acceptance of the prognosis to cause us to overlook progress in the field. We should subscribe to that ontology center's newsletter and keep up on related research. It's high-priced for a quarterly, but I think we should buy it."

He put an unlit cigarette to his lips, then took it away. During their airplane trip Jasper had quit smoking again—for the fourth time—after seven-year-old Leonard had asked him what smoking was for, and Jasper could not come up with a plausible answer. He broke the cigarette in half on the nearest end-table, arranged a tiny hill of shredded tobacco, and swept it all into the wastebasket. On top of the tobacco he placed the pieces of his eyeglass frames, from the floor where he had left them, and then he got the vacuum cleaner out of the closet and watched the shattered fragments of glass disappear into the vacuum tube. Zoom.

—— ❤ ——

The lumberyard where Jasper worked had a severe set-back when popular imported woods became temporarily unobtainable. Jasper was told he could sell for commissions only, with no salary. Though this change decreased his income substantially, he stayed on the job; but in the evenings he combed the help-wanted advertisements and sent out resumes to area restaurants. And he continued to wield his hammer and saw; he had earned a reputation as an able craftsman.

One day when Jasper was depressed over his small commission check, a building contractor proposed a day's work on Saturday. "My regular man is out sick, and I have a deadline clause on a warehouse. Concrete is coming in Monday morning, so the forms have to be finished," explained Mr. Topliani.

On Friday evening, as Jasper was gathering the tools he would need to build Mr. Topliani's forms, he received a long-awaited telephone call offering him a position as buyer-manager of an elite uptown restaurant. But it was mandatory that he start work Saturday and work all day Sunday too, because the manager had left without warning.

Jasper said he was busy on Saturday, but he would be glad to begin early on Sunday. The ensuing conversation made it plain that these terms were not acceptable. Tara, catching the drift of the dialogue, made wild gesticulations to show that she was violently opposed to Jasper's response.

When Jasper hung up the phone, Tara looked at him reprovingly. He answered her unspoken protest: "I made a commitment to Mr. Topliani. He can't get a skilled carpenter on such short notice. I was happy enough to take his job when I needed it; now I have to keep my word."

"You'll keep your word, but we can't eat it," grumbled Tara.

"Something else will turn up. I'd love to take the job as manager, but don't you see? I can't renege on an agreement." Tara was so dolorous that he went on, "Look at it like this—if I didn't show up for Mr. Topliani tomorrow, the manager's job would probably be a washout. We can't be certain, but that's the best way to surmise when there is no choice."

"No choice! Of course you have a choice! Just call up Mr. Topliani and spell out the facts. He doesn't know that a full-time job is hanging in the balance. Tell him you have to feed your wife and three kids."

Jasper shook his head. "Mr. Topliani has more kids than we have—he has six. And he has to pay a sizable penalty if this warehouse isn't built by the date in his contract. He has ordered mixed concrete to be delivered Monday morning, and the forms have to be done so the concrete can be poured. I promised I'd build them, and that's it."

Tara had another thought, "When word gets around that you refused such a rosy offer, you'll be whitewashed from the list of prospects."

Jasper hugged her. She pulled away and asked, "Do you know we have twelve dollars left in our checking account?"

"Swell! I didn't know we had that much."

The next week Jasper landed his present assistant manager's job, which had proved to be far from ideal. Tara sometimes wondered if the other position would have been more desirable; Jasper never gave it another thought, as there was no doubt in his mind that providence had not intended him to have it.

Jasper strode into the living room and picked up the Southericks' Christmas card, which Tara had left on top of the pile for him to peruse. When he read Alex's note about the money, he dropped into a chair, stunned. He was re-reading it when Tara appeared in the doorway.

"That beats the cake, doesn't it?" she remarked pleasantly. "Imagine trying to borrow money from somebody you haven't seen for five years."

Jasper let out his breath in an audible sound of relief. "What a godsend that we have a thousand bucks in our Christmas Club right now," he said. "We've had spells in the past when we wouldn't have been able to swing it."

Tara stood up straighter. "What do you mean, swing it?"

"I mean, what great timing that we happen to have it just when Alex needs it."

Tara's jaw dropped involuntarily.

"What's wrong?" asked Jasper, puzzled by the aghast expression on Tara's face.

"This thousand dollars we have was no windfall. It was sweat and save twenty dollars a week, no matter what. We gave up steaks and movies and concerts. It wasn't easy, but we did it for the Best Christmas Ever for the kids, remember?"

"Yes, I know that, but we're not giving the money away. Alex only wants it for a month. We can explain the whole deal to the kids, they'll understand. Then we can have our own family Christmas celebration on January 15th after Alex returns the loan, and it can still be the Best Christmas Ever. On December 25th we can focus on the birth of Christ, which is what Christmas is all about anyway. The gifts can come later."

Sincerely Yours

Tara looked as if she were going to faint. Though the note from Alex Southerick had been fascinating, she had not considered that there was even a remote possibility of complying with his request. When she spoke, her words came in faltering half-sentences: "We don't have any credit cards—we can't charge anything—and when the boys go back to school—after Christmas vacation—and compare notes—they'll have to say they received nothing—from their parents for Christmas."

"They don't have to word it that way. They can say we decorated a tree with popcorn and candy canes, and we sang carols and went to church; and our family is going to exchange presents in January because gifts are not the most important part of Christmas."

"I don't mind for me, Jasper, you know that. But kids don't think like that. Presents are earthshaking to children."

"Well, they're bound to get packages from their grandparents and relatives."

"Our folks have already bought them clothes—shirts and dungarees and new winter jackets. Heaven knows they need them, but shirts don't make children jump up and down, and shout 'hurray'."

"But it's only for a couple of weeks! How can we say 'no' to an old friend? Let me give you some refreshers about Alex Southerick, though I'm positive I've told you about him before. In college he made straight A's. But instead of leaning back on his laurels, he lent a hand to students who were doing poorly, including me. I think I'd still be there struggling to pass calculus if it weren't for Alex tutoring me. And he didn't play up his brains either. Do you know how he put it? He said he was born with a sixth sense for math, and he didn't mind sharing his genetic heritage. He spent hour after hour with me, and not once did he make me feel dense. And I know he lifted a number of others, too, from the pits of D's and F's."

"But honey, that was in college, almost twenty years ago. Since then you've only gotten together at class reunions. It's been nearly five years since you've seen him."

"If I didn't see him for forty years, I wouldn't forget him. Alex was that kind of a guy. He had it all, but he wasn't conceited about it. Don't you remember him? We sat with him at my reunions."

"Yes, I remember him and his wife, Marcia. They were cordial people and I liked them. But I don't feel on close terms with them after seeing them at three class reunion dinners and three morning-after breakfasts in the course of fifteen years."

"Hey, that reminds me. There must be a reunion coming up in the spring. We should be getting an announcement soon, and I want to go. It will be great to see Alex and Marcia again. And do you remember Chester and Pamela Kovent? He's sort of a blowhard, but she's sweet and extremely shy. They went together in college. He was a football star, and she hung on his every word. She didn't seem to have any backbone of her own, but she was a nice kid. And Gilbert Desston. Can you place him? A likable guy. We both served on the Homecoming Committee. I've lost track of what he's doing, but he was in some type of deadly business five years ago—a stockbroker, I think. I forget his wife's name—is it Isabel? I do recall she was snooty. She asked me my occupation, and when I said I sold lumber she looked down her nose at me as if lumber were on a level with child pornography."

"We haven't been getting Christmas cards from them the past few years, I guess since that last reunion," put in Tara.

"Well, I like Gilbert; keep sending cards to them, will you? I get nostalgic when I think back on my college friends. Sam Norpeg became a construction engineer. He came to the last reunion alone because his wife was away on a seminar. He had pictures of her though—her name was Roberta and she was made up like a movie star. I remember feeling sorry for him because she wasn't with him, then even sorrier when I came up with a snapshot of our kids and he said he didn't have any children. It was hard for me to conceal my emotions, but he smiled and said, 'Don't look so mournful. It's our own option.' I don't know what they opted for, though, he didn't say. Well, I'm straying off the subject. Here's Alex's business card—did you notice he's vice-president in charge of marketing for Kinnelac Corporation? That adds up—Alex was voted 'Most Likely to Succeed'."

"The election didn't foretell very much," said Tara drily. "If he was such a big success, would he be so strapped?"

Jasper brushed aside her query. "It takes a lot of courage to sit down and write to ten of your friends that you're short of cash," he said. "Once when I was a kid I was three cents short for the bus fare to get home. I'd gone downtown Christmas shopping with a pocketful of change that I'd saved up by shoveling sidewalks, and I spent everything but seven cents. This was back when bus fare was a dime. I was by myself, and I thought, I'll just ask a grownup who looks obliging for three cents. I trekked up to a gray-haired lady, and when she glanced down at me I mumbled, 'Uh, uh, uh, do you have the time?' After five stuttering attempts with five people, I knew precisely what time it was, and I also knew I couldn't ask anybody for a handout. I could picture my mom getting frantic at home. I was shaking in my boots when I trudged over to the corner news-stand to negotiate a three-cent loan. I can see that surly owner as if it were yesterday. Thick black mustache, greasy black hair. He grunted when I told him I'd return the three cents the next day—which I did, and it cost me twenty cents in bus fare to

198

do it. And this big gruff guy grunted again—not even a smile. That was in the days when twenty cents meant something to a kid. I'd earn a quarter by mowing an acre of lawn or shoveling snow for a couple of hours. But getting back to Alex, I really feel bad about this."

"I feel bad for Alex too, whatever his problem is," said Tara. "But I feel worse for our own children. A thousand dollars would bring our account down to nothing, and we have no credit. Every single application has been denied because of the Nook loan. We've scrimped and saved for a year so the kids would have a memorable Christmas. Wouldn't you feel dreadful for our own children, not having a real Christmas?"

"If you're talking about their presents—no, I wouldn't. Drew and Lenny are old enough to appreciate that we're helping someone in need with our Christmas money. And it's a short delay for their gifts. Lenny wants a ten-speed bike. If he got it on December 25th, he probably wouldn't be able to ride it that day anyway because of the weather. So what's the difference if he gets it in January? What's tops on Drew's list? A drum set and a walkie-talkie radio— or is it an automatic pitching machine? He changes his mind every week. At any rate, nothing that can't be postponed. Life is more than gratification, and the sooner they learn that the better. Sally is too young to tell December from January, or cheap from expensive. You can get some toys and books at the five-and-ten that will make her overjoyed with Santa Claus. And then we can say Santa is stopping here for another visit on his way back to the North Pole. She'll be merry for Christmas twice, how's that?"

Tara sighed and sat down. She saw the earmarks of a lengthy discussion.

"Aside from the Christmas-present angle," she said, "$1,000 is a lot of money to loan out lightly, at any season."

"Lightly! I wouldn't lend it out lightly! And even though $1,000 strikes us as a lot, it actually isn't, if you know what I mean."

Tara did not know what he meant. "At this stage it's our total savings. And it's taken us an entire year to stow it away. I can't agree that we should write a check to some man we haven't seen for five years just on his word that we'll have it back in a month."

"Some man? I'm not picking a name at random out of the telephone book! This is a person I *know*. He got me through calculus, for heaven's sake. Don't worry, I'm not throwing this money away; I worked too hard for it. I'm merely lending funds for a few weeks to a terrific guy who did me many good turns. I never thought I'd have a chance to do anything for him, yet here it is, right in my lap. I'm sorry he's in a predicament, but I'm glad I can help. I knew Alex for four solid years, and let me tell you that he's not only smart, he has a good heart."

"He could have the world's greatest heart, and still be down on his luck. He could fully intend to pay the loan back, and not be able to do it. If he doesn't have the money, he doesn't have it—you can't get a stone out of blood. You should know how it is when things don't turn out according to plan. That's happened to you a few times."

"It sure has! I know how rough it can be to put your hands on cash in a hurry. That's why I have a sympathy for Alex that goes down to the pit of my stomach. I know we have steep payments on the Nook loan, and we have no credit—but we do have our Christmas Club check. And if Sally hadn't come down with chicken pox, we'd have done our Christmas shopping by now and the money would be gone. It's a miracle how all these things fit together, and it turns out that on the day we get this card we still have the exact sum of $1,000. Isn't that telling you something?"

"Yes. It's telling me it's a rotten shame that Sally got chicken pox."

"And besides, I have a strong feeling that if I ever sent Alex a letter like this, he'd get hold of some cash somehow and send it to me on the double."

"Too bad you never thought of it. There were times we could have used it. Anyhow, I'm afraid that if Alex's plans don't work out, we won't get the money back promptly in January. Then there will be a second letdown for the boys. How can you guarantee that they'll have Christmas in January?"

"I have a gut feeling it will work out. And in addition to everything else, I have a theory that good begets good, and evil begets evil. Because we would be doing a right-minded thing, only good could come out of it."

"That sounds noble on paper, honey, but what about Mrs. Ollderman up the street? She cooks and cleans for the sick, drives people to the doctor's, takes up collections for Thanksgiving baskets, you name it. She's the saint of Ullstra Road. Last month her car was stolen, and Monday she broke her hip. She'll be laid up for the holidays. How come she has such awful luck if good begets good?"

"Because the good isn't always readily discernible, especially to the human eye. Maybe the good is that she'll teach others charity by her example. Or her unselfishness might stir her daughter, or a neighbor, to become a nurse and take care of crippled children, or people stuck in institutions. Blessings like that can be hidden.

"Let's say there are two sons tending to their sick mother with similar amounts of time and work. They take turns preparing her meals, washing her clothes, and so forth. One son is doing it only because he wants to inherit a share of his mother's estate; the other son is caring for his mother because she's old and ailing, and needs help. When the mother dies, each son inherits equally. Offhand, you might say, 'See, it doesn't matter whether a person's thoughts are righteous or mercenary.' But my belief is that the son who ministered to his mother out of greed will never derive any true spiritual benefit out of his deeds, even though he might buy a new car or house with his inheritance. The other son will achieve well-being on the inside even if it isn't evident on the surface.

"Now, in the case of this loan for Alex Southerick, whether we get the money back is not the prime consideration."

Tara looked startled. "It's most assuredly *my* prime consideration!" she said.

"Don't get me wrong, I want to get the money back, that's for sure," Jasper said quickly. But my major concern is that Alex must be desperate to have gone to the extent of writing ten friends for a quick loan; and if it's that critical, we should send it, period. Why he wants it is immaterial. And if the money isn't returned—and I'm confident it will be, this is just for the sake of discussion—that wouldn't necessarily be all bad. The proceeds might wind up being applied to a good cause, far more crucial than drum sets and bicycles. Or this might turn out to be the greatest lesson our kids ever have."

Warming to his hypothesis, Jasper spoke with increasing vim. "You were talking about the Best Christmas Ever—this Christmas may be more memorable than all the rest. The kids get toys every Christmas; that's routine procedure. Years from now they may say, 'Hey, remember that Christmas when our family helped somebody out with the Christmas-club money?' *That's* memorable. I wasn't thinking about it along these lines before, because I was concentrating on Alex, but all at once I feel indebted to him. This is a sensational way for our boys to learn firsthand that Christmas is real and wonderful whether they have presents or not." With a roguish wink he added, "All that's gold doesn't glitter, you know."

"I recognize that old saying," said Tara without blinking an eye. But your theory doesn't appeal to me. If there's any good being accomplished, I want to be able to see it. Maybe *you* could lose $1,000 and console yourself that it might have been spent for a lofty mission, but not me! If we loaned out our Christmas money and didn't get it back, I'd consider the whole affair plenty bad, believe me."

Tara studied Jasper's face and saw an odd combination of hope and despair. She thought, how strange that we can disagree about a weighty issue like this without raising our voices. Our big screaming fights are about dumb little things—a broken dish, or spilled tomato sauce.

She came to an abrupt conclusion. "All right, it's obvious this is vital to you, though I honestly don't know why. I've had my say, and now I'm going to leave it up to you. Anyhow, we're hungry and I should be putting the hamburgers on. Please check and see what the kids are doing—Sally should be sleeping, but I don't hear Lenny or Drew. Will you round them up and tell them to wash up for supper?"

After dinner Jasper explained the situation to the boys.

"But Dad, what if he doesn't send the money back?" was Drew's first misgiving.

"He will. I knew this man very well in college. Don't forget what I told you. He was a very good friend to me, and he helped me out a lot."

"But you said you haven't seen him for a long time."

"Our college has a reunion party every five years, and that's when I see him."

Leonard chimed in. "But what if he doesn't send it back anyway? Will I get my bike?"

"I have no doubt in my mind that he'll return the money, but since you're pressing me for an answer, if he doesn't, wouldn't that really be the very best Christmas present? Standing by a friend who may be in trouble and who needs the money more than we do?"

"Oh," from Drew. Silence from Leonard.

"The main thing I'm telling you is that I have to do this favor for my old friend." There was an awkward pause. After a moment Jasper resumed. "Pretend you were having a hard time with multiplication in school; you were getting bad grades on your papers, and failing your tests. Then a nice boy in your class came over to your house and helped you. He drilled you every day until you learned how to multiply. After that, your marks improved, and the teacher praised you. Then one day this boy's father lost his job and the boy needed a winter coat and his Daddy didn't have enough money to buy it. Now make believe you had money in your piggy bank that you were saving to buy yourself a bike or a drum set. Wouldn't you feel like lending it to this boy who had been kind to you, just until his Daddy found a job?"

"Mommy helps me and Drew with arithmetic. And I made two potholders for Mommy in school," said Lenny, completely missing the point.

A tinge of disenchantment crept into Jasper's voice as he strove to cope with the boys' skepticism. "Let's think of this as a family Christmas project," he said. "This is a chance for you to practice what you're being taught in Sunday School, 'love thy neighbor.' It's a way for us to show love. We're not supposed to be thinking about what we're getting for Christmas, we should be thinking about giving. What I'm asking you to give to me and my friend is three weeks of waiting, three weeks of patience. It's harder than

204

wrapping up potholders for Mommy. You can't wrap this type of present up and put a bow on it, but it's a present just the same. Do you understand?"

Drew, with eyes cast down, answered glumly, "Yes, Papa, I think I understand."

"Well, I don't!" yelped his petulant brother. "I don't love your friend and I don't want to give him any present. He's a grown-up man, he can get a job!"

"You don't have to regard it as a gift to Mr. Southerick," said Jasper. "Think of it as a gift to me, because I am asking this of you, and you are giving it to me."

"I finished your presents already! And I told all the kids I'm getting a ten-speed bike for Christmas! It's okay for you, Papa, you have a car!" Lenny ran out of the room howling.

Jasper's body sagged, along with his spirits. But he was heartened by the next fear that came into Drew's head: "But what about Sally, Dad? She still believes in Santa Claus!" Drew was upset by the thought that his adored baby sister would not get a visit from St. Nick.

"Don't fret about that," said Jasper, giving his son a warm hug. "Santa will come down the chimney right on schedule, and fill Sally's stocking with a bunch of inexpensive toys and coloring books that will make her happy. Sally doesn't know or care what anything costs. And in January she'll get some bigger things, just as you boys will. Why don't you write her a note from Santa Claus saying he's coming back again in three or four weeks, and we'll leave it by the empty hot-chocolate cup on Christmas Eve."

Drew smiled at this conspiracy, and Jasper went into the boys' room to continue talking to Leonard about the joys of Christmas in January. Lenny proved inconsolable, however, and in the end, Jasper lost his temper. When Lenny bawled, "I want my bike for Christmas" for the third time, Jasper yelled, "You get it through your stubborn little head that I'm sending the money to Alex whether you cry or not. And if you don't stop that howling you won't get a bike in January!" He regretted his statement even before he stalked out of the room.

Tara had overheard parts of Jasper's conversation with the boys. She was cleaning the stove in the kitchen and thinking, what's wrong with me? I've agreed to help someone, and from what I've been told, I'm supposed to be tasting sweet satisfaction. But the plain truth is, I feel miserable because my eight-year-old is crying his eyes out in the bedroom.

Later that evening she was comforted when Jasper put his arms around her, held her tight, and said, "Thanks for going along, and not getting mad at me. This is something I have to do; I can't let Alex Southerick down. I love you deeply, Tara. There isn't anyone else on earth who could understand me."

I don't understand you either, thought Tara, but I won't spoil this moment by saying so.

Mr. and Mrs. Ned Packerbey
114 Ryerson St.
Salt Lake City, Utah
                           84118

11

During the very first week of marriage, Ned had decreed
to Harriet that catalogs and advertisements sent to the
Packerbey household should be thrown away unopened so
that no precious time would be wasted reading 'garbage.'
'Time is money' was a platitude that Harriet was to hear
repeated again and again in the course of the next 22 years.

As a newlywed, Harriet broke the rule now and then to
read a colorful piece of junk mail, feeling like a thief
because she was stealing a minute or two from manuscripts
piled high on her desk. At the time she was a home typist,
and Ned was an office clerk, which was the poorest-paid
post in his company. Harriet's minimal earnings were
added to Ned's in a pool that Ned rationed and monitored
alone.

Ned abhorred wasting either time or money. Not that
Harriet advocated wastefulness; the two merely disagreed
on what constituted waste. For example, Harriet did not
think that elegant gift wrappings and ribbons were a waste
of money; or that stopping the car to gaze at a spectacular

sunset was a misuse of time. Ned construed any activity that did not have some relation to the saving or production of income to be a needless loss.

———❦———

When Harriet was eight months pregnant with her first child, and her typewriter seemed to be moving further and further away from her fingers, she expressed her feelings to Ned: "I'd like to give up home typing. Nowadays I'm not comfortable reaching the keyboard, but even after I have the baby, I don't want to be typing when he's crying."

Harriet was nervous. She knew that Ned was looking forward to the coming birth, but she was also aware that he worked for a low salary, and that he extolled savings and thrift. She was pleasantly surprised when he said, "All right. I'm old-fashioned enough to like your suggestion. Mothers are best off watching the children and the budget. Let me see what I can do."

The next evening he had his solution. "We'll have to counterbalance the reduced funds," he said. "The way I've figured it out, you'll be able to economize by sewing the baby things and our own clothes—maybe when the baby's napping. This should net as much as you bring in now, and at least you won't have deadlines to meet. And I've trimmed some minor items off our budget, such as newspapers; we can hear the news on the radio. And another thing. You probably won't believe this, because you've seen how I peck at a typewriter—but I'm going to type address labels for a couple of hours when I come home at night. I brought a batch of them home today."

These measures sounded more than fair; Harriet was eager to cooperate. She acquired a rickety secondhand sewing machine, and a friend's collection of infants' clothing patterns. Ned took over her antediluvian oak desk, which housed an equally antiquated typewriter.

Thus, to the background whir of a treadle sewing machine, Ned started typing addresses, slowly and laboriously, in his spare evenings.

By the time Ricky was five, and a second child, Melanie, was three, the family's monetary position had vastly improved. The Packerbeys had moved from their cramped apartment to their own home, a small house with imitation brickface siding.

Ned's one-finger typing of address labels had expanded from a part-time endeavor into a thriving full-time mailing-list company, located in the basement of the house. With a high-school course in bookkeeping as her lone credential, Harriet had taken care of the business ledgers from the start, carefully recording the swelling profits month after month.

However, Ned did not modify his austere family budget to keep pace with the flourishing company. His one-line test for spending money was, 'Is this purchase absolutely necessary?' This eliminated nine out of ten proposed expenditures. Once when Harriet wanted to buy a book on gardening, her pet hobby, she was not able to prove it was a crucial need.

"Just what is absolutely necessary?" she exclaimed. "Somebody has said death and taxes—is that what you mean? If we did only what's compulsory, what would we do? Would we ever play cards? Would we dance?"

Harriet had become distraught, but Ned remained impassive. He walked quietly over to the telephone, made a call, and came back. "The free public library has that book," he said, "and you have a library card."

Within an hour Harriet was worried that her outburst had been shortsighted.

Now that I've put the thought in his head, we probably won't dance or play cards for the rest of our lives.

But she had no cause for concern—Ned had often speculated about these pastimes himself, without her agitated reminder. He went along with occasional games and dances as a concession to Harriet, not specifically to please her, but to substantiate his long-range view that she needed some relaxation to keep her healthy. Doctors and medicines cost hard-won cash; good health was one of Ned's pursuits because ill health was expensive. He took up tennis to stay in shape so that sickness would not rob him of income-producing time. Though his narrow vision blurred the sheer pleasure of sport, he derived enjoyment from doubly using his athletics time to court new customers.

Harriet would never forget Ricky's sixth birthday. She had wanted to give Ricky a birthday party, but Ned had given a categorical 'no' to her 'whim.' Harriet became unusually headstrong. Complaisant up to this stage in their marriage, she changed face and determined to have the party without Ned's knowledge. She asked a friend for the use of her home, telling her that Ned was redecorating the downstairs rooms. She laughed inwardly at her excuse, thinking of the absurdity of 'Silas Marner' (an unspoken nickname) opening the money-sacks for paint or wallpaper when the house was not even up for sale.

The little celebration was held according to plan. To pay for the modest prizes and refreshments, Harriet had saved a dollar a week out of her budgeted allotment for food. But in the bustle of preparations, she had not looked ahead to the inevitable moment when Ricky and his younger sister Melanie would greet their father on party night.

"Look, Daddy!" cried Ricky. "Jimmy gave me a helicopter that flies! We had cake and ice cream, too!"

"*I* found the most peanuts," interrupted Melanie, vaunting the only moment when Ricky had not been star for the day.

Ned surveyed the gift toys with an affected smile, but Harriet could see that he was white with anger. When the children were asleep, their parents had a bitter quarrel.

"Where did you get the money?" Ned demanded.

When Harriet gave him a straight answer, he said, "Apparently you don't require your total allowance for real food. You know we don't fritter money away on junk food." The result was a decrease of one dollar a week in the already stringent food disbursement.

Later, when Harriet calmed down, she reflected with a feeling of shock that Ned was more outraged by her supposed extravagance than by her duplicity. After that, she gradually became more adroit at executing petty deceptions about money. She took advantage of food coupons and rebates, and guiltily pocketed a few dimes and quarters for her own use. Sometimes she wore old dresses—altered for Ned's eyes with buttons or scarves—and spent her fabric dole on little extras for her home or her children. But she despised herself when she cautioned the youngsters 'Don't tell Daddy' if she scraped up the means to buy them a trinket.

Several weeks after Ricky's party she bought and planted some flower seeds, and then brooded about the repercussions ahead when Ned spied brilliant marigolds along the front walk. On her worst days she hoped they would not come up at all; on her better days she hoped he would think the seeds were spread by the wind or the birds.

With the inadequate data from library books on beginning psychology, Harriet had tried to analyze Ned. He was
a considerate husband in many ways: on Sunday mornings
he brought her waffles and coffee in bed; he openly praised
her cooking and her other capabilities; when she was over-
tired or had a headache, he tended the children.

But why was he so intent on accumulating money, and
so stingy when he had some? She knew his parents had
been compelled to scrimp, bringing up six children during
the Great Depression. Ned's mother would cut two oranges
in quarters, and each family member would eat one-fourth
of an orange. "Mom never spent a penny on a candy bar,"
he said with pride. When Ricky or Melanie asked for a new
toy—anything that might strain the paltry sum meted out
for playthings—he would declare that he and his siblings
had made their own toys out of scrap containers and packing boxes.

Yet Harriet recalled that her own parents had likewise
been tightfisted in the Depression era. She had worn her
sisters' hand-me-downs throughout her childhood, and she
could not recall a single store-bought game. But as an adult
she had veered in the opposite direction: she was inclined
to spend money freely. She wondered how this antithesis
could be logically explained. It was a riddle that she would
have liked to ask a psychiatrist if she ever happened to meet
one, but it did not seem important enough for an office
consultation. Or was it? But Ned would not have paid for
such a session anyway, no matter what the grounds.

Ned had become extremely investment-conscious. After a few years of togetherness, Packerbey Mailing Lists moved downtown into the business district, and the family moved to a fine Tudor home in a prestigious section of the city, solely because Ned believed that the property would rise in value. "When we retire we'll make money on the resale," he said. Rugs and furniture did not fit into this master plan, however ('they wear out and have to be replaced'), so they lived in the house with bare floors and the cheap unsightly furniture they had bought as newly-weds.

Harriet's initial excitement at buying the house waned considerably when it became clear that the handful of inexpensive decorative items she was able to gather did not begin to offset the shabby furniture. Old and childworn, the small pieces took up half the space where furniture belonged, making the house seem cold and uninviting. She was ashamed to have guests over for coffee; hospitality on the broader scale she would have liked was unthinkable. But, Harriet told herself, the deplorable state of the furnishings was of no real consequence. Her yearning to have social get-togethers had always been defeated anyway, because Ned had never wanted to buy even limited party fare. It was cause for conflict just to ask a few relatives— brothers and sisters, and Ned's father—to an infrequent lunch or dinner.

Harriet busied herself with raising the children and sewing the family clothing. She raked leaves, and mowed the lawn, and attacked the overgrown shrubbery in the backyard with her pruning shears. But Ned's single-mindedness wormed its way into her busy days, and sometimes disheartened her, as on one summer Sunday when she and Ned were riding on a deserted country road. He braked the car abruptly and cried out, "Look at that!" Harriet saw a deer with her fawn, motionless as statues, partially camouflaged by tree shadows and flora. "What a sight!" she whispered, awestruck.

"Yes!" Ned chimed in. "A stretch of property like this, out here in the wilderness, could accelerate in price by ten."

Harriet noticed the 'For Sale' sign then, but Ned never saw the animals, nor the tears in Harriet's eyes.

At that instant Harriet's mind flashed back to a crossword puzzle she and Ned had filled in together while on their honeymoon. The puzzle required an eight-letter noun beginning with 's' for 'a fundamental of life.' She had called out 'sunshine,' and Ned had laughed in a patronizing manner, as if amused by her childishness, while he wrote in 'security.'

⎯⎯ ⚹✦⚹ ⎯⎯

When Packerbey Mailing Lists had been in full-time operation almost ten years, and boasted computerization and a staff of fourteen employees, Harriet armed herself with ledgers and confronted Ned in what she hoped would be his own language. She made her points in rapid-fire succession, as if she wanted to dispose of an unpleasant task in quick order.

"Ned, we both know that the company's profits are getting higher every year, and this has been an exceptionally good spring. I've been taking care of the books without pay since you started out twelve years ago. I'm sure you'll agree that if you didn't have me, it would cost quite a lot for a bookkeeper. Starting next month I would like to have a very small salary, no more than a tiny fraction of what an outside part-time bookkeeper would receive." She finished somewhat out of breath.

Ned gaped at her as if she had suddenly lost her faculties. It took him a full thirty seconds to speak.

"You are standing right there in front of me and saying that you want to willfully decrease the assets of the business that is your own bread-and-butter? The business that will provide for your children's college education? I can't believe this is happening!"

She had foreseen opposition, even a burst of temper, but not his stunned look of incredulity. "But Ned," she stammered, "I only want six dollars a week." She sounded feeble; her pinpricked balloon was losing its air.

"Six dollars a week!" he echoed. "Whatever for? Everything you need is included in the household budget— food and shelter and clothing."

The last word in his sentence revived her. "Clothing!" she yelped. "I'm still sewing every stitch of all our clothes. Are you sure you don't want me to weave the material? Maybe we should invest in a spinning wheel." She laughed derisively.

Ned was not smiling. His eyes studied her, as if he were gauging her sanity level.

She persevered bravely, in a lower voice. "I could use the money to perk up the house a little." His silence made her tense. She bit her upper lip and added, less boldly, "And for gifts."

"Harriet, you're being frivolous. Those things aren't necessities, as you well know. Furthermore, gifts are adequately covered in the budget under 'Miscellaneous'."

"I could contest the word 'adequately'," she said between gritted teeth. "But this request has nothing to do with the household budget. This is money that I am earning, over and above running the household."

She appeared so forlorn and close to tears that his mood shifted to patient forbearance. He walked over to her desk, and patted her on the head. Harriet felt that she was being treated like a child who has staged a foolish tantrum.

"I thought you had assimilated some key principles," he said gently. "The reason we are progressing is that I operate my whole organization in a judicious manner. Naturally the employees must be paid salaries—you can't get strangers to work for nothing." He looked wistful, as if he had revealed one of life's saddest realities. "But under no conditions would I take money out of the till to perk up the house or run around buying nonsense gifts. I don't take a cent out of the business unless it's absolutely necessary."

Harriet could not dispute that claim because she knew it was true. Ned had no illusions of grandeur, even as president/owner of a prosperous establishment. Harriet had made a recent joke that Ned's car and topcoat were nonidentical twins—they were both nine years old. She had certainly not intended, by her small petition, to impugn her husband's business acumen.

She could think of nothing more to say. She never brought the subject of salary up again.

———⟨≡◇≡⟩———

The Packerbey family had lived in their spacious, rugless, sparsely furnished home for eight years when Melanie entered the local high school, where Ricky was already a junior. For several years, Harriet had been plotting a novel idea. By the time she introduced it to Ned, she had a carefully worded proposition.

"I want to get a regular job as a bookkeeper; I think I can qualify, after keeping Packerbey's books for sixteen years. This is my proposal: when I find a job, I'll put fifty percent of my net income into our joint savings for you to invest however you wish, and the remaining fifty percent I will spend as I choose. For your part you would agree to make no suggestions or reprimands about anything I do with my share, even if I go up to the corner and throw dollar bills down the sewer. And I wouldn't question you about your half, either."

She had made her fifty-fifty master stroke to win her husband's compliance. She was familiar with Ned's sentiments about working wives, which he now repeated: "Wives who are employed consume as much money as they earn—on restaurant lunches, baby-sitters, expensive fast-food meals at home, clothes to wear to the office, and transportation. On top of that, household efficiency declines." He made no mention of her remark about enriching the sewer system, although it had caused him to turn a shade of red that was just a tinge below purple. After a pause he said slowly, "Of course, a baby-sitter is no longer a prerequisite for us—and you would be taking care of your expenses out of your half..."

"What about Packerbey's books?" he inquired.

"I'll continue to do them part-time without pay."

Ned nodded approvingly. "I believe 75-25 in favor of the savings account would be a more suitable percentage," he haggled.

"Definitely not."

"Sixty-forty then. That's a fair compromise."

"No."

She had steeled herself against negotiation, and she stood firm for another twenty minutes before Ned decided that 'half a loaf is better than none,' and using those words, he finally accepted her terms.

Harriet's sister and confidante, Imogene, told Harriet that this entire procedure was ludicrous. "Why did you have to win Ned's consent?" she asked Harriet. "Is Ned going to help you with the cooking and laundry? Go get a job and do what you want with everything you earn, just as I do," said Imogene.

But Harriet had the wisdom that came from years of closeness with Ned, and she loved him in spite of his preoccupation with thrift. Imogene's husband, Harriet thought ruefully, is very openhanded indeed, but he drinks too much, and his generosity extends to his secretary and the cashier at the Eat-and-Pub.

Ned did not drink or have affairs with other women, and Harriet was confident that he never would. Her self-assurance did not stem from his sterling moral character, or from her own attractiveness, but from the fact that such proclivities cost money. She also knew that once Ned had agreed to a deal, he could be depended on to abide by it.

Imogene was correct about one issue: Harriet did not seek household help from Ned as part of her scheme. When Ned was at home, he was occupied with business, not leisure. In the evenings he pored over reports while she read fiction; or he worked on contracts while she watched television. She planned to sacrifice both novels and television as soon as she restyled her life. "I'd rather see deep plush rugs on the floor than any program on television," she said. She was convinced that she had made a wise move toward living her middle-aged years in peace.

———— ⚔ ————

Though Harriet had never collected a nickel for handling the Packerbey ledgers, she had gained marketable knowledge; she found a fine position because of her expertise. A few months and a few dollars later, she started to emerge from her tight cocoon; now, after five years, she was a fully developed social butterfly.

In those five years her home had been transformed. Harriet's first step was to order beautiful new sofas, followed by cabinets, tables, and chairs. Then she created a background with various window and flooring materials. Displaying talent that had been smothered, she combined accessories in fanciful arrangements. On one wall in the family room she hung multi-shaped wicker baskets, with assorted plantings in several of them. In the dining area she employed spotlights to accentuate imaginative groupings of family photographs. Her tastes were not expensive, and she often found serviceable odds and ends at garage sales. The prodigious changes in the Packerbey home owed as much to her artistic flair as to her paycheck.

In this setting Harriet could have the dinner festivities and after-theater soirées she enjoyed hostessing, and she set about revolutionizing her life as well as her house. She got in touch with old friends, and cultivated new ones wherever she went.

Even though both children were in college now, she was busier than she had ever been. She coordinated a full-time job with Packerbey's bookkeeping and a crowded social calendar. It was not her nature to be deceitful, thus another dimension of joy was added because she no longer had to be surreptitious about every piddling expenditure.

Ned was happy too. Computing the details, he knew he had actually received at least the 75-25 percent salary distribution from Harriet to which he had originally aspired. Harriet subscribed to plays and concerts by the season, instead of asking Ned about sporadic performances. And she supplied most of her own wardrobe, as well as many special clothing articles for the children. Ned now paid out zero dollars for recreation, and a pittance for clothing.

Harriet was not stupid; she realized that Ned was saving money on things he had purchased in the past. She also knew that nothing could have made him happier, and a happy husband was nice to have around the house. Burgeoning investment accounts kept Ned in a mellow humor, and he was satisfied to stick to his part of the bargain, saying nothing about what he honestly considered to be his wife's wanton spending.

Harriet underwrote vacations, too. Never before had Ned been able to luxuriate in a weekend away, because his mind was constantly focused on the bill. But when Harriet paid, he relaxed with the mental justification that she would have squandered the money anyway.

Ned loathed shopping, but Harriet wallowed in it. She bought lavish birthday and Christmas presents for Ricky, Melanie, and Ned's elderly father. Harriet always signed the gift tags 'Mom and Dad' or 'Ned and Harriet,' though she knew Ned would not have paid for, or even countenanced, a single package.

She also gave exorbitant gifts to Ned. Last Christmas she had presented him with a solid mahogany desk for his business office, a furnishing she knew he would not have provided for himself. He was still using the gouged, scratched desk she had picked up for next to nothing at an auction over twenty years before. Ned's first utterance after "Thank you" was, "I hope you've saved the receipt; this can be deducted as a business expense." She had the feeling he was more titillated by the tax deduction than the desk. She chuckled and thought, oh well, he liked it, one way or another.

That same year, his present for her was a new toaster. The old wedding-shower model had broken, and he had taken it to a repair shop and found out that fixing it was not practical. It was an item that would have been replaced in any case, Christmas or not.

Once in a while, Harriet wondered if she was truly generous, or if her gifts were efforts to compensate for her humiliation in prior years, when Ned's notion of a Christmas present was a clearance-sale tie for his father. But most of the time she was content to spend her money without self-analysis. She even allowed that her husband's frugality had produced many beneficial side effects. She and Ned had the lean, firm cast of teenagers. After 22 years of

220

marriage, she was positive she could slip into her wedding gown with ease. On my former fabric allowance, she thought, I couldn't afford half a yard more material for the next larger size.

There were other contributing factors. Ned had not permitted Harriet to buy soda, cakes, candy, or cookies, because they were an irresponsible waste of money. Alcoholic beverages were so clearly gainless that they had not rated discussion. The family had never gone hungry, but Harriet was obliged to buy nothing but 'real' food. She cooked all her meals from basic ingredients, because processed foods cost more.

It was a dark day if she had a momentary lapse at the grocery store, and Ned found forbidden food on the kitchen shelf. She still remembered the storm over a box of chocolate-chip cookies she had bought for the children. But one day, months later, when she remarked that Ricky and Melanie had no cavities, he stared at her as if she were an imbecile.

"Don't you understand?" he asked. "That's one reason we don't buy cookies. First, the cookies are a waste because they are not a food requirement; second, they can lead to cavities; third, doctor and dental bills are high and therefore to be avoided."

If Ned's primary incentive had been to spare the children the ordeals of toothaches or obesity, Harriet would not have been so piqued. Yet she had to acknowledge that the end results were the same: the whole family had developed sound food practices along the way.

When Melanie was a junior in high school she had gorged on a pound of chocolates, and then hid for days with a bout of blemishes on her face. Now, three years later, she had a peach-velvet complexion. She had become a natural-foods devotee who brought books and pamphlets home from college to persuade her father that some foods merit-

ed their extra cost in terms of superior health. Since childhood she had known how to capture Ned's attention.
Rather than stating, "This is better," she would begin by
saying, "Dad, you know how doctors' fees have climbed."
She was so successful in inducing Ned—the toughest customer on earth—to buy brewer's yeast, raw wheat germ,
and cod liver oil, that Harriet thought her daughter should
go into sales.

Melanie was seventeen when she had disclosed that she
wanted to become a nurse, and Ricky had commented,
"Lucky sick people!" Coming from a brother who had
teased her all her life about every real or imagined flaw, it
was the highest compliment.

Ricky, meanwhile, was majoring in Business Adminis-
tration with the expectation of working in the family business. Ricky was tall and muscular, with a slender frame
that was distinctly unrelated to his voracious appetite.
Usually he appeased his frequent hunger pangs with large
quantities of fruit, and after college breaks Harriet always
sent him off with a bounteous supply. He was generally eating by the time he waved good-bye.

Harriet had spent years squelching the urge to sneak
candy to her children so they would be like the other
youngsters on the block. The lack of lollipops to lick had
seemed so salient to her then, but now that her son and
daughter were grown, she championed their mettle in
making unconventional food choices while their peers
flocked to fast food.

And when Harriet looked in the mirror, she knew that
Ned's food code was responsible for her own youthful
appearance. Most of her acquaintances were developing
'middle-age spread'—she was delighted to be the exception. As her friends ran in vain from diet centers to exer-
cise classes, she was already settled in the eating pattern
they were all struggling to attain.

She was amused by the irony: now that she was at liberty to buy fudge, cheesecake, butterscotch pudding—any prohibited treat she had craved in earlier years—she found to her own amazement that she would rather have melon or strawberries for dessert.

Harriet could think of other bonuses that had been well- disguised as trials during her life with Ned. For one thing, she had learned to cut and set her own hair, thanks to Ned. She had not thanked Ned at the time, however—quite the contrary. In the early months of marriage, when she was told that trips to beauty salons were taboo, she was indignant.

"You can take an evening-school course in hair-cutting and setting," Ned had said after her second professional haircut.

"How kind of you, sir," she had retorted sarcastically.

Ned had estimated the cost of haircuts for them both over a period of thirty years, and he had concluded that the charge for a course would be worth the prospective savings. She had bridled at taking the lessons, but today she prized the dividends: she was forever released from the inconvenience of making appointments and waiting her turn at beauty parlors. She had not opted to return to them, even with her present spending arrangement.

The beauty-course episode had taken place long before Ricky and Melanie were born, so Ned's investment had yielded much greater compensation than he had originally tallied: all the children's haircuts from babyhood through adolescence. With practice, Harriet had become remarkably proficient. She had recently received a letter from Melanie at college: *I hope you'll have a chance to cut my hair when I'm home for Christmas. I hate the way the beautician here cuts it.*

And Harriet had burst into laughter. The wounds of the past were healed.

Sincerely Yours

On Thursday evening, December 14th, when Harriet brought in the mail, she quickly discarded the advertisements and then handed the economics magazines to Ned. Next she started to open Christmas cards. In a few minutes she unsealed a fine manger-scene card from Alex and Marcia Southerick, former neighbors who had moved away ten years ago. Turning over the picture in anticipation of a newsy message, she was dismayed to read Alex's note requesting a speedy loan of $1,000.

Oh, Alex! You're barking up the wrong tree. You're not going to get that kind of loan from this source. You picked the wrong person when you chose Ned as one of your ten friends to contact for money.

"Ned," she said, "do you remember the Southericks?"

"Uh-huh." Ned was poring over his favorite business newsletter, and the inquiry did not raise either his eyes or his curiosity.

"Alex wants to borrow $1,000." If any statement could have diverted Ned's attention from a current financial publication, that was it.

"What?" he said, almost in a shout.

"Look at this Christmas card."

Ned read Alex's brief letter twice. Harriet expected him to show scorn or distaste before tossing it back to her. She was confounded to hear him say musingly, "What do you think?"

Unaccustomed to being asked her opinion about money matters, she was disconcerted by his question. "I don't know what to think," she hedged. Her uppermost thought was, why are you bothering to ask me? *My recommendation wouldn't make you part with $1,000 in 1,000 years.*

A kaleidoscope of memories passed swiftly through her brain. Alex and Marcia Southerick had been newcomers to this street on the same day that she and Ned had moved here, thirteen years ago. Meeting each other as they did—two couples standing exhausted next to their respective moving vans—Harriet had not felt overly uncomfortable with her meager furnishings. It was obvious that she was making a move to a larger home; spectators could presume, albeit mistakenly, that redecoration would follow.

The Packerbeys and the Southericks became friends on moving day; in the subsequent weeks and months they shared many jovial evenings, playing cribbage and rummy, even poker—with chips only, because Ned vetoed penny stakes. Each couple were parents of a boy and a girl, and the youngsters had gotten along well also. Harriet had cut the Southerick children's hair periodically, and she had given Marcia a flattering new hairstyle—and Ned had decried Harriet's refusal to take payment for these neighborly favors. Though the two couples had not met since the Southericks moved away, they had kept in contact with annual notes on Christmas cards.

"Since you're asking me," Harriet said at length, "I think it would be nice to lend Alex the money. The Southericks were good friends, even though it was a long time ago. What a shame—he must be in a jam."

Ned did not reply, and it occurred to Harriet that perhaps he had sought her judgment because he meant for *her* to make the loan, so she added, "I've already done my Christmas shopping, and frankly I don't have ten dollars to my name." This was not a guess, but a precise account of her fiscal condition. With Ned for security, Harriet had no qualms about emptying her wallet as fast as it was filled.

Ned remained mum, but by his vacant stare Harriet knew he was absorbed in thought. After a while he strode over to the phone and dialed a number, while she proceeded to the kitchen to make dinner. She overheard the clipped end of a conversation: "That's great. Yeah. 'Bye."

"Who did you call?"

225

"My tax accountant. I'm going to send Alex the money."

Harriet dropped the package of lamb chops she was holding. Ignoring the scattered chops, she lowered herself into a chair and gasped, "You are going to do *what?*" She would not have been more staggered if Ned had offered her a yacht for her birthday. In fact, she would have wagered a year of her salary that Ned would thrust Alex's note aside within half a minute of reading it. The idea that Ned, of all people, would send $1,000—with no legal contract—to someone he had not seen in ten years, was beyond credibility.

"Don't throw out the lamb chops," said Ned matter-of-factly. "Just wash them off before you broil them. But yes, I'll be sending out the thousand now, before my tax year ends on December 31st. In the meantime, I'm in the process of selling some real estate with the proviso that I don't receive any money until January. My accountant said the sale will most likely put me in a higher tax bracket next year, so I'll need to work out a number of transactions—like this worthless bad debt of Alex's—to offset the capital gain in the new year."

Harriet was confused. "What do you mean, worthless bad debt?" she asked. "Alex is going to pay this loan back in January."

"Nah. I'm not counting on getting the money back. If Alex is impoverished to such an extent that he can't go to a bank—and has to borrow money from friends—I don't think he'll be able to come up with any fast money. To me this sounds like a last-ditch effort before personal bankruptcy. My accountant says this thousand-dollar loss will serve me rather than hinder me." He pushed his glasses down to the tip of his nose and smiled. He had the look of a man who has just landed a ten-pound mackerel.

Still numb at the unexpected turn of events, Harriet made no response. In predicting how Ned would react to

Alex's letter, she had not considered that he might think of a way that a loan could have redemptive value. If she had thought of that, she would have known it would interest him.

Ned was talkative. "I also get brownie points with an executive of Kinnelac, in case I ever want them," he crowed. "Did you see Alex's business card? He's a vice-president at Kinnelac Corporation, and I've heard persistent rumors that they may open an office here in Salt Lake City. But I'm not planning on it; if Alex goes bankrupt, he may get sacked."

Though Harriet seldom made reference to Ned's 'business first' attitude—especially since she had liberated herself from its yoke—she could not resist saying, "But you wouldn't have helped him unless the loan was advantageous to you."

"Of course not; I'm not a dunce. What difference does that make? You wanted to send the thousand, and I didn't at first glance. Now we're sending it, so be happy."

Ned's one-track outlook had never made Harriet happy, but she was glad that her husband was lending Alex Southerick the money. She placed the thousand-dollar check in the mailbox the following morning with unsettled emotions. She knew that Ned's actions often produced coincidental benefits, and in this case the money would be helpful to Alex. Yet she wished that Ned's motives were purer.

Unaware that the act of spending money was the salve that softened her scars, she turned her thoughts to shopping for Christmas decorations. She had seen some gilded angels at a department store yesterday, painted a lustrous gold. She decided she would buy a few and hang them on the higher branches of the Christmas tree, where they would be partially hidden in the shadows of the flickering lights. They would look nice, and no one would know they were made of hollow tin.

12

Alex Southerick was pacing at home in his favorite location—the long center-hall corridor—while mentally composing his next note to his friends. Marcia knew everything now, about the Christmas-card notes and the money, so there was no need to hide from her by walking in circles around the tiny den.

His old dog Barkle followed him slowly back and forth, up and down the hallway, imitating his gait. When Alex paused, Barkle paused; if Alex quickened his step, so did Barkle. Marcia said that the big English sheepdog must be solving some tricky posers in the animal world, because he wore the same contemplative expression as Alex.

After a half-hour, Alex and the dog traipsed solemnly into the den. Barkle was not one to dwell on his problems—he curled up in a corner and went to sleep. Alex sat down at his desk and grinned at five checks spread out like a fan in front of him. Out of the list of ten names he had compiled so carefully four weeks before, half of the couples had responded. He had received $1,000 from each couple, a total of $5,000. I wonder what motivated some people to send the money, and others not, he mused.

In a mood of elation he started to write.

January 8, 1983

Dear Friends:

When you open this letter you will be surprised to see a check for $10,000, written not by me but by

228

Humphrey Wattsindorf, a name you have probably never seen or heard. First, let me assure you that the check is good. Second, here is the full explanation.

Humphrey and I are cronies who love to talk about life, philosophy, and the fascinating facets of the human race in general. Although we are close friends, we have many dissimilar views, and I am quick to point out to Humphrey that I think some of his convictions are downright cynical. He is just as quick to let me know that he thinks my opinions are naive and simplistic. He believes that 'dog eat dog' is the prevailing attitude in the world; I believe that the roses outnumber the thorns. We are constantly sending each other newspaper clippings that illustrate our opposing viewpoints.

For example, I recently mailed him an article about a mother and her two young sons who take a shopping bag filled with groceries to the poorest section of their large city every Saturday, and distribute the food to unsavory-looking beggars and vagrants. Humphrey, in turn, sent me a story about a well-to-do businessman who persuaded 57 elderly low-income widows to invest their life savings in counterfeit gold-mine stocks. You get the picture.

Well, late one evening in early December, while we were debating my firm belief in the inherent goodness of people, I came up with an idea to prove my case. I told Humphrey that I would address my Christmas cards the following weekend, and I would include a brief note on ten cards asking old friends I had not seen in years to lend me $1,000, no questions asked. I would give no reason as to why I wanted the money, and I would clearly state that no papers or contracts would be signed. It would be a loan on faith alone.

My contention was that if I wrote such a note to ten couples, at least one couple would come up with the money. Humphrey said, "Not a chance. Nobody will lend you a nickel on that basis." The notion appealed to Humphrey as an easy means to shut me up forever on the subject of human relations. "For a man your age, you don't know much about people," he said, shaking his head sympathetically.

Our final pact covered these additional requirements: I would write only to friends I had not seen in four years or longer, and had not contacted by letter or telephone since last year's Christmas cards. And I would select people who were middle income like myself, no one particularly wealthy to my knowledge.

My original plan did not include a bet of any kind; it was simply an experiment to win Humphrey over to the concept that most people are essentially compassionate. If one couple out of ten met the conditions of this loan, then it would be logical to assume that the majority of people would help friends-in-need under more reasonable circumstances. For my part, I decided to send interest on whatever money I received, so that no one would lose a dime.

But Humphrey happens to be very rich, and once in a while he likes to make a far-out bet on a 'sure thing.' He was so positive he was right that he spoke hastily, and, as it turned out, rashly. He said that if I wrote these letters, he would pay out ten times any money I received, to anyone who sent it, and it wouldn't cost me a cent for interest. Don't misunderstand—he wasn't trying to throw money away. He was dead certain that this promise wouldn't cost him a cent either. "When nobody sends you any money, you can take me to dinner in a restaurant of my choice, how's that? I can taste it now!" Those were his sentiments at the time.

Humphrey added two stipulations: he had to approve the phrasing of the note; and no one else was to know about the bet, not even our wives. If word leaked out, the deal was off.

You, my dear friends, have reaffirmed my faith in human nature; in fact, your response surpassed my wildest dreams. I had thought that one answer—ten percent—would be a superlative return. Many direct-mail selling campaigns, using all the lures known to advertising, are considered successful if they attract a mere one percent response. Therefore I am overjoyed to report that not only one, but five couples—fifty percent of those I wrote—sent me $1,000 within a week.

Lest you benevolent people feel badly because my friend had to pay out so much money, let me interject here that Humphrey is a millionaire (which I decidedly am not). Though he is by no means fond of losing a wager, the $50,000 is not as momentous a factor to him as the brilliant redness of his face.

This little test of human goodwill could hardly be called a survey, since only ten couples were involved. There were many variables, and the out- come does not denigrate the other five couples who were petitioned. My Christmas card was not sent by certified mail, and could have been lost. Addresses can change, and families can be away on vacation. Some people might not have had the money to spare, but nevertheless be just as good-hearted as the ones who had it available.

My practical friend Humphrey is still shaking his bald head and reviewing the unscientific aspects of the whole affair. But I am happy to say that when all was said and done he had to agree that the outcome was sig-

nificant. We may make a philanthropist out of him yet!

My dear friends, I want to thank you ardently for lending me this money. I am very touched that you were willing to help me on such obscure terms, and I am glad that Humphrey made this pledge so you will be rewarded for your kindness in a way I could not have afforded.

Sincerely yours,

Alex

This letter, with a $10,000 check enclosed, was sent to addresses in five states. In New York, Vivian started to think of a new scheme to conquer the midwestern sales territory, especially since Sidney was, indeed, about to be transferred to Chicago. I'll have to find out Humphrey Wattsindorf's line of business, she thought.

In Arizona, Chester, for once, stopped laughing. With no joke on Mr. Most Likely to Succeed, and no adoring wife as a traveling companion, he decided not to attend the class reunion in the spring.

In Colorado, Isabel ordered the most splendid mink stole she could find, more luxurious than any she had ever seen worn to a class reunion or anywhere else. "Maybe we should sit with the Southericks after all," she murmured to Gilbert.

In Utah, Ned raced to the phone and called his accountant. "Is this a short-term capital gain or a tax-free gift?" he shouted.

And in New Jersey, Tara and Jasper and the children had the merriest Christmas any family ever enjoyed in the middle of January.